Descendants of Rust

K. A. Gandy

THIGPEN-
GANDY
PUBLISHING

Thigpen-Gandy Publishing

Contents

DEDICATION

For my mom, for being so proud of my books
that you tell every single person you know that
your daughter's an author.

And for Lia, my editor. Your work is impeccable,
and your advice not to put the first section of
chapter one as the ending of the last book kept
people from hunting me down. You're a gem!

Last, but certainly not least, for my readers.
Thank you for continuing to come back and
trust me to provide a great story, even with
my beloved cliffhangers. I appreciate each and
every one of you spending your time with me
and my stories, and . . .

I hope you love this book.

One

SHTF

S creams echoed off the arched dome as people darted in every direction—some still
charged the stage, despite Officer Kutsuki's
threats of capital punishment, while others fled
into the walls. The sounds of more gunshots
rang out, knocking me from my state of frozen
shock.

"We need to get out of here, River. I think
we should head to the lifeside, see if we can
find Morgan or somebody who knows what the
track is going on here. A *spaceship*?"

River tensed at my side, but when I looked
over, his eyes were rolling back in his head, not
locked onto the spaceship like mine had been.

"River!" His name tore out of my lips as I spun
to face him, and saw the electric net wrapped
around his chest. Before I could do something
stupid—like try to grab it and pull it off of

1

him—hands like vice grips latched onto my upper arms and dragged me back.

"No, stop! What the frack are you doing?!" I spat at the guards and tried to knee the one on my right in the groin. He blocked the blow with his thigh and snatched upward on my arm to put me off balance.

"Subdue her. The commandant wants her in medical." Gabriel's cold words surged like icy water down my back as two more guards grabbed River, his body falling limp as soon as the electric pulse stopped. His head dangled from his shoulders as they dragged him through the crowd, and I fought and scratched harder at the men holding me, desperation pushing me against impossible odds.

"You just don't learn, do you?" Nanette's voice was loud in my ear as I felt a sharp prick in the side of my neck, and hot lead filled my veins.

My body grew heavy, and the world around me began to distort, the colors garish and awful as I frantically whipped my head back and forth, trying to clear it.

"River, River!" I sob-screamed, and fruitlessly tried to blink away the intrusive colors. Once, twice, and the whole world dissolved into a neon blur.

For the second time in my life, when I woke up my mouth tasted like rotten cactus. Everything was blurry, and it took several long seconds for me to remember where I was, and how I'd gotten there. I was flat on my back, staring at an unfamiliar ceiling. When the awful memories clicked back into place, I jerked upright, or tried, but was stopped by bands around my chest, wrists, and ankles.

They'd strapped me to a table. The glaring whiteness of the medical bay's ceiling overhead finally came into focus, adrenaline and panic pushing the rest of the drug from my system. The familiar antiseptic scent hit me next, and a wave of nausea threatened.

I whipped my head left and right, finally spotting River. He was also strapped down, but to a chair in the corner of the room.

"You're awake! Thank the sweet oasis," River said in relief.

"How long have I been out? What's going on?"

"I'm not sure. So far all they've done is restrain you, and hook you up to that." He pointed with his chin, and I craned my neck the other direction to see what he was talking about. "I've been awake at least four hours, I'd guess, and I don't know how long we were both out before that."

The sight of a tube sucking blood from my arm and feeding it into a device containing several large syringes made me feel lightheaded, and I sucked in several deep breaths through my nose.

"Why are these freaks so obsessed with my blood, River?" I was proud of how even my voice sounded, given how badly I was shaking inside my restraints.

"'These freaks,' really?" Miriam—the same medical worker who'd taken care of us on our first visit here—walked in behind the commandant. "Such rudeness, when we took you in and offered you your brother's freedom. The younger generation has no appreciation, anymore."

She tsked softly. "Don't jerk around, Nyx. You'll pull out the IV line."

Her ultra-soothing vibes weren't doing it for me today. Something about being drugged and strapped to an exam table didn't give me the warm fuzzies.

"You can't do this. You can't strap people down and do medical procedures on them without their consent."

"That's where you're wrong." The commandant stopped at the foot of the exam table, looking down his nose at me with his hands clasped behind his back in military parade rest. "With martial law established, we can do anything we deem necessary to preserve the greater good."

"How the hell is taking her blood for the greater good?"

4

The commandant grinned, the expression more wolfish than joyful, as if he'd been waiting for that question. "I think we'll keep that a lovely surprise. Miriam, do we have what we need? The captain would like an introduction to the patient as soon as we're done here."

Bastard. The captain of what? The *spaceship*? Why would he know I existed, let alone want to meet me? I shot a worried look at River, and found his expression every bit as grim.

"Yes, Commandant. I just need a few minutes to detach everything and clean her up. She may be a bit wobbly, but anything lingering from the dosage should burn off quickly."

"Very well. Excursion Team One knows where to take her. Make sure they're in here before you unhook her. Their report said she fought like a wildcat."

"Yes, Commandant." Her voice never lost the flat, pleasant tenor, and I loathed her for it.

Weren't medical people supposed to have taken a vow to *help* others?

Drawers rattled and the sounds of boxes opening and closing right over my shoulder where I couldn't see made me itchy, but River still looked calm from his position. Miriam appeared at my side again a moment later, bandages and tubes of something in hand.

"How can you do this? Aren't you supposed to help people?"

"Please don't be upset, Nyx. If you hadn't fought, they would have brought you to me so I could explain the procedure."

"If I hadn't fought? Are you serious? They attacked my—" I faltered, eyes landing on River. He wasn't just a friend anymore, but I didn't want to clue them in to the changing nature of our relationship.

The sharp pinch in my arm as she removed the tube caused me to hiss, saving me from having to finish the sentence.

"Given your refusal to come in for further medical treatment as recommended, they thought it would be best if you were both restrained."

"That's bogus, and you know it. Why do they even want my blood? They already took a sample."

She smiled patronizingly down as she dabbed something gooey in the crook of my arm, and began wrapping a stretchy bandage around it.

"I'm not authorized to say."

"In what world—" I started to rant, but River smoothly cut me off.

"Nyx, save your strength. She's not going to talk. I've been trying to get her to every time she's come in to check on the pump."

I ground my back teeth together, but let it go. Miriam might have been as good as a piece of camel dung stuck to one of the Bronco's wheels, but she wasn't in charge. Even if she told me *something*, I doubted many people below the commandant knew what was really going on here.

"Nanette, she's ready for you," Miriam called, then began humming as she cleared away the supplies, pressing buttons on the pump full of my blood. The machine beeped and clicked, and then she gathered the four large, capped syringes and pressed them each into a padded case.

It snicked shut with a sickening finality, as Nanette pushed the door open. She took the case from Miriam as four more members of Excursion Team One walked in behind her.

"Would you like me to—" Miriam began.

"We'll take it from here." Nanette dismissed her with a nod.

Two of the soldiers undid my restraints while the other two worked on River's. Then it was a march down familiar hallways until we were thrown into a room in Barracks C.

I could only hope, as the door clanged shut on our heels, that Chace hadn't been dumped into the desert to die while I was locked in this room, unable to get out and meet him.

Two

Revelations

Two long days passed in near-complete silence. Unlike the last time we were locked in this god-forsaken room, Morgan didn't come back. One of Excursion Team One delivered our meals, and other than a larger delivery the first day where all of our things from our small apartment were dumped just inside the doorway, it had been monotonous.

On day three, just when I was good and losing it about Chace, the door opened to reveal Gabriel looming on the other side.

"Get your things. You're needed." He spun on his heel and left, not waiting for a response.

"These fracking people," River muttered, but began shoving his personal items into a bag, regardless.

Five minutes later, we were being half escorted, half herded down the halls to one of the conference rooms, when a ruckus broke out and the sounds of running boots echoed off the walls.

Gabriel put his hand to his ear, and then spun, barking orders to our guard at lightning speed. "Lock them down in room three, and then the rest of you with me. We've got a situation."

Our casual escort turned rough, and a hand banded around my upper arm.

"Keep your hands off her!" River snapped as I was shoved hard through the nearest doorway, only instinct keeping me on my feet. The door to the conference room slammed shut, and things fell eerily silent.

"You okay?" River asked, and I gave him an exasperated look.

"I'm fine. A little manhandling isn't going to break me."

He nodded but didn't apologize for checking on me. My feelings were all over the map now, and I most desperately didn't want things to change between us. Something inside me bristled at his concern, and that probably meant that I was very screwed up on a deeper level.

"Shouldn't we hear if there was some big threat?" River stood right inside the door, looming in a position to knock somebody off their feet if they came charging back in.

"Depends on the problem. The *fracking spaceship* was hard to miss." I sounded bitter, even to myself.

And I *was* bitter. I was tired of being shoved in closets while other people ran off to the action. I was not a "sit around and wait for somebody else to figure out my life" kind of woman. I broke stuff for a living, and right now, their shiny one-way mirrors were a tempting target. I already knew how that turned out, though, so there was nothing to do but wait. River kept his position by the door, and I positioned myself a few feet inside, in case we were able to get a drop on whoever came in next.

A scuffle broke out outside the door, nothing but quiet grunts and the sounds of shoes scraping alerting us to the change. When the door flung open, River lunged forward, prepared to defend us.

"Stop!" I shouted, something clicking in my brain as River made contact with the black-clad man.

Black-clad man. Not Excursion Team One.

The man defended, putting himself between River and whoever was outside, but River still landed a solid punch to his shoulder, knocking him back before he heard me.

They both froze, fists raised, chests heaving.

"Why are you here?" I asked, and another man in black appeared at the first's shoulder. His eyes were piercing, and I'd never forget them as long as I lived.

Hema.

"To speak with you, while the guards are detained. May we sit?"

Always so cultured, so reserved. River stood strangely stiff as he waited for me to answer.

"Yes, please come in. I can't say that this won't have consequences, though." I gestured vaguely to the hall, where I could see a booted foot sticking past the open doorway.

"Wouldn't it be better if we *left* instead of standing around talking?" River asked, and I couldn't help but agree. I needed to find out if Chace was still inside the walls, and then we needed to get the frack out of here. But . . . without Hema, neither of us would have been alive to make it this far. So, we'd talk.

"I am prepared to deal with the consequences," Hema said with a shrug.

"Okay." I gestured toward the table and resumed my seat.

He glided through the room, presence as calm as I remembered from the cave, when he'd saved my life.

We sat at a table, River and I on one side, Hema on the other. His man stood at his shoulder, dutifully ignoring us while constantly scanning for nonexistent threats. River was straight as a board, and a frisson of worry tingled down

11

my spine. They surely wouldn't have come all this way to cause trouble for him, would they?

They barely glanced his way, as if they didn't recognize him.

"Why are you here, Hema, really?"

"There is much you do not know. I find myself . . . unsure of how to tell you."

He was visibly hesitant, his eyes hooded. I didn't know what to say, so I stayed silent. Every muscle in my body was locked down tight, frozen between leaping into action and true calm.

He reached for his facial covering, and for a moment, I thought he was adjusting it—surely the thing was hot, and itched from time to time, though I'd never seen him touch his covering before—until the front panel dropped, revealing his face.

I stared in confused silence. How could a face I'd never seen before be *familiar*?

"Holy camel's humps. You two could be twins. How is that possible?" River asked, raking a hand through his blond locks and staring between us.

Hema nodded once, slowly, then re-covered his face with practiced fingers. "I am a bit too old to be her twin, but it is a question I asked myself, when I found you collapsed in the desert on my doorstep. A simple blood test from my medical team revealed the truth. You are my παιδί. My child."

My jaw dropped. I couldn't help it. Here, sitting across the table from me was a man who shared my face, and he was . . . my father?

"How—how is that possible?" I stammered, not processing quickly enough to ask a more elegant question.

His eyes dropped, and for the first time ever, I sensed discomfort from him.

"When I was a young man, and not yet the ηγέτης of the Nightbloods, I was a true nomad. Wandering from place to place, rootless. I had no family, no friends save one." He gestured behind him, to where his lone guard still pretended he couldn't hear his leader—best friend?—spilling his life secrets.

"We ran afoul of a gang, and barely made it out with our lives. We took the risk of approaching the nearest city, for we had no choice. Our wounds were grievous, requiring medical supplies. Back in those days, any new entry into the city was approved or rejected by the leader, a bald-headed man in a coyote jacket. He took one look at us, stripped us of all our coin, and assigned one of his kept women to look after us. Her name was Jaen, and she was kind to us."

Frackity-fracking-frack.

Jaen.

My mother.

"Nyx, you, uh, okay over there?" River rested a hand gently on my shoulder, but I flinched back from the contact. I didn't do this; I didn't break down in front of people. My trader mask was my greatest asset, and I had never fought so hard to wrench it back into place as I did now.

I ignored the hurt look on River's face as I straightened, because I couldn't handle his emotions *and* mine right then.

"So, you used her, like everyone else in her life?" I snapped, bitter. It was my only defense to the feelings threatening to pull me under. Later I might regret it. But I couldn't stop the words, not with all the willpower I possessed.

He looked ashamed, so I had my answer. I shoved back from the table with a loud screeching scrape and paced away from the table, unable to look at him another second. At those eyes so similar to my own.

I hated who Jaen was.

I hated how she put me aside, abandoned me to the streets to eke out an existence on the blade's edge of death.

I hated the way she looked through me, to the very end, instead of *at me*.

But she was a product of her life. The accumulation of every tiny abuse, every tiny stripping away of self, of worth. She was the husk that was left after the world took what it wanted, day in and day out, giving nothing back.

Empty survival was all she had left. For all I loathed her—loathed her life, loathed her for not having anything to give me except rejection and indifference—I still knew it wasn't her fault. Deep down, as an adult, I could see that the best she could do for me was to not sell me to a keeper. She didn't have anything left to give me, except a life on my own two feet.

Maybe one day, when the pain had all been drained away by time, I could find gratefulness for that. But now, all I felt was hate. Hate for another man who'd used my mother instead of helping her.

I dropped my hands to my hips and glared at the white wall. Hating its clean solidity. Hating everything about this place.

"It was not like that, Nyx. Your mother was a light in a very dark time. We came to care for each other, but in the end, I had to leave. I could not support myself, let alone afford her price, or help her care for her young son. We parted as friends, and I never knew of your existence. Not until I found you."

"You should leave," I whispered. I couldn't look at him.

"I understand. I will go. But first, I need you to hear me; now that I have found you, I will not allow them to harm you, to take you from me again. The Nightbloods are here. We have their city surrounded. We will breach this dome and take you by force if need be, but for now we're in negotiations to come along on the journey with you. It seems it would be beneficial to us all, if what they say is true."

"What they say about what? And where are they taking us?" River asked the questions that my throat was too clogged to ask. *Journey?*

"They are taking us underground, to the water generator. Our time grows short. Come, Rahlise." The sounds of shuffling feet and a door clicking softly shut didn't move me from my position.

It wasn't until River stepped up behind me, offering silent support but not touching me, that I turned, and let myself be folded into his arms. For the first time in the very long span of my life, I let my tears flow, and silently soaked the fabric of his shirt.

Three

WHEELING

I sat and stared numbly at the nearest wall, tired of pacing, completely over being shoved to the side like an object to be pulled out when I'm useful again. It was better than being one of King's favorite playthings, but not by much. River stood behind my chair, arms crossed and significantly more alert—but less on edge, as usual—than I was.

The door to the conference room slammed open. The commandant strolled in, flanked by two excursion team members I didn't recognize, and straightening his jacket cuff as he pointedly ignored us. It wasn't until he stood directly across the small table from us that he deigned to look up, acknowledging our presence.

"It's been a long day already, so I'll get straight to the point. We're about to undertake a journey, and your presence is required."

He stared straight at me, completely ignoring River's grunt of annoyance beside me.

I didn't respond because I could already tell it wasn't necessary. The commandant liked to hear himself talk, so if I waited, he'd tell me the pertinent bits on his own.

His jaw ticked as he waited for me to speak, but after a few long beats of silence he launched back into his speech as I expected.

"This is a joint mission. The space contingent has sent down a representative, as they're also interested in the outcome. What I need from you is a promise that you'll be a contributing party member along the way, and not cause problems."

Contributing sounded a lot like it meant *obedient* and I wasn't good with that.

"And why would I agree to that after you violated our last deal, and threw me back into your cell under guard?" I kept the words neutral, but it cost me dearly. My trader mask was firmly in place, but the aching numbness in my breastbone wouldn't be ignored forever.

"Believe it or not, that was for your protection."

"Are you fracking kidding me? Your goons were the ones *shooting people*, and you want to

18

claim protection?" River's outburst was explosive. He slammed both hands down on the table separating us from the commandant, the hollow sound ringing out and putting the guards on alert.

I moved quickly but silently, putting my hand on his knee under the table and squeezing gently, hoping he got the message to back off and let this play out. We needed information. You can't trade effectively if you don't know the other person's motivations, and I was getting *so close* to figuring it out.

The commandant's lip lifted in a sneer at River's outburst. "See, this? This is exactly what can't happen. You're *not* crucial to this mission, and I'm more than happy to take out the trash before we leave."

Fury boiled my guts at the insinuation that River was nothing more than trash, but I kept it locked down tight.

"But you won't do that, because you know that I can cause a lot more trouble than River." My stare was indifferent, but he flinched back, nonetheless.

I still didn't know *why* they needed my blood—a fact that rankled—but I knew it meant bargaining power. If I could figure out the *why*, then I'd have all the cards.

"There's no need for trouble. I've got a generous offer for you, and I think you'll both be pleased."

"Let's hear it."

River crossed his arms stonily over his chest, but kept his jaw clenched tightly shut.

"Yes, of course. Your brother will be freed, effective immediately." Commandant Kieran waved a hand as if this was a boring discussion and not our very lives on the line. "He can remain here, as a free citizen with River while we undertake the mission. You are also released from your prior obligation to deliver seed stock to Bastion City. You will be given a place as an equal member of the mission, and will receive credit as a member, to go down in history as one of the people who changed the trajectory of humanity's future."

"I see." I wasn't sure if I should be relieved at the confirmation that Chace was still securely inside the walls and hadn't been left outside alone in the midst of the chaos, or disappointed that he didn't make it out. He wouldn't be safe until we were out of these walls, and out from under Commandant Kieran's thumb.

"You don't look pleased, Nyx. Truly, I thought you would be overjoyed to have secured your brother's freedom, since that was your entire goal upon arrival. Has that changed, or are you concerned because your lover and your brother don't get along?" There was a sharp glint to his gaze, and I knew I had to tread more carefully. Any hint that I had my own plan to release Chace would have consequences for everyone involved. I didn't want blood on my hands; just my brother freed.

"Of course not, but I know a crap offer when I hear one, just like you knew it was crap when it spewed out of your mouth."

River barely suppressed a grin as he popped a hip and leaned against the table.

"I take offense—" Commandant Kieran began, but I held up a hand, stopping him in his tracks.

"Here's how this is going to go. Chace *and* River will also be given a place at my side on the mission. I don't know what it is you want from me yet, but I've got a feeling it'll be unpleasant, given your obsession with my blood. I'm not about to let them out of my sight—you keep locking us up."

He glared but gestured for me to go on.

"As equal members of the mission, I expect to be fully debriefed on what the mission is, alongside everyone else. And finally, as soon as the mission is completed, the three of us will be given our freedom. Immediately, with no further strings attached." I held his gaze, unblinking as I delivered my demands.

His jaw ticked, but he didn't look surprised. He was a self-important jerk, but he wasn't stupid.

"You realize this is entirely a gesture of good will; I don't have to give you anything. Under martial law, I can drug you and take you on this mission the same as my luggage, and you'd have no choice."

I drummed my fingers on my thigh under the table, the desire to pace again nearly overwhelming. It was true. He could have kept me drugged, so why didn't he?

An idea struck me. I cocked my head and studied him more closely.

He was arrogant as usual, yes. Perfectly dressed and styled, same as always. The guard was new, but there was something else *different* about him, and I couldn't put my finger on it. His shoulders were tense, his eyes tight at the corners.

Anxiety.

Was that because of the unrest in the city, though, or because of the spaceship? He wouldn't tell me, so I'd have to take a stab and hope for the best.

"If you could have kept me drugged and still completed your mission, you would have. It probably doesn't look good to have the spacefarers land, and find your house isn't in order. Rioting in the streets and blood on your hands doesn't say much about your skill as a leader, now does it?"

The commandant took a menacing step forward, his eyes narrowed to slits as he glared down his nose at me, while I remained seated at the table.

"You listen here, little girl. You don't know anything about me, or my people. You're a scrappy *nothing* from the Wastes, and when I'm done with you, you'll be right back out there until some gang-banger does us all a favor and dispatches you. I might even be willing to pull the strings to make it happen myself, if it meant I didn't have to listen to your lip anymore." He pulled his jacket sleeve down again—the motion sharper, more agitated this time.

"I think you struck a nerve, Nyx."

"Seems so. And I think he needs us to cooperate more than we need to cooperate."

"Yes, he does." River smiled, and later I'd chide him for letting his emotions play so freely on his face. But right now? Right now, I was reveling in figuring out the commandant's weakness, and didn't care.

"You'll have your man-friend and your brother on the journey. But remember, Nyx—one wrong move, and I can make all of your lives a living hell. You've put them directly in my line of fire, and if you make me look bad, I'll make sure you regret it."

He made a circling motion with two fingers to his guards, and they formed up to take him out of the room.

The door closed with a soft *snick* behind them. River turned to me with an incredulous look on his face.

"I don't know how you do it, but you can read people like nobody I've ever met before. You're something else." One side of his mouth lifted in a crooked grin, popping that dimple in his right cheek that always drew me in like a thirsting woman to a cool drink.

I shrugged one shoulder, embarrassed by the praise and the scrutiny. I wasn't used to anyone paying me such close attention. Nanette saved me from responding by pulling the door back open.

"Time to move."

I rose, and followed River out the door, possibilities and questions swirling in my head. Only time would tell the answers, and something in my gut told me that mine was running out, faster than sand in an hourglass.

Four

Space Rangers

To my surprise we were led, by a now-intact Excursion Team One, away from our cell. Instead, we continued down the hall to a twisting side-passage we hadn't been in since the very first day when we were taken to the decontamination chamber. My insides clenched at the reminder of *that* unpleasantry, but thankfully we were led past it. Gabriel palmed the scanner to let us into an even smaller passage, where the sounds of many people talking reached us.

We stopped about fifteen feet from a doorway being held open by another member of an excursion team. Gabriel turned to address us.

"I'm on strict orders from the commandant. You two are to blend into the group and act like you're honored to be here. If you cause *any* trouble, my team members will remove you from the meeting, and we drop the pretense."

And drop my brother . . . down a deep, dark hole, I'm sure.

"We understand."

He nodded, then led us through the doorway.

It was oddly reminiscent of the family dinner turned resistance meeting Morgan had brought us to just a few short weeks ago. Chairs filled the out-of-the-way space in tidy rows, most of them occupied. Except this time, there were plenty of heavily armed and armored people mixed into the crowd, instead of the hard working but simpler inhabitants of the lifeside.

We were ushered inside, but then our guards dispersed; only Nanette stayed near and led us to open seats in a row toward the back of the room.

No one paid us any mind, most of them already involved in intense conversation.

"I heard the commandant himself is coming," a uniformed man two rows in front of us said.

"That's absurd. The commandant never comes on missions. He likes to stay in his cushy apartment and let us all go out into danger for him," his companion argued.

Someone behind us pushed between me and River, completely unconcerned with invading our personal space, to interject, "Rainey's right. Kieran himself is coming along. But it's not out of the goodness of his heart. I heard the captain of the space vessel is a real ball-buster, and he wouldn't come if Kieran didn't."

"Good. It's ridiculous to put yourself up as a leader, throw the whole fracked city into chaos, and then hide in your office while *we* deal with the fallout. *Cowardly*, some might say."

"Some might be wise to keep their mouths shut," Nanette said, and all three of the uniformed men snapped straight in their seats.

"Yes, officer," they all said. It was in perfect time, like a creepy puppet master was pulling their strings simultaneously.

She sniffed, the sound indignant, but didn't give them any further attention.

A hush fell over the crowd, and when I looked up, a group of people in darkly gleaming metallic space suits were pouring in. They were taller than most, and every single one of them was trim and muscular. A fact I could tell because instead of the bulky white suits in pictures of the astronauts before the meteor strike, these were fitted and slim, skimming every plane of their perfect bodies. Every single one of them was armed with high-tech weapons, some strapped to thighs or hips, others with large grips sticking up over their shoulders from back harnesses.

It was intimidating, and suddenly I was glad to be a nameless face in the large crowd. The commandant's words from before, about me being *a scrappy little nothing from the Wastes* echoed in my mind. But I wasn't ashamed of who I was. Not of the scars on my body, or the hard life of survival that put them there.

I might not look like the next evolution of human biology, but I had grit, and it had gotten me farther in life than good looks ever could have. Nothing anybody said could take that from me.

River, though, could have been one of them, if he grew another inch or two and lost fifty pounds of muscle. The last one through the door was a woman, a stunning blonde with features chiseled from fine porcelain. One of the soldiers in front of us whistled low and elbowed his neighbor, nodding toward her.

But she didn't filter into the empty front row like the rest of her party. She crossed to the podium and met Commandant Kieran. They spoke a few quiet words, and then exchanged a handshake. They stood side by side as he addressed the crowd.

"My people, I thank you all for coming." He was reserved, much less flamboyant than his usual address style for crowds—at least that I'd seen. "It's my honor and pleasure to introduce you today to Captain Jacira. She has brought a contingent of her best and brightest, and through the rigors of this shared mission, we hope to forge a new bond between the people of space and earth."

There was a general rumbling of people shifting in seats. Some leaning forward in interest, some sitting bolt upright in surprise.

Captain Jacira beamed at us, but something about the expression was off. Her eyes were almost hungry, as she looked over us. "While we know it will not be easy accessing your water supply and repairing it, we have the most talented engineers in the universe. I have every confidence that we can pull it off, and build something beneficial here."

She paused for the smattering of applause, then continued, "We leave in twenty-four hours. Suits will be delivered to each of your accommodations when we arrive. Pack light, because there will be less than four hundred cubic inches per person of personal space."

"CK acting like we know what the camel's hump *four hundred cubic inches* is," one of the soldiers in front of us joked, and he and his companion burst into laughter. Sporadic laughter broke over the crowd, but I was watching the two leaders. Jacira's eyes had landed on the jokester. They were lit with a strange light as she sashayed down the aisle.

"What's your name, soldier?" There was an underlying purr to the words, clearly meant to draw him in, but I wanted nothing more than to *run*. Something was off with her, in a big way. The young man didn't get that, though, or he didn't care. He was on his feet in a flash, a sexy smile parting his lips.

"It's Xandy. The ladies call me Candy, though." He brushed a thumb over his bottom lip and winked at her.

"Candy—I like that. You must be *extra* sweet. I think I'd like you assigned to my personal vehicle . . . as long as you're amenable to that?"

"Hell yeah, I'll ride with you."

"Excellent." She smiled, the picture of innocence, and leaned forward. The room felt frozen as we all watched the strange exchange between this space captain and the young soldier.

Captain Jacira whispered something in his ear. When she pulled back, she caressed his neck tenderly, like one would a lover.

But all the joviality was gone from his face. His caramel skin had gone deathly pale, fear rounded his eyes, and all trace of the youthful cockiness had vanished.

He tried to take a step back, but her caress turned into a vice-like grip, her hand a claw-like vise on his neck. "What's wrong, Candy? I thought we understood each other," she purred again, sidling her body up against the front of his. She locked her left arm around his neck so he couldn't move, and then snapped toward the front row with her other hand.

"Alix. What is four hundred cubic inches, in earth terms? Give *Candy* here an idea."

One of her people sprang lithely to his feet and held up his hands less than a foot apart. "Four hundred cubic inches is roughly the size of a standard rations box, Captain."

"Excellent, Alix." She gestured for him to take his seat. All the sensual purring was gone from her voice—nothing but cold, hard threat left behind when she spoke again. "You see, Candy, I'm new to earth. So, I don't know how things are run around here. But where we're from? Incompetence has consequences."

With speed I could barely track, she shook her right hand; the sparkle of something appearing inside it was all I could catch before she whipped it up, and then Candy was screaming as blood poured down the side of his face. A wet plop drew my eyes down to the floor, where the top half of his ear lay limply. Bile burned the back of my throat as I looked away.

"You'll need to get that seen to before we leave," she tutted and released him, taking a few steps back to watch as two other soldiers rallied around Xandy, quickly hauling him out the exit and hopefully straight to medical. His screams echoed in the tiny hallways, and nobody moved as the sounds faded.

Captain Jaric strode back to the front of the room to resume her position next to Commandant Kieran. His expression was grim as she wiped what I now saw was a glowing blade against the material of her pants, before sliding it back up inside the sleeve of the suit.

"Where were we, Commandant?"

"Mole assignments will be given when you arrive tomorrow. Be at bay six by nine a.m. Dismissed."

Motion resumed like a dam breaking, a small trickle followed by everyone leaving at once, anxious to get away from the captain.

I exchanged grim looks with River as we escaped into the hallway. Commandant Kieran was one thing, but Captain Jacira? She was deadly.

Five

STUMBLING

R iver and I had little to no personal possessions—inside the city, at least—so packing was a breeze. I only owned one spare set of under-clothing, so *in* that went. I wore the locket—so it didn't take up any of my miniscule allotment of space for personal items—and slipped my Bronco key into my under-shorts pocket. Even though we were going underground, I wasn't parting with that for any reason. Because yes, they delivered actual boxes to our room. If it didn't fit, it didn't get to make the journey.

Half an hour after the meeting, we had both collapsed to our backs on the rug to talk and stare at the ceiling, trying to process the strange events of the day. Our elbows touched, and the tiny bit of contact did something to my insides.

"So, your 'dad,'" River said. "How are you feeling about that?"

My mind had been spinning in circles ever since Hema's big reveal, and I still wasn't sure how I felt about him.

"I feel like 'dad' is maybe a stretch. I don't know the man, so—" I blew out a long breath, trying to find words to voice the mixed-up knot of emotions that had replaced the emptiness behind my breastbone. "I don't know. I mean, I guess I'm glad he's alive. That's how I'm feeling. Glad he's not a skeleton out in the desert somewhere. Also, confused about why he's here."

"Fair enough. Do you not think he's really here to get the water generator technology for the people outside the city?"

A thought occurred to me, and I flipped onto my side, so I could see River's face better. "I don't know how that could even work. Generators make electricity, not water. But you were part of the Nightbloods. Did you know Hema? How is he as a person?"

He rolled to mirror my position, and I stared into his eyes, the clear blue sucking me in, as always.

"I only knew him by reputation, and . . ."

"It's okay, River, I'm not fragile. You can tell me the truth."

He gave me a sad smile. "I know you're not fragile, Nyx. You're the strongest person I know.

That doesn't make any of this *easy*, and I wish you'd beat yourself up a little less. It feels like you're pulling away from me, and I want you to know that you don't have to. You *can*, but you don't have to. I'm not going anywhere."

The lump that rose in my throat at his words was really fracking inconvenient.

"You can't say that, though, can you?" I rolled onto my back, breaking the eye contact between us. It was too intense, too close. Staring at the ceiling was safer.

"Of course I can. Why couldn't I?" He reached over and twined his fingers with mine, tugging gently until I reluctantly looked back over.

"Because *everyone* leaves." Hot shame and embarrassment flooded me. What a thing to admit. *Everyone leaves.* The worst, most horrible thing wasn't how hard it was to survive in the Wastes. It wasn't the heat or the hunger or the thirst.

It was that simple, knife-in-the-gut truth.

Everyone leaves. Even if they didn't want to.

"Nyx, come here."

"No, River. I don't need you to coddle me!" I shoved away the well-muscled arm that tried to scoop me up, but he was persistent, not put off by my halfhearted efforts to shoo him away.

He swept past my batting hands, looping his arm around my waist, and sliding me over so that I was pressed against his chest.

He stroked the back of my tightly balled fist as he spoke. "You're right, and you're wrong." The words were soft, ruffling my hair, and I held my breath as I waited for him to continue.

"There are some things I can't control. I could get killed tomorrow. I could be forcibly separated from you. The whole dang city could collapse and fall down around our ears. All of that's outside of my control, as much as it is yours. But where you're wrong, is that I don't *want* to leave. You don't scare me, Nyx. I know you've had a hard life—hell, who hasn't anymore? But it's not *coddling* you to be by your side through the hard times. It doesn't make you weak to lean on me, any more than it makes me weak to lean on you."

Didn't it, though? All my life I'd had to stand on my own two feet. Chace was the only exception; he had been the only shield between me and the bitter realities of being a lone woman in the desert. Having had him taken from me—stolen from under my nose back in Coyote Springs—was a wound I wasn't ready to examine this closely yet.

It was piled on top of a lifetime of hurts, big and small. Never knowing my father. My mother abandoning me to the streets when I was seven. Hoss—the only man I ever *considered* before River—wanting to own me, not love me. Every other man saw me as a *possession*, not a living breathing person with thoughts and feelings.

It made me feel small.

That difference was why I was so drawn to River. He'd never treated me like less. Less than a man, less than a free woman, less than him. We were equals. On a level playing field, no matter the situation. And maybe that was the real truth behind why I was pulling back from him. Because something about the way he was standing up for me, trying to protect me . . . it made me feel weak.

And I couldn't afford to feel weak.

But should I? Was he right? Was it *okay* for him to help me, and could I allow him to without feeling like I was somehow less?

I didn't know.

"I don't want to push you away. But maybe that hurts less than you leaving."

He sighed, and cupped my face in his big, warm palm. His thumb was gentle as it stroked over my cheekbone, his eyes sincere when they bored into mine. It felt like he saw every bit of me that I tried to hide, every flaw, every weakness, straight down to my soul. But he still didn't pull away.

"Nyx, I've fallen in love with you. You are the one bright spot in this sucky world. And I don't care what our day holds, I don't care what crap sandwich the world tries to feed us next. If I'm with you, we'll figure it out. And you can push and deflect and not let me get close, if that's what you want. But I'm not going anywhere. Not unless you look me dead in the eyes, and tell me to go, that you don't want to be with me anymore. Because I love you. And love means sticking it out, even when it's hard."

My mouth was dry, my throat more barren than the whole sand-filled pit that was the Wastes.

He loved me.

I threw my arms around him, words completely failing me. He rubbed my back, the gentle circles soothing in a way I didn't understand. And I let him, because he loved me.

And even if I wasn't ready to admit it, I was pretty sure I loved him, too.

The sound of the door being flung open pulled us from our bubble, and I groaned. It wasn't the normal mealtime, so whatever the guards wanted, it wouldn't be good.

"Couldn't you people just leave us alone for like . . . a day?" I groused, loath to leave River's arms.

"Not the reception I expected, but then again, I also didn't expect to find you shacked up with some guy while I was imprisoned."

Chace's cold tone had me springing off the ground with speed I didn't know I possessed. We stared at each other for a heartbeat before I threw myself at him, our arms tangling briefly before squeezing each other in a bone-rattling hug.

"You're here? What . . . They locked us in here and I didn't know—"

"I was informed that you negotiated to have me dragged along on a mission. I don't care what it is, it'll be better than being stuck in the chain gang."

Chace pulled back, studying my face intently before looking over my shoulder at River, who now stood awkwardly, watching our reunion.

"I'm so sorry I couldn't get you out sooner. I tried, but then—"

"A spaceship landed? Yeah, that tidbit made it all the way to the peons breaking the rocks."

"Yeah. That. And I don't think we're out of the dunes yet, but I don't know if I care, as long as they keep their word and let you come with us." I squeezed him again, scared to let him go, scared to *breathe* wrong, in case he vanished again.

Eventually he got tired of me squishing him, and tickled my ribs until I let go, swatting at his hands.

"So . . . you going to introduce me to your man, for real this time and without the guard's uniform?" He cocked an eyebrow and stared at River expectantly.

Six

BLOODY SHIELD

"I — Yes. Of course. River, this is Chace, my brother. Chace, this is River, my—" I paused, brain blanking on what to call him. Boyfriend felt wildly inadequate yet also somehow embarrassing to declare. We hadn't discussed what we were to each other, and calling him a friend felt dismissive. What the heck did you call the guy you'd traveled through the desert with, whose life you'd saved and who'd saved your life, but also you had feelings for and had slept with exactly once?

River stepped forward and extended his hand, an easy grin on his face. "I'm her boyfriend. It's nice to meet you, man. You should know your sister has been single-minded about finding you, and she's been through hell and a half to find you."

Chace stared at River's hand, letting it hang awkwardly in the air.

"How did you two meet, boyfriend? I don't recognize you, so I know you're not a Sidewinder, and yet that tattoo says you are." He nodded to River's forearm, where the cottonmouth leered threateningly.

"Chace! Don't look at him like that. We met in the Wastes, okay? He had some bad history with the Nightbloods, and the tattoo was, well—"

"Hey, it's okay, Nyx. I can explain myself." He settled a warm hand on my shoulder, giving me a little squeeze.

Chace glared at the touch. "Why don't you do it with your hands *off* my sister, huh?" He let his shoulder bag drop to the floor with an ominous thud.

River tensed, but didn't drop his hand. "Hey man, I've got no issues with you right now, but your sister is a grown woman, and I'm not going to stop touching her unless *she* asks me to."

Chace's eyes bored into mine, and the disappointment I could see carved on his familiar features felt like a knife to the gut. Of all the things I expected when I finally got him back, it certainly wasn't this.

"What is the problem, Chace? River has been a true friend to me for months now while we looked for you. I don't understand why you're so mad to find I'm not alone!"

"You think he's the first dickhead to come sniffing around you over the years? No! He's just the first leech that got to you without me to stand in the way. I'm disappointed you couldn't see through that, Nyx. You're *special*, okay? You've got the chance to make something different for yourself, find real freedom. What happened to that dream? Me and you, going north. Instead, I'm gone for *five minutes* and you're shacked up with the first pretty face that doesn't try to shackle you up? News flash, Nyx: that's still coming. Any minute now, he'll show his true colors."

I staggered back a step, horrified by the venom in my brother's tone, how he saw my relationship with River—everything. If he'd whipped out his boot knife and stabbed me in the gut, I couldn't have been more surprised than I was right now.

"I would *never* hurt Nyx. And she's been very clear what she wants in life—and only an idiot would think she'd accept being kept. By anyone, even *you*," River said, uncharacteristic ice in his tone as he stepped toward Chace.

"What the hell did you just say to me?"

"You heard me. You're mad because she's living on her own terms, and it turns out she didn't need you to be her keeper, any more than she needed anyone else. She's capable, and strong, and she's done fine with you locked up."

"You arrogant bastard. I'm not her keeper, I'm her *shield*. You know how hard it is to keep a free woman free? She was seven when I started looking after her. I was nine. Nine years old when I had to start fighting off *grown men* who wanted to snatch her out from under my nose. I had to drag her on jobs into the Wastes to keep her from getting stolen while I worked to keep us in water credits. I was barely ten when I had to kill the first one who thought he could take her, and I was lucky if three or four months passed before the next one showed up thinking he was bad enough to do what the ones before him had failed to do, and I'd have to get my hands bloody again. But I've got news for you, dipstick—none of them succeeded, and you won't either. I'll take the blood, and the pain, and hurt—I'll take it all and then some to keep her free of the hell-hole life our mother lived."

Nausea, hot and thick, threatened to consume me. How did I not know this? I knew Chace looked out for me, but I didn't know he'd been *killing for me*. Blood rushed in my ears, the room seeming to narrow around me as I let his words sink in. How many men's blood was on his hands for me?

"Why didn't you say anything, Chace? I had no idea" My words were quiet, those of a broken little girl, not the strong woman I was today.

Chace held me by the shoulders, eyes burning with regret and sorrow. "You think I wanted to put that on you? No! I protected you then, and I'll protect you with every breath I have left. You don't need this guy, Nyx. He's just a distraction. When we head north—"

"I'll be at her side. I've told her, and I'll tell you. I'm not out to use and abuse your sister. We're in this together, and I hope you can accept that. If she wants me gone, she can say the words. But until then, I'm never leaving her again. You don't have to believe me, but you do have to respect her wishes."

The two men I cared most about in the world squared off, glaring like one of them was about to throw a punch, and I knew I had to do something.

I stepped between them, laying a hand on each of their chests and shoving them back a step. Chace tried to maneuver me to the side, but I held my ground, looking back and forth between them.

"Chace, I know this is hard, but I need you to trust me, like I've always trusted you. I'm sorry, *so sorry*"—my voice cracked, and I had to clear my throat to continue—"that you had to do that for me. I didn't know, and I owe you my life. But I *also* owe River my life."

Chace stiffened under my palm, finally dropping his gaze to mine. I continued, "I wouldn't

45

be *alive* right now, let alone standing here with you, if it wasn't for him. Do you understand that? He's never once suggested that he should be my keeper. And we're equals. Truly. I hope you know me well enough that I'd never accept anything less. You taught me better. You taught me to value myself, and I do, Chace. I promise I do."

I sucked in a fortifying breath, and forced myself to say the words I knew he needed to hear. "I love him, Chace." River froze, his heart hammering a mile a minute under my palm. "This is not a fling, or a manipulation."

Chace's eyes closed and he rocked back on his heels at my words.

"Don't pull away from me, Chace. We all need to work together if we're going to get out of here alive. So much has happened since you've been gone. Will you sit down with us, and let me tell you? Explain it all?"

"Fine. But I'm not sold, Nyx. You need to know that." He looked over my shoulder at River then, a new resolve in his eyes. "I'm going to be keeping an eye on you, and if you take one step out of place, I'll put a knife in you just like all the arrogant bastards that came before you."

"I love your sister, and I have no intention of being anything but friends with you." River was steady; calm, even, in the face of Chace's ire. He once again extended his hand, and I let out a relieved breath when Chace reluctantly shook it. He dropped it like it burned him, but it was still a step in the right direction.

We all sat, River on the edge of the bed while Chace and I took the two chairs across from each other. And I told him everything, making sure to keep my voice low and my back to the camera, should anyone decide to try reading lips. All the things I hadn't had time to say before, in the tiny room where we had been under observation. About my huge score, the journey south, Chrysanthe's home, Hema saving me from dehydration, running into River. How the Bronco got struck by lightning and upgraded by Hog; then how River and I found Wolf Well together; that Bastion City had bombed Coyote Springs and we didn't know who besides Marl was still alive.

The part where we escaped the Nightbloods by River pretending to be my kept man got an eyebrow raise, and by the time I told him about the Red Riders and their many wounded, his mouth was set into a grim line.

River squeezed my hand as I finished the harrowing tale with our time inside Bastion City, the resistance, and Hema's shocking revelation that he was my father.

A single quirk of his eyebrow was Chace's only reply.

"Yeah."

Chace leaned back in the chair, arms flung wide over the sides, a brooding look on his face as he considered me and River, and the way we'd gravitated together through the telling.

"It probably makes me a selfish bastard, but I'm glad you found me, Nyx."

"There was never any other option." I smiled, but emotional exhaustion weighed down my shoulders.

"I know." He smiled back, the familiar expression softening the hard edge that had been on his face since he'd walked in and found me with River. "It sounds to me like there's more than speculation to the idea that you're Chrysanthe's real descendant."

"It's such a long shot, Chace. And even if I am, I don't see why it matters. They already let us in and exiled two of their elderly citizens to make room for us." A lump rose in my throat at the terrible memory.

"I can see you putting that on your shoulders, Nyx, and it wasn't your fault. The commandant killed them, not you."

"I know, but it was *because* of us, River."

"For once, I agree with him. The decisions of evil men aren't your fault." Chace shifted in his seat, steepling his fingers together. "What we need now is a plan. I don't trust that they'll honor the deal they made with you. Whatever reason they need a descendant of Chrysanthe's,

I can't believe they'll really let you go when this is all over. For now, we'll have to stick together, and make sure they can't separate us again. And any chance we get to find out more, we have to take it."

I nodded, but I had no idea how we'd manage it. "We've been cut off from all of our contacts ever since the spaceship landed. We might not know anyone on the journey besides our guards, and they've got no particular love for us."

River snorted. "We're not particularly easy to guard."

Chace cracked a smile at that. "Good. They *should* have to work for it. We'll figure something out, but for now I think we could all use a good night's sleep."

"Agreed. We've only got two beds, though." I looked mournfully at the single-width bunks, knowing that even if we wanted to share we'd never fit two to a bed.

"I'll take the floor tonight," River offered, dropping a casual kiss on the top of my head. I ducked my head to hide the blush burning in my cheeks at my brother's disgruntled stare and hurried into the bathroom to clean my teeth.

As soon as it clicked shut, I pressed my shoulders back into the cool metal, and my eyes fell shut. It was going to be a major adjustment having Chace and River in the same space, and we were about to go on a mystery mission, under guard.

What could possibly go wrong?

Seven

SUBTERRANEAN

A bevy of shiny hover vehicles waited at the eastern edge of Bastion City. It was already hot, though we'd been escorted here as soon as the sun rose. The crowd of people waiting was larger than I'd expected, based on the meeting, and we were funneled to the front of it. I saw plenty of marshmallow-suit-wearing soldiers, as well as the sleeker suits of the spacefaring contingent. What I really didn't expect to see was nearly forty black-clad Nightbloods.

Had Hema successfully negotiated to be let on the trip? I couldn't imagine what he'd had to use as leverage, but the man held many secrets.

My father.

A fact Chace hadn't seemed surprised at yesterday. I glanced over at him, standing two feet away from me. His arms were crossed tightly over his chest, the white jumpsuit he wore a stark indicator that he didn't belong with all the soldiers jogging back and forth, loading supplies into the vehicles. He watched them all with an eagle eye; a quick glance at River found him doing much the same on my other side.

I was bookended by the two of them—my bodyguards—inside the ring of *actual* guards formed by Excursion Team One. It rankled after being independent for so long, but they meant well, so I tried not to be annoyed. Mostly, I was just glad to have them both with me and safe, even if they were suffocating me.

A mechanical bell intoned once, twice; and people started funneling into the vehicles like ants into an anthill.

"This way. We're in the third transport," one of the soldiers told us, jerking his head toward the front of the line, indicating we should follow. A last look over my shoulder showed that the Nightbloods didn't move, and weren't funneling into the vehicles.

Maybe he failed at negotiating to get brought along?

I wasn't sure whether I should be happy or sad about that.

The transports were cramped, clearly carrying more people than originally designed for. The seats had all been removed, so we all stood, holding onto overhead loops, and I ended up wedged in next to a window between River and one of our guards' shoulders. There wasn't any-where to put our small bags, either, so we con-tinued to hold them as it rocked into motion.

"I don't know how long this mission is, but if this is how we're traveling, I have to hope it'll be short," Chace muttered under his breath, glaring at the rest of the transport's occupants.

"This part's only about an hour." A weirdly jovial voice filtered through the tightly packed bodies, but I couldn't see who spoke. I wasn't short for a woman, but in this crowd, I may as well have been a toddler.

"That's good to know," I said back in the gen-eral direction of the voice.

"Excuse me. Yes, I'm trying to get over there. Could you just, ah— Oof!" A short, bespectacled man in a silver space suit nearly bowled me over as he popped free of the crowd.

"Oh, good, I was hoping it was you." He shoved his glasses up his nose and squinted at me while nodding. "Yes, it is you. Nyx Brandt, right?"

"Uhm, yes?"

"Oh dear, did I get it wrong? Apologies. But I'll keep standing here, if it's all the same to you. I got quite a few dirty looks getting over here, and in my experience it's best not to rock the ship when you're the smallest on board."

"No, no—I'm Nyx. And you are . . . ?"

"Oh! Wonderful. I'm Guffey. Bernard Guffey, engineer extraordinaire at your service!" He sneezed into his sleeve, then offered me his hand to shake.

"Nice to meet you, Guffey." I shook his hand gingerly, trying to ignore the damp sneeze overspray I could feel on my palm. "I admit, I'm confused how you've heard of me, though. I'm nobody special." My smile felt tight, but he didn't seem to notice. River watched our interaction, lips twitching in amusement as he tried not to smile.

Being *notorious* was akin to a death sentence, in the Wastes. So, the fact that someone presumably from space knew me by name was worrisome.

Though he was possibly the nicest, strangest fellow I'd ever met. Three inches of salt-and-pepper hair poked out from his head all willy-nilly, and he seemed wholly unconcerned with the somber attitude inside the shuttle. Even Chace glowering over my shoulder at him didn't seem to faze him.

"Nobody special! Why, you're the only known living descendant of Chrysanthe Kokinos-Diaz, the brightest engineering mind to live since the crash! Please tell me you share your progenitor's knack for engineering." His eyes pled with mine, larger than they should have been behind his round frames when he looked up at me.

"I'm sorry to disappoint, Guffey, but I know nothing about engineering." His shoulders fell, and I hurried to add, "Unless you count break-ing it. I'm pretty good at breaking stuff."

That did not cheer him up. "Oh, dear. Well, I'm afraid our journey to the aquifer just got one thousand times more difficult. Neverthe-less, you may have a latent talent, and just think, I shall be the one to pull it out in you! You'll be a grand challenge." He sneezed again and lifted his glasses to wipe watering eyes.

"You know what they don't tell you in space? That earth is positively teeming with allergens. It's horrendous. Once we fix the water supply, I believe I shall petition to be taken back up, post-haste."

Shock rocked through me, and I gaped at the strange man. Aquifer? Water supply? "Did you just say *fix* the water supply? That's not even possible, is it? Also, what's an aqui—"

The transport rocked violently, and ground to a halt. The *literal* ground met us a sec-ond later as the transport touched down with a none-too-gentle cracking sound that sent me sideways into River's arms. He caught mc, steadying me before letting me go.

Please walk calmly to the nearest exit. Emer-gency protocol activated. Please walk calmly to the nearest exit. Emergency protocol activated.

The AI-voice repeated its message, ground-level lights flickering as they came on all around the shuttle. As an apprehensive murmur rose, and people began shifting on their feet in the tightly confined space.

"Nobody move, nobody panic! We had to come to an emergency stop, but we're not disembarking." The authoritative tone from the driver's compartment had the soldiers around us at ease, but not our little group.

I turned away from Guffey toward the window at my back, and gasped at what I saw.

Chace swore under his breath. "Nightbloods. *Thousands* of them. We've got to get out of this tin can."

Gabriel pointed an accusing finger at his chest. "Don't try it, dirt-boy. You're not crucial to this mission, and if you cause trouble, we'll be more than happy to drop you back into this forsaken sand-pit."

I ignored the standoff that ensued between them, instead doing mental math as my gaze skipped down the line of Nightbloods—their black linen clothing whipping in the wind—forming a line across the dunes as far as I could see. There were so many of them—*too many* of them. They stood, weapons in hand, in front of numerous trucks and transports of their own.

This had to be Hema's doing. I looked up at River, then over at Chace, and wondered if Hema was on their minds, too.

Was Hema really here for me? Or was it something else? And why had he brought so many of his people? Bastion City blew people up for *no* reason, and here he'd trotted his people out and put them directly into the line of fire. It didn't make sense.

"This is not good, Nyx." River's words were low, an inch from my ear. "If a fight breaks out, we should head back, try to get to the Bronco."

I nodded, too overwhelmed by the enormity of what was going on around us to speak. An elbow to my ribs broke me out of my shocked trance.

"Pardon, I'd like to see— Oh. Oh my." Guffey pressed his forehead to the glass, trying to get a better view. "Are these native desert dwellers? Very interesting. You wouldn't think anyone would willingly wear black in this heat, but it seems to be what they've adopted as a society. Do you know the name of this particular group? Are they friendly?"

"Nightbloods," Chace spat. "And no, they're not friendly. They'll cut your throat as soon as look at you."

Not Hema, a little voice whispered in the back of my mind. But I didn't say it out loud; didn't air that connection when surrounded by Bastion soldiers.

"Oh look, one of them is heading this way." Guffey pointed, and I craned to see who was approaching.

It was impossible to know from this distance, but I'd bet my last water credit it was Hema. He walked with his head high, not bothered by the sands shifting and sliding under his feet. He was bold and strong, and some deep part of me felt a sense of pride that he was my father.

It made no sense, none whatsoever, given what I knew of both him and the Nightbloods, but it was still there, a tiny coal burning in my chest.

I couldn't bear to put it out, and that was the crux of it. Jaen was gone, and even alive she'd never been family. But if Hema was really going to show up, shouldn't I give him a chance?

I didn't know.

He walked out of sight of our window, and the transport was too packed to cross to the other side to see more. I gritted my teeth as I waited for the people on the hill to move, to attack, to get blown up—but none of that happened. Time ticked on, every muscle in my body tense, until the Nightbloods began to pull back, the impassable line parting.

The speaker overhead crackled to life. "All right, folks. Our last few transport vehicles have joined the fray, and we're back on our way. T minus thirty minutes until disembarkation."

Joined the fray? He's really negotiated to come along.

My mind whirled with the what and why and how, but there was no one to ask, so I kept them to myself. Only time would tell what Hema's intentions were, and what the future would hold.

Our hovercraft sped over the Wastes until we rocked to a stop just under an hour later. The doors slid open and soldiers filed out in an orderly fashion, but Guffey stayed with us, hanging back.

"I believe the four of us are slated to ride together, so I'll wait with you, if you don't mind." He adjusted his spectacles before giving us a questioning look.

Chace scowled but didn't protest, too busy scanning out the open doorway for some nonexistent chance to escape.

"May as well, until they herd us where we're meant to be." River's jovial tone had Guffey giving him a wide smile.

"Too true, too true."

When it was no one but us and Excursion Team One, one of them gestured for us to go first.

What I saw on the other side blew my mind. In all my life of wandering the desert, I'd never seen anything like it—the gaping maw of a great rocky cave sloping down into the earth. The roof was smooth rock which blended into the surroundings, but inside, the walls were natural, tan stone. Bumpy and rough, uncarved by mankind. The floor was a level road with piles of stone on the edges, dusty red grit coating much of them.

Rugged vehicles with nubby tires waited at the mouth of the cave. These vehicles were smaller but more numerous than the transports we'd been squeezed into.

Chace laid a hand on the back of my arm, eyes peeled and calculating. I knew *exactly* what he was thinking—one of those could get us out of here, back to the Bronco and then away, to freedom. But Excursion Team One didn't give us a second to breathe, let alone escape, before forming up in a tight circle around us. We were escorted to the front of the group.

"The UTVs are smaller than the transports, so your group is going to be split. Nyx and River, you'll be over here with half of us." Gabriel rested his hand on one of the black-and-tan UTVs. "Chace and Guffey, you're riding there, with the rest of your escort. You'll have line of sight the entire trip, until we reach base camp." His tone brooked no nonsense, and we didn't fight it. Curiosity warred with fear as we climbed into the UTVs. The bucket seats had five-point harnesses, which we warily strapped ourselves into. The road looked wide and flat, so why all this fuss?

River settled in next to me and squeezed my hand. We were both silent as we watched the huge crowd of soldiers, spacefarers, and black-clad Nightbloods load into the UTVs. Within minutes, the lead vehicle pulled out, and we slotted in right behind it. A quick glance over my shoulder showed Chace's UTV right behind ours, and we locked eyes for a second before I turned back around, too curious about what was ahead to keep looking back.

In no time at all, the ever-burning sun faded, swallowed up by the dim interior of the cave.

Eight

Shaken, Not Stirred

M y heart pounded and my palms sweated as the road wound deeper and deeper into the earth. Lights were spaced overhead every few feet, but something in my brain kept going, *what if those fail? What if the lights go out?*

What if, what if, what if...

The farthest I'd ever been underground before was the time I fell through the mall roof, and that familiar fear was spiking through me as we continued our steady trek underground. Tunnels branched off every so often, but we never turned.

"Would you look at that," River said, pointing to his side. Part of the cavern went up so high, we couldn't see the top. There had been a collapse at some point; rocks were piled willy-nilly wherever they landed, and the sight made my blood run cold. All that cold, heavy rock, and it was looming over our heads right now.

"This doesn't freak you out at all?" I asked River, my voice sounding thin.

"No, it's pretty sweet. And do you feel how cool it is? I could totally be a cave man."

He was right, it was cool. The feeling washed over me, my skin pebbling as if my body had belatedly realized it as well. The smell was strange, too. My pulse slowed as it all started to sink in, and nothing terrible happened to me.

I could still feel the *weight* of all that rock overhead, but my eyes had adjusted, and I looked at my surroundings with new clarity.

"What are those black dots on the ceiling between the lights?" I ask.

River shrugged. "No idea. Do any of you know?" He looked around at our guards, who mostly ignored us. But one turned, propping his arm on the back of the seat so he could see us.

"Communication nodes. The rock is so thick where we're heading, without the repeaters there's no way to get any signal to the surface. I'm Perry, by the way."

We exchanged nods, and he turned back around. It was weird thinking of our guards as individuals, because up until now, they'd been stony-faced sentinels, silent and unbending.

Though, to be fair, we hadn't *tried* to strike up a friendship with any of them. Maybe that had been a mistake.

River and I exchanged a long look, but his eyes dropped to my water meter. I was confused for a second, but then he worked his jaw, and I realized the wordless message he was sending me. I had a comm device built into my water meter with a connection to the Sidewinders, and he still had the dental-implant radio which contacted the Red Riders. They were both across the desert by now, but . . . *would they be able to help us? Could something we would learn down there help them?*

I gave him a subtle nod, so he knew I'd caught on. Hopefully somewhere along this journey, we would have enough privacy to make use of our resources.

We zipped along until the pavement ended, smooth road giving way to bumpy rock, and the twisting of natural cave formations. We slowly wound around and down, teeth jarring until I gave up and clenched my jaw, trying to stop it.

I couldn't tell you how long it took or how far we'd traveled over the rough terrain, only that by the time we stopped, my head was *pounding*. Exiting the UTVs and being able to stand and stretch was a luxury, though none of us were very excited at the pervasive chill in the air down here. Even River was subdued, rubbing his lower back as he looked around the cave.

"Is this it?" I asked Perry, the guard who stood closest to us as everyone stretched, bending over and reaching high overhead.

He laughed. "No, but we are about halfway to the base. This is the only spot from here out that's wide enough for us to park, and use the facilities." He pointed across the small cavern to a couple of doors. A part of my body I'd been studiously ignoring decided to remind me it existed and was none too pleased about being jarred around all morning.

We made quick use of the bathrooms, the water in the sinks shockingly cold. I was shivering when I walked out, my breath puffing strangely in the air.

Our guards escorted us to where Chace and Guffey waited. The engineer was talking a mile a minute.

"Do you see the striations in the walls? Those are different types of sediment, which are typically water resistant. Much of this cavern and tunnel would have once been limestone, and was slowly washed away by the rain over the course of millennia, back when rain was still a regular occurrence. The ceiling appears to be shale, which is why it's so flat. Some caves made of different minerals form long, pointed structures, called stalactites and stalagmites. It's possible we'll see some of that, but this cave is rather dry. You can still taste the minerals in the air, though, if you try."

He sucked in several deep breaths through his mouth and gestured for us to do the same.

"The air does smell strange down here," I said, trying to be friendly.

I'd never met a person as effusive as Guffey and wasn't quite sure how to act around him.

"That's the minerals! It was once believed to be quite good for you, to breathe in cave air. Now we know that there are also pockets of trapped gas that can be quite deadly. Though I assume the path we're traveling has been tested and found safe, otherwise we'd be in enclosed suits." He quirked an eyebrow as he looked around, as if waiting for someone to confirm, but Excursion Team One was once again ignoring us.

"Are we allowed to switch up the seating arrangements?" Chace asked, a wry expression on his face as he pointed to me.

"You have to stay two and two, but yes you're allowed to swap," Gabriel answered this time.

"Great. Nyx—"

"Oh, I'm afraid I *must* monopolize your sister. I want to quiz her on her knowledge of engineering. See how much she shares with her brilliant ancestor."

Chace rolled his eyes and shot a questioning look at River. River shrugged, but didn't step away from my side.

"I was quite disappointed, you see, to find that you and Chace are only *half* siblings. Such a shame. He has *no* interest in engineering, can you believe that? I'm sure you and I will have much more to talk about." Guffey looped his arm through mine, already talking a mile a minute about something called *karst* and how he was quite certain that he could calculate the *something* about this cavern if he only had an hour and a *something*-ometer.

It was all flying over my head, but I nodded along, trying to follow him.

"Oh boy, this is going to be a fun trip," Perry muttered from the seat in front of us as the driver pulled back into line after the lead car. I resumed jaw clenching, but Guffey barely slowed his lecture as the bouncing and bucking of the UTV resumed.

My body had gone numb from sheer necessity, by the time we rolled to another stop and got out. Everything that wasn't numb hurt, I was starving, and the roof of my mouth felt scuzzy. I did appreciate the facilities again, but the cold was seeping into my bones. I needed a tooth tablet, a meal bar, and the almost-horizontal Bronco seat, *stat.*

Unfortunately, we were in yet another cavern with the Bronco nowhere in sight and the temperature was still dropping. I scanned the ever-present overhead lights and wondered if they gave off any heat. As soon as I unclenched my jaw, my teeth began to chatter.

Guffey turned to me and said, "Oh dear, you don't have much padding on you. We'll have to get you into a thermal suit quickly. I'm sure they've got one around here somewhere." He patted me on the shoulder, and I could only consider the gesture to be fatherly. That thought sent my eyes skittering over his head until I found the group of Nightbloods at the very back of the pack. None of the rest of the party acknowledged or spoke to them. They stood loosely, but also on alert as they eyed the cave.

And me, I realized. A startling number of them had their eyes trained on *me* and not the cave.

Perry approached and pointed to a bend in the cavern, pulling me back to our conversation. "All of the thermal gear is inside your tent, and they've been pre-assigned. We're going to be waiting here a few days while the details are sorted out for the last leg of the journey."

We waited for River and Chace's group to also unload before heading that way. River wrapped his arm around me immediately, and I had to resist the urge to burrow into his side to soak in the warmth as we walked. I *did* dig my fingers in under the hem of his shirt, the tiny skin contact helping some of the feeling come back.

Maybe it was the cold, as much as the endless jarring, that had made my body go numb.

"I'm really not looking forward to spending the night down here," I said, the fabric of River's shirt swallowing the words.

"Ah, don't worry. I'll warm you up. It won't be so bad."

"Gross," Chace said under his breath.

"Pipe down. You've had girlfriends." I jabbed an accusing finger over my shoulder at him.

"Yeah, sure, but you're my baby sister. Just . . . no touching outside your tent."

I sighed louder, burrowing further into River's toasty warmth, which elicited a chuckle from him and a groan from Chace.

"Keep it up, and you'll be sharing a tent with *me* instead of lover boy."

River chortled, tossing a challenging look over his shoulder at Chace when he answered. "Sure, man. I'd love to see you square off against the most stubborn female on the planet. I'm sure we'd all die of exposure before you two worked out the sleeping arrangements."

"Tent assignments have already been made and are not negotiable," Nanette said, her boredom evident as she marched around the corner with us.

My retort died on my lips, though, because as soon as we rounded the bend, it was into the mouth of the most massive cavern we'd seen yet. The roof was still mostly flat, but it was high, high above our heads—even if I stacked three of our UTVs on top of each other, I wouldn't make it halfway up. This one didn't have the overhead lights; instead, they were all drilled into the cavern walls, thirty or forty feet up.

"Oh, extraordinary! It's an engineering marvel," Guffey cooed and darted off, leaving a couple of weary guards to sigh and jog after him.

"Why do you think they brought that guy along?" River asked close to my ear, low enough to avoid the guards' hearing.

"Who knows. He seems excited about it, though. I guess after living in space your entire life, this is a grand Earth adventure."

River snorted but didn't disagree. "If it wasn't for the whole non-voluntary thing, this *would* be pretty cool."

I raised an eyebrow skeptically at him.

"Okay, fine, it's *still* cool. I mean, did you ever think you'd get to see what was *under* the desert? I didn't."

"No, can't say I ever thought beyond trying not to die."

"So practical. But that's why I love you."

Warmth filled me at his words, and I burrowed a little further into his side, ignoring Chace making exaggerated gagging sounds behind us.

Okay, so I might have flipped him the bird behind River's back.

Nine

Base Camp

"Nyx and River, you're here. You have guards stationed at all four sides, so don't try anything funny." Gabriel pointed.

Our tent was indeed that; one low, narrow tent out of a field of them inside the enormous cavern. The party had split up almost as soon as we'd walked into the main cavern. To my surprise, there was a squat, hulking stone-block building off to one side of the cavern. The commandant, Captain Jacira, and their entourage had immediately ensconced themselves inside.

Half the group stayed with us, while the other half led Chace a few rows down, and escorted him into a tent. I watched until he was inside, still in disbelief as I gazed around at all that was hidden down here.

"You ready? Supposedly we have suits in there that will warm us up." River chafed the sides of my arms with his hands but didn't push.

We slid into the tent, the flap magnetically closing behind us. It felt like a weight being taken off my shoulders, being out from under the watchful eyes of our guards, even though logically I knew they were still right outside.

The privacy, the cocoon of peace; it reminded me of Marl's place. Though, I didn't truly have that same safety.

The click of the door locking behind me at Marl's always signified something. That for a little while, no one and nothing could touch me. Here . . . I had a flimsy tent flap, surrounded by guards, and they weren't here for my protection.

For now, it was enough.

There were two cots, each with a folded blue suit sitting on the end. River lifted the first one up, then the other, and passed me the smaller suit. With numb fingers, I stripped down to my underclothes, hastily stepping into the strangely woven fabric. It was stiff on the outside, but the inside was velvety against my chilled skin.

To my relief, the instant I zipped it up, heat blossomed. I sighed, my eyes sinking closed as warmth even better than that of River's skin suffused me.

"That good, huh?"

My eyes cracked open, too blissed out by the heat to do more. He was also in his suit, but unlike me he was taking me in, a soft smile on his finely-carved lips.

"What is it? You're staring." Heat of a different kind crept up the back of my neck as embarrassment tried to take hold.

"No, just glad to see you happy, even for a second. Things have been hard for a while, so we've got to grab every moment. A wise woman once told me that."

The memory had me returning his smile, a tiny pocket of happiness, true happiness, in the middle of so much struggle.

"She sounds incredibly wise. Probably beautiful, and if I had to guess, a real fighter."

"She is. Super tough, and, man, is she a hottie." He winked and stepped forward, surprising me when he wrapped me in a hug.

My heart fluttered at the closeness, but he didn't try to take it further.

"My suit's a bit on the small side, so I'm going to see if they can switch it out. I'll be right back. There are tooth tablets and some meal bars in the chest."

"'Mmkay," I murmured, already climbing into my cot, the warm cocoon lulling me toward much-needed sleep. I'd eat and freshen up in the morning.

He was back a few minutes later. After slipping into a different suit they'd given him, he crawled into his cot next to mine. We laid on our sides, facing one another. Sleep didn't take long to find me, now that I was finally warm and somewhat safe.

And when it did, I was holding River's hand.

"Let's go, up and out! The commandant wants to see you." The unforgiving voice belonged to Nanette, our sole female guard.

When my eyes cracked open, it took me a minute to remember that we were no longer inside the city. The pale blue canvas filtered the overhead cave lighting, and the unique smell of earth and dirt finally made it all click.

We were underground, in the cave full of technology with . . . everybody.

I lurched upright to find River already out of bed, hair combed, and with suit and boots on.

"Take a minute, I'll stall them."

His voice soothed my ruffled feathers, and I nodded. I *definitely* didn't ogle his backside in his fitted suit as he stooped to exit the tent.

Okay, so maybe I did. But as soon as the flap magnetized shut behind him, I slipped to the end of the bed and pulled on my own matching boots, and hastily scraped my wild flyaway hair into a fresh braid. It wasn't my usual level of precision, but hopefully it was passable.

When I stepped outside, everything was both the same, and different. Where last night everyone had immediately dispersed, this morning the enormous cavern buzzed with activity.

Everywhere you looked, people were moving and working, like ants in a hill. Supplies were being hauled to the far end of the cavern, food trays being carried from an open-air central kitchen, and people queuing up at one side of the cavern for what I hoped was a bathroom.

Our full escort led us there and cut the line so we could go first. They must have already taken care of their morning preparations, because as soon as River and I were done, we strode straight across the cavern toward the command building.

Good thing I inhaled that meal bar before we came out.

Gabriel palmed an access panel, and let us inside with a beep. The lights were near-blinding after the soft glow of the cave's sparse lighting. The harsh glare left me squinting, and I was shuffled forward with a hand on my arm, down a hallway.

I could mostly see again by the time they shoved us both through a door, into a small, cozy sitting room. Bookshelves lined the walls, and it was furnished with creamy white club chairs. I was pushed down into one—Nanette was getting more hands-on the longer we spent together—and the fuzzy looped fabric felt strange under my fingertips.

Seconds after we were seated with Excursion Team One fanned out behind us, the door opened again, and Captain Jacira glided in, Commandant Kieran hot on her heels.

"So," she cooed, "which one of them is the descendant?" Her eyes held a fervent light as she settled into her own chair across from us, examining both River and me expectantly.

A shiver rolled over my skin, and I had to resist the urge to bolt. She was the big bad wolf, and I was the little girl in the red coat. Her expression said I was tasty, and it left me terrified of what lengths the woman would go to. I wanted to leave this cave with both of my ears—and the rest of my body parts, for that matter—intact.

"Nyx is a direct descendant of Chrysanthe," the commandant answered, a barely perceptible frown on his lips.

"Interesting, so interesting. She's diminutive, for the one who's going to save us all. So much potential in such a . . . squat package."

Shock had me rocking back in the overly plush seat, and I nearly tipped over. The one who was going to save *who* all? And how?

"The question is, can she tell us how, or is she as in the dark as the rest of us?" When she leaned forward, bracing her elbow on the arm of her chair, it was with blatant curiosity. "What can you tell us about your ancestress?"

"Uhm, she was a scientist, married to a gardener?" I stammered lamely, but I didn't want to tell them about her message inside the locket, and it was the first thing that had come to mind.

"Fascinating. So it's normal in your family to marry the common man." I caught River stiffening out of the corner of my eye, but for once he was the one silently observing while I was reacting on the back foot. "What else can you tell us about the nanites?"

"The . . . what?"

She rolled her eyes and snapped blood-red-tipped fingers toward my face. "Catch up, girl, it's not cute to be stupid. Your blood has nanites that have never been found in anyone except a direct descendant of Chrysanthe's. We suspect they're somehow related to all of this, but what we don't know is *how* or why."

Nanites in my blood? My head was spinning. I had no idea how *or* why—or what the frack a nanite was—but my mind was flipping back through what I'd read in her journal, what she'd left in the locket message. She had seemed skeptical that her family would be given safe harbor, without her direct interference. Was that why my blood was the key? Had she done something to alter her descendants?

"I don't know anything about nanites. The only thing I do know is that Chrysanthe didn't believe that her family would be allowed to stay safely inside the city." The words felt right as I said them, and I lifted my chin as I met her eyes, then the commandant's.

He shifted uneasily in his seat, tugging at his collar.

"Interesting." Captain Jacira swiveled her gaze to the commandant. "Were these reservations founded? How has her line been treated over the years?"

"I'd prefer to discuss that separately, if you please."

"I don't please." She was out of the seat in seconds, and he leapt up reflexively. The guards shuffled behind us, but nobody moved, nobody *breathed* in their direction as the two leaders stared each other down, nose to nose and toe to toe.

"There have been none of her descendants inside the walls for more than a century. Her eldest grandchild was exiled, and Nyx is the first of her line that we've found in all our years of recruitment. She also has nanites. It could be that one of her *other* ancestors had access to advanced technology; you have medical nanites in space, after all."

Despite my suit's warming capabilities, cold began to leach into my fingertips. My ancestors

had been exiled to the Wastes, and they'd survived. *Still* survived, if Hema was to be believed
about being my father. Exactly what Chrysanthe had feared had come to pass.

My mind spun with questions. And did this
mean that Hema could also serve as the key?
Did he carry the nanites? But why did they need
me and my nanite-laden blood, and could we be
sure the two things were even related?

I still wasn't sure, and I had no confidence I'd
get the truth if I asked them. The captain was
unhinged enough she'd tell me *something*, but
would it be the truth?

Jacira's cold, dead eyes swiveled back to
where I sat, still in stunned silence. "And how
have you been treated since you've been inside
the city?"

Commandant Kieran's eyes rounded, pinning
me to my seat. The answer mattered to the two
of them, somehow. But how?

The frustration of working with no information was driving me insane.

"We were allowed inside, but I wouldn't consider the welcome warm." I hedged my bets,
giving as little detail as possible.

"I see," she purred, a cocky half smile tilting
her painted lips. "You're diplomatic. Stupid, but
diplomatic." Jacira shook her head, and then
pinned a finger to the commandant's chest. "If
I hear one complaint from the girl, or from my

80

man, I'll be taking her under my protection. And if I don't need you anymore, well . . . that wouldn't be good for you, or any of *your* men, now, would it?"

"She's here and well, as you can see for yourself. I won't have you using some false reports of mistreatment against me, as if you're some white knight riding in to save us all. You don't fool me, Jacira, not for a second." He turned his back on her, and sank into his own fuzzy chair once more, a bored expression on his face when he spoke again.

"Leave us, all of you. I've got preparations to attend to." His tone was bored, but the stiffness in his spine told me that the captain's threat was real, and he was none too pleased.

We were escorted out of the sitting room, nothing but the ringing of boots on stone floors echoing in my ears to beat back the questions that plagued me.

Ten

RUMBLES

My hands were shaking when we stopped just outside the command building. Why were my hands shaking? I balled them into fists, then thought better of it and shoved them into my pockets instead.

"Do you want to be taken to the gathering area, or back to your tent? Nyx?" River squeezed my arm. The gentle urging in his tone confused me. Had I missed a question?

"Where's Chace?" I sounded hoarse, so I cleared my throat.

"Gathering area."

"Take us there, please."

Gabriel nodded and led the way. The gathering area was a large, bowl-shaped depression in the cavern floor. Too sloped for easy building, but not too steep for people to traverse easily. People clustered in groups all over the space, many talking and laughing, others having what appeared to be more serious discussions. The sounds echoed in the vast rock space, but the weight of the earth constantly hanging over our heads kept my shoulders knotted tightly.

"Come on, Nyx. He's over there." River pointed with his chin, and I followed. When there were only ten feet left between us, I half jogged to close the distance. Chace looked up, surprised, seconds before I barreled into him. But he caught me and held me tight against his chest.

"What happened?" he asked quietly, but the threatening edge to his voice wasn't lost on me.

"We were called to a meeting," River answered but looked pointedly over the two of us to the small crowd of people Chace had been talking to.

"Let's step to the side, Nyxy." Chace's tone had turned soothing, like it used to be when we were little. I hadn't needed that voice in a long, long time. But today was one knock too many, after a long line of blows. I was fragile, and I hated it. But it had been so *long* since I really let myself feel; process all that had happened in the last few months.

We shuffled to an empty area, and nobody batted an eye. Our guards all lined the rim of the bowl, but really . . . where would we go, even if we ran?

"Tell me everything."

River rattled off the details. I winced when he got to the part about the nanites in my blood.

"What the frack is a nanite?"

"A microcomputer. Smaller than visible by the human eye. Clearly they're not harmful, given Nyx is alive and well, and presumably has had them for . . . some time. Her whole life, maybe."

"So these nanites mean that your blood is special somehow, and they need you specifically for their project."

"Apparently," I muttered, finally leaning back from his arms. My eyes stung, but no tears fell. River chafed the back of my arm lightly with his palm and gave me a supportive smile, but it didn't reach his eyes.

"How is blood, even special nanite-infused blood, supposed to fix a water generator? Do you even know what that is?" He looked down at me.

"No, I've got no clue. And we don't know if Hema was right, either. So, we suspect that's the mission . . . but our debriefing didn't exactly contain all the details."

Chace ran a frustrated hand over his shorn hair. "This is maddening. I just want to be on the surface, driving away from these lunatics. Or even better, their dead bodies."

I elbowed him in the ribs, eliciting a grunt.

"I'm not going to apologize for it, Nyx. They kidnapped me. They won't let you leave. These are *not* good people, and I would have no regrets lighting a match, and watching their fancy little city burn to the ground in my rearview mirror."

"Lower your voice, Chace!" I snapped, letting my gaze rove over the echoing cavern.

"So, what do we do? Is there anything we can do?" River asked.

"I don't know." The admission grated, and now that the shaking had stopped, anger was quickly rising up in its place. I was sick of being controlled, sick of being kept in the dark and dragged around like a rag doll. Unlike Chace, I didn't want to light a match to the city—there were too many innocent people inside it—but that didn't mean I wanted things to continue like before. I had already been trying to get the lifeside resistance out, and I hadn't forgotten them.

Something had to change, but what could we do? We were trapped deep underground, where they controlled all the equipment, food, and water.

"I can contact the Red Riders. They won't be able to do anything down here, but at least someone friendly on the surface would know what was going on. Maybe they like us enough to send Bramily back with more of that T-4 if things go sideways."

"If they're smart, they're nearly to Wolf Well by now." But he had a point. We weren't without friends, if we broadened our definitions. And Hema had quite a few forces surrounding the city—at least on that point, we knew he'd told the truth.

There had to be something we could do. *Something* to change our trajectory.

"Well met," a voice called, and we all turned.

It was a black-clad man, one of Hema's Night-bloods.

"Well met," I called back, a plan suddenly clicking into place.

"Hema wishes to inquire after your health after the long journey. Have you been well provided for?" The man stopped a respectful distance away, hands clasped politely behind his back.

"My health is fine, but I'd like to request an audience. Is that possible? Have you been given safe quarters where a private conversation may be held?"

"Yes, of course. I will relay your request and bring word when it is arranged."

He turned and left, not bothering with any further small talk.

"Nyx, is it wise to lay our cards on the table with them? What are you thinking?" River asked.

I clenched my jaw. "Wise? Maybe not. But a tiger's got *us* by the tail. I think it's time for a stick of dynamite. You should make your call to the Red Riders while we wait. I think they'll be happy to hear what we have to say."

The rest of the day passed in quiet contemplation, with an edge of unease. We ate three meals, kept our thoughts to ourselves, and then retired to our tent when our guards indicated it was time. River's call to the Red Riders went unanswered, which wasn't ideal.

A scuffle of boots on stone woke me sometime in the night. Barely a whisper, but I slowly rose, ears straining for a repeat noise. It never came.

But when the tent flap began to lift, I was ready. I grabbed the hand, folding it back over the wrist and steered the person backwards by their palm. When I followed them out of the tent, three things came to me with crystal clarity—River jolting out of bed behind me, my guards unconscious—*please, let them only be unconscious*—on the ground, and that I was surrounded.

It took longer for me to process that the people circling me were all men in black clothing, faces covered in the Nightbloods' style. I looked into the eyes of our would-be intruder as River emerged behind me, his warmth at my back reassuring. This morning's messenger stared back at me, and I slowly released his arm.

He never grunted, never winced at what I knew to be a painful hold; he merely bowed and gestured that we should walk with them. River squeezed my shoulder, lending me quiet strength as we walked into the unknown.

We slowly threaded through the cavern, picking up Chace along the way to the Nightbloods' portion of the underground tent city. They must have brought their own sleeping accommodations and set them up after I was asleep last night, because their tents were much larger than any we'd seen in the rest of the tent sea. A large central pavilion made of canvas sat at the center of it all, too large for me to have missed otherwise.

The rest of their tents were set out in a large circle ringing the largest, centermost pavilion. That was where they led us, and the flaps were held open as our group walked inside. Lamps in a gorgeous array of colors, and in all shapes and sizes, set the space aglow. Cushions covered the floor, many occupied with men, their hoods and face coverings dropped inside their private space. It was strange to actually *see* them, after they'd been shrouded in mystery for so long.

They were just men, like any other, and that strengthened my resolve.

Hema stood at the end of the pavilion, surrounded by advisors, in deep conversation. They broke apart as we approached, and Hema spread his arms wide in welcome.

"My παιδί, *daughter*, I am so pleased you've come. The Nightbloods welcome you and your companions."

"Αγαπημένη του αίματος." As one, the room spoke together, and I nearly jumped out of my skin.

"What does that mean, Hema?" I asked quietly.

"It means you are one of us and will always have a place here." He smiled, little crinkles forming around his eyes with the action. It made him seem warmer than his reputation warranted, and my stomach flip-flopped as I considered him; who he was. "But that's not why you've come. What brings you to us tonight, παιδί μου?"

I blew out a breath through my nose. "I want to change things, and I think you can help."

"Go on," he murmured, an unreadable look in his eyes.

"The leadership of Bastion City has been a bane on the desert for too long. They hoard their resources, and instead of helping, they hurt. Kidnapping. Killing. *Bombing*, maiming innocents and children—they've proven that they are not good people."

Chace grunted his agreement as a murmur of assent moved through the tent, but Hema held up a hand and it once again fell silent.

"You wish us to wipe them out?"

The question made my blood run cold, for there was no judgment or hesitation in it; only possibility.

"No. To destroy the city would be to destroy a precious resource that humanity can't afford to lose. We need to work together, forge peace."

He nodded slowly, so I took it as encouragement to continue.

"There is unrest between the space captain and the commandant. If we can band together the people of the desert, perhaps now while their attention is divided, we could change things. Make the city what I believe it was always meant to be—a place of hope, and safety."

"These are pretty words, παιδί μου, but what you speak of will not be easy. It will be a bloody insurrection, and I'm not sure you're prepared for that."

"I am." Chace stepped forward, tugging gently on my ponytail before focusing on Hema. "Nyx is right. We can't allow them to continue ravaging the desert and killing us all, city by city. There is unrest in the city, and there are factions inside who would like to see the commandant fall. If the Nightbloods are willing to work with the other desert dwellers, and we can get even a portion of the people inside the city to help . . . we could remove them from power."

Hema pursed his lips. "And put who in their place? You? No matter how divided the city may be, they won't accept a desert wanderer as their new leadership."

I raised a hand in a placating gesture. "No, we wouldn't just put Chace in power—or any of us, for that matter. There would be time to figure out a new system, a new way of moving forward that all could accept," I answered. Better not to give my hot-headed brother too much rope with Hema.

He nodded slightly. "There is much wisdom in you, for one so young. We must discuss this matter, and we will. But for now, let us break bread together." Hema gestured, and people with trays poured in from a side flap, circuiting the room.

There was indeed bread, with sticky-sweet jams, cheeses, and pearls of red fruit. I had no idea how the Nightbloods came to have such delicacies, but the fruit burst on my tongue, sending sweet-tart juice down my throat, and the cheese was better than anything I'd ever tasted.

It was many hours later that they led us back to our tents, yawning and our heads full of possibility.

Eleven

Precipice

"Nyx Brandt, on your feet!" An angry shout had River and me both scrambling out of our tiny cots. "Let's go, let's go!"

I pushed out the tent flap and came nose-to-chest with Gabriel, and he was angry.

"River, you're not needed," was all he said as he grabbed my upper arm and practically dragged me from the tent. River tried to leap forward, tried to get Gabriel's hands off me, but the rest of Excursion Team One surged forward, making an impenetrable wall of flesh.

"Let her go!" His angry shouts echoed off the ceiling, and people started pouring out of their own tents, eager to catch a glimpse of the show.

My mind spun, wondering what this was about. It could only be about our meeting with the Nightbloods last night; but did they *know* what the meeting was about, or were they just angry we'd evaded their guards? I would have to be careful not to tell them more than they knew.

"Nyx!" Chace's furious shout made me snap out of indecision.

"Hey! We made a deal; we stay together! Chace, too!" I shoved at Gabriel's iron grip, but all my might wouldn't budge his fingers, and my donkey kick to the side of his knee didn't even make him falter.

Once we'd gained some distance from the sleeping area, he stopped briefly, glaring down at me with uncharacteristic venom. "I don't think you want your big brother to see this." I felt the blood drain from my face as I scanned the set of his jaw, the angry tick just below his temple. It wasn't a threat, it was just fact.

"Don't hurt them, whatever you do to me."

"Nobody's going to get hurt. Yet."

He didn't ease up the entire way across the cavern and into the low command building. I didn't get the cushy sitting room this time. I was surrounded by bare cement walls, and shoved down into a solitary steel chair. Until my suit caught up and regulated to the change, it was cold against my thighs—a vivid reminder that I wasn't actually a guest here. I was still a prisoner, with Gabriel standing guard at my shoulder. I sat straight, though, and stayed sharp.

When people were angry, they let things slip. One tiny thing could be the difference between us successfully taking them down, or failing.

The commandant strode in a few moments later, not making me wait. He adjusted the cuffs of his jacket before pulling a tablet out of a breast pocket. He twirled it idly in his hands, but didn't turn it on.

"I'd hoped, Nyx, that you and I understood each other. You see, I need you, and whether you realize it or not, you need me."

I gritted my teeth to stop myself from saying something stupid.

"Still going to play tough, huh? How about we start with what happened last night? Four of your guards were knocked out. When the morning shift came to relieve them, you were in your cots. Would you care to tell me where you ran off to while you were unsupervised?"

Did he really not know, or was he trying to catch me in a lie?

"There's nowhere to *go* inside the cavern, and I didn't knock out the guards. How could I?"

"A question I've asked myself several times since I received the news. How could you, even with your two men, take out four of my well-trained, fully armed guards? And do you know what I came up with, Nyx?"

"No," I said, keeping my tone airy. "Why don't you enlighten me?"

"You've got help—more than I realized. That *is* a problem, but I'll quash it if I need to." He stopped spinning the tablet, pressing his thumb to a point on the bottom which made it light up.

A few taps later, he turned it toward me and handed it over.

It took me a few seconds to realize what I was watching, because the angle was strange. It was the back of my head, but my long, dark braid was pretty easy to recognize. And there was River, seated on the mattress in front of me.

The two mattresses we'd pushed together on the floor of our room.

Bile rose in the back of my throat as we kissed, and his fingers threaded into my hair.

"What is this?"

"Oh, I think you know *exactly* what it is."

River pulled away from me onscreen and said the words I remembered oh so well.

"Tell me to stop, Nyx." The low rumble of his voice had soothed me then, but now my stomach turned, because I knew that our moment was polluted, tainted.

"Don't stop," I blurted on the tablet. "Stay with me."

I screwed my eyes tightly shut as we kissed again, and he removed his shirt.

"Turn it off," I said, and he ignored me. The sounds of our kissing echoed in the empty, soulless room, so I demanded again, "Turn it off!"

"Tsk, tsk. Not proud of yourself, are you? That's what happens when we slum around." Sheer fury had me leaning forward in the chair, ready to spring at him, but Gabriel's hand clamped down on my shoulder, forcing me against the hard back of the chair and knocking me breathless in the process.

I wasn't *slumming* with River. But I didn't want the tender moments between us sullied by their eyes. A moment so private and beautiful wasn't for them, and something inside me felt like it was tearing to pieces at the fact that they not only knew, but clearly had seen it all. I bit my lip to stop it trembling. I couldn't break down, not now, not ever while we were down here, no matter how much it burned me up inside.

Keeping my head was all that mattered, no matter how bad it stung.

"I could make your life very miserable, Nyx, in more ways than you realize. I don't want to, of course. How do you think your dear Chace would feel about this video, hmm? What if we strapped him to that chair, and played it on a loop? Twenty-four hours or so should have him ready to tear River's head off his shoulders, and never look you in the eye again."

"What does that do for you, Commandant? You'd humiliate me, is that it? If you think a little embarrassment is enough to get me to stay in line, you're dead wrong. Embarrassment won't kill me."

It might feel like it, but who was counting?

"That is true, but you and I both know there are worse things than death. I don't want you dead, or to be your enemy. But an act of rebellion like this can't go unpunished. You and I had a deal, and you violated those terms."

"Once again, I didn't knock out the guards."

"No, probably not. But you weren't surprised. You know what happened, and that's enough. We leave in twenty-four hours, and you have a choice. Option one, Chace gets strapped to that chair, and we project your home movie on the wall on a loop until it's time to leave. Option two, your brother stays here. He won't be harmed, and so long as you cooperate *fully* from here on out, we'll keep this ugliness between the two of us. But if any more trouble happens, well . . . I think you get the idea."

I nodded tightly, watching as he twirled the tablet between his palms, and willed it to crash to the floor and shatter.

Alas, I didn't have any psychic powers, for he tucked it safely back into his jacket pocket.

"You can notify Gabriel of your decision when you're back at your tent." He nodded to Gabriel, and headed for the door, but stopped at the last second. "And Nyx? No more field trips. I promise you—it's never going to work out in your favor."

His boots echoed down the hall, his words pulsing through my head in time with the staccato beats while anger, hot and liquid, burned me up from the inside out.

I was done being a pawn, and no matter how this ended, I never wanted to be under someone else's control again, as long as I lived.

I'd changed my mind. I would burn the whole city down around the commandant's ears, if that's what it took to free myself.

Twelve

Ingress

"Chace is going to be staying here, in the base camp." The words were bitter on my tongue, but the slow walk back to the tents had given me time to run through the options, and it was the best way forward.

"Like hell I am!" He grabbed me by both shoulders, shaking me lightly.

"Hey, settle down and let her finish." River moved to knock Chace's hands off me, and he rounded on him, jabbing a finger to River's chest.

"You can back off, buddy. I don't care what my sister thinks, I'm not sold on you, yet."

"Chace! Knock it off." I grabbed him by the arm, and he let me tug it away from River. "This isn't River's fault, and us fighting is *exactly* what they want. Trust me, please?"

"Talk." His eyes were dead as he listened, but he didn't go after River again, at least.

"They know we left our tents last night, and this is the punishment. He made threats, and frankly, I'm not willing to push him. If we get into an outright war right here, we'll lose, and we'll never find out why they dragged us down here. If there's technology down here that can really generate water and help save us all, we have to know about it."

River whistled low, scuffing his palm over the back of his neck. "Nyx . . . you know it's not your job to save us all, right? You're one person. And I'm on your side, but you don't have to be the hero. You don't owe anybody your life."

"River—" My throat clogged. When the frack did I get so emotional? Apparently sometime between the kidnapping and the blackmail. I swallowed hard.

"I know that, and I'm not trying to be a hero. But if there's a way to help the water problem on the surface, that helps us, too." I spun to Chace. "We've always dreamed of going north, finding somewhere green. What if that place doesn't exist?"

"Don't talk like that, Nyx. Out there you're *free*, and that's more important than wherever they're taking us. Even if the north isn't what we hoped, anything is better than being under the commandant's thumb. Trust me." His eyes were haunted, pleading with me to listen, not to leave him behind.

"One step at a time. He's still honoring the deal, in his own, twisted way. We defied him, so he's taking something from us. And it might be better this way—we don't know how good the communication is further down, but if you stay here, you might be able to contact the Red Riders, or even some of the Resistance inside the city. I have a friend named Morgan we've lost contact with, and I really want to know she's okay. Maybe you could snoop around and find out. If you could connect with her . . . together you could let them know what's going on. This is bigger than just the three of us. If we can win the Nightbloods around to our side, we've got a chance for change."

As hard as it was to consider separating from him again when we still weren't safe, the words felt right as I said them. I did want to know that Morgan was okay. I did want to gather more allies to our side. One person couldn't change the world; but maybe I could be the first grain of sand that started the landslide.

"Is that change worth the risk to you?"

"I'm not some fragile flower who can't take a risk, Chace. What do you think I've been doing since they took you?"

He snorted. "I'd hoped you'd stay under the radar so you could live out your life safely."

River clapped him on the shoulder, ignoring the incredulous look Chace shot him. "Dude, your sister doesn't know what *under the radar* means."

"I know. You have no idea how hard it was keeping her alive when we were kids," Chace said, cracking a wry grin at me.

"Okay, I think I liked it better when you two weren't on speaking terms."

I waved them off, as if separating would stop them from ganging up on me.

"All members of the incursion party, please report to the gathering area for instructions. All members of the incursion party, please report to the gathering area for instructions." The lilting, feminine voice echoed in the cavern, and cut through our blue canvas like it was nothing.

The jovial moment in the tent evaporated as Chace's anger at being separated from me rose again faster than the sun on a clear morning.

"Nyx, I think they're trying to isolate you. Are you sure there's no alternative?" His words were sincere, with none of the hotheaded temper I was so used to from him.

There *was* an alternative, but I couldn't bear to tell him what it was.

"The alternative is worse. Do you trust me? I really think this will work in our favor, having you here."

"But I can't protect you from here, Nyx. It will kill me if something happens to you down there, when I should have been there to stop it."

My eyes sank closed, because I knew exactly what he meant. If he'd been killed before I got to him, I'd never have forgiven myself, either. But he hadn't, and I'd found my way back to him. I had to believe this would be the same.

Not because I was a hero, or a martyr. Because the possibility of a water generator . . . a real, working water generator would be the most amazing thing I'd ever discovered. Life-changing. And I couldn't pass that up.

"Nyx, we should probably—" River started.

"One more second." I leaned forward, wrapping Chace in a tight hug. And then I followed River out of the tent, and into the next phase of our journey. Something inside me settled, now that the decision was made.

The organizer was Sakura, from the leadership panel. She looked tiny and petite, as she stood next to Commandant Kieran, but held herself and spoke with authority. "The supplies are nearly loaded, and the moles will be leaving in exactly six hours. Get some rest, stretch your legs—whatever you need to do. Once you leave, quarters will be tight for the duration of the mission. Seating assignments are here," she said, indicating a stack of tablets, "and if you'll tap your water meters where indicated, they'll be transferred to you directly." A few volunteers began passing out tablets, which were then passed from person to person to distribute the plans.

"The moles are equipped with heat shielding, as the temperature at the depths where we'll be going can reach upwards of a hundred and forty degrees, which is dangerous for long-term exposure. Your suits have some temperature regulating capabilities, but should only be considered a backup in case of vehicular failure. When you've arrived at your destination, strict shifts will be enforced, so that no one is outside of their mole for too long, or exposed to excessive heat. If you have any questions, I'll be stationed here until departure."

A tablet was pressed into my hands, so I tapped my water meter to get the seating charts, and then passed it to the next person with a hand out.

A tiny diagram appeared, showing an eight-man configuration. I only recognized four of the names in our mole; myself, River, Nanette, and Guffey.

"You know, we haven't seen Guffey since we got here. He wandered off, and that was it," River said, mirroring my own thoughts.

"Well, I guess we'll be seeing him again in a few hours. I wonder who the rest of these people are?"

"Probably just Excursion Team One members who never bothered to introduce themselves. Although, I think Quinn is the guy who switched suits with me. Remember, mine was too small?"

"Vaguely? I was so exhausted it's all kind of a blur. There's a lot of people down here, but it seems likely it's the same guy." I sighed and dropped my wrist. "We'd better get back. We've got a lot to do in six hours."

He sent me a quizzical look but didn't argue. That probably wouldn't start until we had to dig the radio implant out of his tooth to leave with my brother.

Six hours later, River was still shooting me dirty looks as we waited to be sorted into our mole. Nervous anticipation jangled through me, and I was bouncing on the balls of my feet. I didn't do well with confined spaces, or lack of activity, so this was going to be a challenge for me.

"Mole three! Fletcher Grenkel, Jameson Kutsuki, Consultant Nyx Brandt, Consultant River Zeer, Engineer James Guffey, Kindred Ayala, Quinn Urvit, and Nanette Smythe." Sakura's smooth voice carried over the crowd.

I blew out my breath. This was it.

River reached over and twined his fingers with mine, and I didn't pull away. Mole three was a long, narrow vehicle, almost like a cylindrical train car on tracks instead of wheels. The exterior was a lustrous blue, which matched our suits. The front had a hulking drill attachment, each of the swirls lined with metal nubs. Underneath the drill was a cow catcher, and various other implements, presumably in case of trouble. The front hatch was open, with a narrow set of stairs built into the inside of it for loading.

I'd had no idea what to expect, but visions of furry underground rodents were happily banished from my mind as I climbed into the sleek vehicle. It was thankfully spacious on the inside, and I wasn't able to reach the top of the rounded ceiling, even on my tiptoes. The air inside was cool, if a little stale, and there were eight plush seats, in four rows. The center was open, so that you could walk from the front to the back without crouching, and a narrow window ran down the length of the mole on both sides, allowing us to see out into the milling crowds we were about to leave behind.

"Please take your seats in the order your names were called. Stow your belongings in the compartment, and get strapped in. The sooner everyone's in place, the sooner we leave."

Nanette spoke from the end of our line, and I had to work hard not to roll my eyes. *Of course*, she'd be in my group.

The desert gods were just giving with both hands, lately.

River and I were in the second row, so it only took a second to sink down into our seats and stow our tiny allotment of personal belongings inside the compartment. It was built into the wall, with a press-button design that let it disappear when closed.

The seat was comfortable, but not too cushy so that you sank in and couldn't move. The strap-in part was more elusive, though. I looked across the aisle at River, but he was equally confused.

Guffey stopped in the aisle, a vacant look on his face.

"The schematics for this unit show a harness system stored over your head. If you reach up and run your fingertips along the back of your seat, you should locate it." He smiled at the two of us, and then quickly settled in behind us.

Sure enough, there were two cold metal buckles protruding from the top of the seat. I pulled first one down, and inserted it into the receiver, then the other. And that's when things got weird.

The two straps stiffened over my torso, and snapped together in the middle, forming an X over me. Then a whirring noise overhead started, and they slowly cinched themselves back until I was firmly pressed back into the seat.

I hastily snatched the straps away from the sides of my neck as my heart pounded in my chest.

"How long are we on this journey, exactly?" My voice cracked in the middle, as I asked the question to anyone who might actually give me an answer.

After a beat of silence, Guffey once again helped me out.

"Oh, in theory it could be undertaken in a day, on the surface over flat terrain. But as we descend lower, things get trickier. These vehicles are also built for safety, rather than speed. Best case scenario, it's a seven- to ten-day journey. But any setbacks, and it will take longer."

"So you know how far down we're going?" River asked, not in the least perturbed by being ratchet-strapped into a seat against his will.

"Of course, don't you?" Nanette was waiting in the entryway and gave me a sharp look over the seatback between us.

"Uh, let's just say the specifics are a little fuzzy," I hedged. Her nod of approval was near-imperceptible, but the message was clear. She was still policing us, every step of the way. One toe out of line . . . I shuddered, and not because of the chill, or the creepy harness system.

A few minutes later, everyone was ready, and the door slowly rose and seated itself into the frame, sealing us inside the mole. A radio crackled up front, and our operator rose from his seat to check controls at the front before responding and turning around to face the rest of us.

"We'll be leaving in less than five minutes. Lav's in the back, and we'll be traveling approximately seven hours per day, with a lunch break in the middle. It's preferred that you stay strapped in, given the grade, but not mandatory. You're all adults, so do what you want."

With that little tidbit, he sat back down, and clicked his harness into place. We all waited in anticipatory silence until the mole jolted forward, and the sound of metal tracks crunching on bare rock filled the small cylindrical space.

I watched through the window as the airy cavern disappeared, replaced by rough-hewn tunnel walls. My chest constricted and my heart pounded as the light slowly faded to blackness, as if we were being swallowed by a large beast, rather than the earth itself.

Thirteen

Get to Mole You

Day One

The sound was the worst part. The darkness was eerie, the six-point harness was a drag, and staring out the window into infinite blackness? It straight up sucked. But the *worst* part was the noise. It never stopped.

I would have sworn we'd been in these fracking tunnels for ten hours, but my water meter stubbornly insisted it was only one. *One hour.* Out of seven hours *per day.*

This was it, I was going to die, insane, inside a weirdly-named pod vehicle deep in the earth, because I couldn't handle the noise.

I turned to River, and ground my back teeth at how relaxed he looked. He'd figured out how to recline his seat, and a small smile played over his lips as he napped. *Napped.* Like this wasn't a form of torture directly out of Dante's Inferno.

Huffing my annoyance, I considered waking him up, but went back to picking at my nails, instead. I didn't usually give myself the luxury of showing my fears, but down here, everyone was otherwise occupied, so there was no one to judge me.

Guffey's bespectacled face appeared in the aisle, startling me so badly I screeched and shoved him back with a palm to the forehead.

"I'm so sorry!" I gasped as he landed hard on his backside in the aisle. Snatching at my straps did nothing but cause them to tighten further, and I let out a strangled moan of distress before River's hand appeared. He flicked a lever I hadn't yet found, which caused the straps to disengage and retract.

My sigh of relief was drowned out by the rustle of my suit as I jumped into the aisle to help the engineer back to his feet.

"I'm so sorry, you just startled me. Are you okay?" I resisted the urge to babble nervously, using him as a distraction from how much I hated every single thing about this fancy death trap.

"Oh, my, yes. I'm quite fine. I'd forgotten how much better the reflexes are on my younger colleagues." He adjusted his glasses—which now sat lopsided on his round face—and smoothed a shaky hand through his wild white hair. "I mere-ly wanted to ask your thoughts on the journey so far. Everyone has been so quiet; it's feeling a bit tomb-like in here."

I nodded, biting my bottom lip way harder than was necessary. "So far I'm not a fan."

"A fan? How could you be? You have nei-ther blades nor a motor mechanism." His brows arched down in confusion. I thought he was joking at first, but there was no crack of a smile.

"Uh—" I stared blankly, and River came to my rescue.

"She means an enthusiast. 'Fan' is short for 'fanatic.'" He bumped my shoulder with his, jostling me out of my stupor.

"Oh, interesting. Is this an earth-bound slang? I will have to update my personal dictio-nary." His eyes glazed over, and . . . was that text, scrolling on the *inside* of his glasses?

"Personal dictionary?" River asked, sounding much more enthused about the idea than I had been at any point since we'd come under-ground.

"Why, yes. Surely you all have them. My neural chip stores it, and I can update it at any time, as I encounter new languages and regional slang. Though it comes programmed with all twelve standard Mars dialects."

River and I just blinked at him, completely ignorant of the technology he took for granted. He wasn't put off by our blank stares.

"Okay, I've updated my dictionary. Now, I'm sure you've got some thoughts of your own about the water generation technology we're going to assess, but do you feel the geographical placement is as significant as your ancestress did? I can't think of any other reason she'd have placed it inside an aquifer, given how hard it is to access one."

"The water generator is inside an aquifer? Is that where we're going?"

He blinked rapidly, then shook his head and turned to his companion, a tall, thin man with white-blonde hair and frigid blue-green eyes. "Kindred, can you believe this? How do they expect us to get anything accomplished in a timely fashion, if they keep their own specialists in the dark?"

The man shrugged but kept his silence.

Guffey turned back to us, a determined light in his eyes, and his shoulders squared. "Our first task, then, is to get you up to speed. We can't afford to waste time while we're there, as our time outside will be limited. There's a button to turn your chairs, on the left armrest. Turn toward the wall here, and I'll do my best to draw it for you."

He stepped back into his row, and dug around in his personal compartment, pulling out a white marker. Once I figured out how to swivel my seat, I sat back down, eager for someone to *finally* fill me in on what the frack we were doing down here. A quick glance over my shoulder showed River, forearms crossed on the back of my seat, and to my surprise, Nanette and the other soldier from the back row were also gathered, watching with interest as Guffey began to draw right onto the window.

"This is the earth's surface." He drew a slightly curved line. "In years prior to the meteor strike, surface water was abundant, if not all potable. Lakes, Rivers, streams, ponds. You name it, earth had it." He dotted the surface with what were presumably pools of water.

But underneath that, we have many different smaller layers of the earth's crust, and under many parts of the earth's land mass, there are layers of water, water-porous rock, and even silt. Many of these components together create aquifers. These water stores under the ground have been slowly depleting as the centuries passed since the strike, because rain cycles stopped, the temperature increased on the surface, and they stopped being replenished."

Sadness stole over me. I didn't understand a hundred percent of what he was talking about, but one thing was very, very clear. We used to have *so much*, and over time, it had steadily been stripped away. The devastation on the surface was mirrored even here, deep down in the earth itself, where the last stores of water were slowly vanishing.

How long did humanity have left? Was there any way to tell? Eventually, it would all be gone, or we'd have no way to access it. Then it wouldn't matter who you were or how many credits you had; we would all die.

I thought of the cities floating from one place to the next, leaving what once were good, strong water sources, to flee north, away from the equator as it grew ever drier and more dead. How did the water supply fare up north, though? We didn't really know.

Guffey had continued talking while I went down my mental side-trip, so I tried to school my thoughts and pay attention to his impromptu geography lesson.

"We believe the generator has been placed here, in an attempt to work with the natural infrastructure of earth. If you refill the well from the bottom, it can't be contaminated by the ocean or the meteorites, and eventually, with *enough* volume, you might even be able to achieve a return of limited bodies of surface water."

I blinked, trying to imagine a river, or a lake. I couldn't, not even after having seen the tiny, wild stream that Hema had shown me. It was small, confined. A *lake* sounded vast. Bigger than I could comprehend.

The ocean didn't feel like water, given its color and the noxious fumes wafting off of it. And the explosions. My lizard brain refused to acknowledge water *exploding*.

"Are you listening?"

River bopped me on the head, so I shot him a glare before focusing back on Guffey. "Of course! It's just . . . a lot to take in."

"I'm sure most of it was covered by your basic science curriculum." He adjusted his glasses and drew a little X over the spot on the diagram where he'd been pointing.

I didn't respond, *couldn't* respond. There had been no science curriculum. No loving family who sent me off to school in the mornings—not ever—and the fact that I could read and write were due to a bored kept woman who decided that the street children would be her project in the mornings while her keeper slept off the night's activities.

Math had been drilled into me by Chace, because it was necessary for a trader.

But science? Science didn't exist in Coyote Springs. I'd had no idea that water lived under our feet—deeper than a basic well, at least—or how it could be accessed, let alone created.

A sick feeling crept through me as I watched Guffey continue to talk and gesture and teach. Because there was only one possible outcome for him, when we got down to the generator. And it was big, fat disappointment.

Because I didn't know a dang thing about engineering, science, or how one could make water out of dry rock. And in that moment, it occurred to me that just having the right bloodline might not be even *close* to enough to fix a centuries-old water generator made by a brilliant engineer.

Fourteen

Rock and a Hard Place

I kept to myself the rest of the ride. Guffey's audience had run out of steam long before he'd run out of knowledge to share, so I used that excuse to spin my chair back around and bury my face in my arms. I'd felt so sure when the excursion began, and less than three hours later, all of that confidence had drained away like water from a pierced orb.

I was dry of everything but disappointment and the unlimited conviction that I was going to make a disaster out of this mission. The endless whirring sound ground to a halt, and my head jerked up on reflex.

A beeping came from the front console, and the soldier seated in front of me got up to check it.

"Looks like there's some debris in the tunnel, and the first mole has a loose panel, or something. Quinn, can you hop out and check? The whole motorcade has stopped, and two and four are also sending over a mechanic to assist one."

"Sure thing." The soldier seated across from Nanette at the back hopped up and jogged toward the front. He grabbed a helmet from a cabinet and pulled it on. His suit made a hissing sound as it sealed, and then the stairs lowered. As soon as he was out, the door closed softly behind him.

"You can all take a few minutes to stretch and visit the lav. This should take less than an hour, with four of them working on it."

Two hours later, we were still stopped, all of us restless.

"Hey, man, what's the ruling on getting out? I'd love to take a jog, stretch my legs a little," River asked.

"It's Fletcher. And no, you can't get out. Jogging in the tunnels is a bad idea for a lot of reasons, but we're already hitting temperature increases. Your suit's cooling capabilities will have to work a lot harder if you're actively running."

"Is that what the helmet was for?" I asked.

"Partially, and to filter any fumes. The tunnels were tested with drones before we headed down, but small pockets of noxious gases are always a possibility. The suits have a lot of capability, but it's best not to tax them more than necessary."

"Thanks, Fletcher." River frowned over at me. "I'm going to lose my mind before we get there, if I can't run or get out of this sardine tin."

"Just do some push-ups in the aisle." I waved at the open floor space, curious if he'd rise to the challenge, or be embarrassed to exercise with an audience of strangers.

He considered it briefly, then dropped down and started counting his reps as he levered up and down off the floor. That spurred the other front-row soldier—Jameson, he informed us—to drop down to the front section of the aisle for a push-up contest. We were all snickering at their back-and-forth insults as they tried to outdo each other, when Fletcher swore loudly from the front.

"Nanette, you've got some medical training, right? You're needed. Something's happened, and Quinn's collapsed. They're getting the actual medical officer, but you're closer."

Nanette was on her feet in a flash, and leap-frogged across the two men, still on the floor from their push-up contest. She smashed a palm on the helmet cabinet to open it, and already had her helmet fastened when the door was at half-mast. She didn't wait for it to finish descending, instead taking two steps across the corners of the still-horizontal stairs and jumping down to the rocks below before being swallowed up by the gloom. Fletcher did something to stop the stairs' descent, and stood tensely listening at the comm device while we waited.

River and Jameson both returned to their seats, and an air of thick tension permeated the small vehicle.

"Yes, sir. I understand. Yes, sir." Fletcher swore again, dropping the comm back into its cradle. "Quinn's down for the count. His suit malfunctioned, he overheated, and he's being transferred to the very last mole, where the medical officer is, for monitoring. We can't be down a man, so we're getting a transfer after the community dinner tonight."

He dropped to his seat woodenly, and everyone remained silent for a beat, processing, before the talking started up with the speed of a sandstorm.

"How did the suit malfunction?"

"They've all been tested. Our team reviewed the records."

"But what was *wrong* with it? These can't develop holes, so—"

The speculation blurred into background noise, but I did my best to pick out the differing opinions, watch for any signs of division between our three groups.

River, however, remained strangely silent, his face pale. When things started to die down, I nodded toward the bathroom. It was big enough for two, barely. We squeezed in, and I turned the lock before focusing in on him.

"What's wrong? You look like you've seen a ghost."

"That was my suit. Quinn was the one who traded with me."

I blinked, trying to work through the implications. "You don't think it was an accident."

He shook his head. "The accident was that my suit was the wrong size. Nyx, I think Chace was right. What if they *are* trying to isolate you?"

I ground my back teeth together, frustration and stress rising inside me.

We had no way to contact him, no way to warn him—though Chace was paranoid, so he'd probably be fine—but if things got worse down here, we were well and truly on our own. The Nightbloods had also been relegated to the back of the motorcade.

If River was right—and it seemed very likely, given the general shocked response up front to what had happened—they wanted me completely alone from here on out.

But now that they'd failed to remove River, what would they try next?

I looked up at him, regret pouring through me. He'd been so worried about being a target of the Nightbloods when we first left Coyote Springs. And because of his loyalty to me, I'd dragged him straight through their territory, and into the lap of an even worse enemy. He was going to be collateral damage, if we weren't very, very careful from here on out.

"Don't look at me like that, Nyx. I can see the wheels turning. Whatever you're planning, the answer is *no*. I'm not running scared."

"That's not what I'm thinking. Back me up when we stop for dinner tonight."

He nodded, but it was plain as day that he hated being left in the dark. My plan hadn't fully formed, but I had an idea to secure another ally.

Nanette returned and we got back on the road. All the while River remained quiet and with-drawn. Just before we stopped for dinner, we received the bad news over the comm that Quinn had suffered a seizure and was now un-responsive. The look River had given me . . . it was guilt like I'd never seen.

I tried to convey with my eyes that it was *not* his fault; he didn't sabotage the suit, he didn't know that would happen. And I refused to regret the fact that he was still here with me, with all the turmoil surrounding us at every moment. It might have been selfish, but my sadness for Quinn was miniscule in comparison to my relief that it wasn't River.

When we all donned helmets and climbed off the mole for dinner, I kept my eyes peeled. I walked as slowly as possible without drawing suspicion. People were mingling and talking before we made it ten feet, so I grabbed River's arm and hunkered against the wall, waiting.

They were hard to make out through the deep shadows created by the few portable lights that had been assembled to point us toward the dining setup, but eventually I spotted the first of the Nightbloods. Hooking River's arm through mine, we pushed off the wall and strolled slowly, letting them catch up to us.

The first two dozen or so passed, in a stream of humanity, intent only on food and escaping the claustrophobic transportation. But within moments, one stepped up beside us and hooked my other arm.

"What do you need?"

The voice was low, measured.

"There has been a sabotage inside our mole, and we are now down a man. I thought Hema would want this information."

"They sabotaged one of their own?"

"Accidentally. The target was River."

A sharp inhale was the only response, then the man let go of my arm, and disappeared into the small sea of black clothing.

River still held his tongue, and I was starting to worry about him as we entered the strange enclosure where dinner was being served.

It looked like a giant plastic bubble. It was molded against the walls of the tunnel, giant fans built into each end kept it inflated, and when we removed our helmets inside, the air was cool and crisp. Two people on the left were passing out bowls of stew, so we got into line to get our bowls. There were no seats, simply people milling about or sitting on the ground, talking and eating.

I kept hold of River's arm as I made a beeline to an empty area and cornered him against the edge of the bubble. I set down my bowl next to our helmets.

He was eating his stew, looking studiously at the small chunks of carrot and potato floating in the dark broth and pointedly avoiding my eyes.

"River."

He grunted, not looking up.

"*River*." I tried again.

His eyes were misty when they finally met mine. "What do you want, Nyx?"

"I want you to not avoid me. You're the only friend I have here, the only one I can trust.

I'm sorry that happened today. I'm sorry about Quinn. But I'm not sorry that it *wasn't you*. I can never be sorry about that, do you understand?"

"Am I really your friend? Or was I just convenient?"

I reeled back like he'd slapped me. "How could you *say* that? After all we've been through?"

"Are you ever going to tell me why you asked Chace to stay behind, or should I keep pretending nothing happened, after chasing you across half the continent to find him, just to leave him five minutes later?"

The angry rush of blood to my cheeks probably gave away too much, but it was River. He wouldn't use it against me, or at least I hadn't thought so until forty-five seconds ago.

"You really want to know?" Even I could hear the taunt in my voice, and I knew it was wrong. But I was hot under the collar. Hot with fury, and with resentment that he'd blindside me about it, instead of just asking. No, I hadn't told him, but there was a *lot* going on.

"Of course I do, Nyx! I know you've got trust issues. Hell, so do I. But I put them aside with you. I trust you, and I just keep waiting for the day you're going to trust me back. And after today, my patience is wearing thin. There's blood on my hands, however much you don't seem to think so."

"They filmed us. In our room." I blurted it out, then lowered my volume. "They showed me the video and threatened to lock Chace in a room with it playing on repeat for an entire day." My voice shook, and nothing I tried stopped it. "Are you happy? They violated our privacy and blackmailed me with it. What was I *supposed* to do in that situation, River?" I buried my face in my hands and turned away from him.

This was stupid. I wasn't even hungry, so what was I still doing in this weird bubble? I could go clean up for the night while everyone ate.

But before I took a single step, River's arms swept around me, hauling me back into his chest.

"I'm sorry." His voice was tight with the strain of it all. "I'm so, so sorry, Nyx."

"For what? That you ever met me, and got pulled into this ridiculous mess?" I couldn't keep the bitterness inside, not for all the water orbs in the world.

"No, I'm sorry for taking out my anger on you, the least deserving person. I'm sorry that a man got seriously hurt, might *die*, because of me. I'm sorry that something special between us was twisted into a threat. I'm just sorry. And furious, because that is not even a little bit okay." He rested his cheek against the top of my hair, and I let my eyes sink closed for just a second. One blissful second of shutting it all out—a second we really couldn't afford when we were sur-rounded by enemies.

"I'm sorry too. I should have told you; I know that. But it was so mortifying. I couldn't bring myself to say the words," I whispered.

He squeezed me a little tighter, just for a sec-ond, before leaning down and pressing a kiss to my cheek. "It's going to be okay, Nyx. We'll get through it."

"Will we? Or are we even going to like each other when this is over?" Dejection had stolen away the anger, however briefly. They'd told me not to be a hero, but what if my trying to save us all turned into losing him, losing Chace? I didn't want to be alone with no one I could trust left in the world. Frack, I still didn't even know if Hoss had lived.

"Hey, look—" He spun me around, and I al-lowed it, even though I was still questioning everything. "We're good. Or, I'm good. I got into my head. If I were in your shoes, and one of my relatives was still alive, I would have made the same choice. No way would I expect you to put yourself or Chace through that, okay? You made the right decision. You've made *all* the right decisions, even when I didn't."

"It's not wrong to be upset, River. We're just upset for different reasons. Them targeting you, that's what got to me. I'm sorry for Quinn, of course. But if it had been *you*, I'd be trying to blow up a whole cavalcade full of moles."

He smirked, just the tiniest twist of the lips, but I was so relieved to see the hint of his old humor coming back.

We'd never really fought before this. Sure, there was that time he left me, because he didn't want to go through Nightbloods territory. But he came back, and we'd come so far since then.

He rubbed the skin between my eyebrows lightly. "Don't frown. It's going to be okay, one way or another. You keep using that brilliantly devious brain of yours, and I'll keep backing you up. We can't let these guys win."

"They're going to keep fighting dirty," I whispered, feeling like I had to warn him. As much as it hurt when he pulled away, I didn't want to prolong it if he was going to ultimately leave, when they did something worse.

"I know. But we're going to win anyways." He dropped a teasing kiss on my nose, then patted my shoulders. "Eat. It's a shame to waste real food."

With a sigh, I reached for my bowl, and propped myself against the wall next to him, so I could people-watch while I shoveled it down. We chatted as we observed and ate, normalcy slowly returning between us despite the untenable situation. And just as slowly, the knot between my shoulder blades loosened.

Fifteen

HAB'S THE LIMIT

Day Two

Morning brought news of Quinn's death over the comm, which soured the mood in mole three. Morning ablutions were done in silence, none of Guffey's endless chatter to keep us all occupied. I'd fallen asleep last night to a soliloquy on the different types of rock we had passed through so far on our journey.

But today, it was all sad silence. River was holding it together surprisingly well, given how upset he'd been about things last night.

We were eating our morning meal bars when the stairs began to lower. Fletcher leapt to his feet, standing at attention as the commandant was slowly revealed, wearing a spotless white thermal regulation suit. He climbed the steps, a potent scowl scraping over each of us before settling on me briefly.

"Mr. Grenkel! I've brought your new member."

Grenkel. I recognize that name, but I've never seen Fletcher before this mission.

I held my breath, eyes trained on the stairs. A man clad in the typical Nightblood garb stepped up behind the commandant, and a few sharp inhalations echoed around the space.

"This is Rahlise, a highly esteemed member of the Nightbloods." He gestured impassively to the silent man looming at his back like an ominous shadow. "I expect him to be a great asset to this journey going forward, and your team specifically."

"But, sir—" Fletcher spluttered, "he's one of *them*. How do you expect us to sleep at night, with an enemy in our midst?"

Rahlise was unmoved by the direct opposition, instead, scanning the interior of our vehicle with a critical eye.

"Silence!" the commandant snapped. "You'll sleep lightly, as good soldiers do. For the purposes of this mission, we are all allied, and I won't hear another word of dissent out of your mouth, or Lieutenant Kutsuki can take over as first chair."

Fletcher's jaw snapped shut, angry red splotches dotting his cheeks.

"I take it that a change to the chain of command won't be necessary?"

"No, Commandant."

"Excellent. Show him to his seat, and let's get this motorcade back on the road." He turned on his heel, not waiting for a response before descending the stairs. They closed silently behind him, and it was like the entire mole held its breath to see what would happen next.

"Rear left seat, soldier." Fletcher ground out the words, the sound like broken glass on old cement.

Rahlise nodded and took his seat without comment. He didn't make eye contact with me as he passed or do anything to give away the reason he'd been subbed in, instead of another Excursion Team soldier.

But I knew, and bit back a smile as River and I locked eyes across the aisle. Every tiny collapse of the commandant's totalitarian control felt like a win, and this one was particularly sweet, after the blackmail.

Our rolling lunch was a tense affair, but Rahlise remained silent in the back row; the air of disdain rolled off him like dry sand, blowing away in the wind.

Today it was a dried meal inside a foil pouch, and I shuddered as I tore it open, and held it carefully as Kindred poured boiling water into it from a large kettle. It had a recent date stamped on the side, but after the ancient ones we'd found, I was a skeptic. River looked a little green as he stirred his with a fork.

"Is this something you eat frequently in space?" I asked, and received a bland nod in return, before he moved on to Guffey, behind me.

He was unusually subdued today, and the chatter had been kept to a minimum. I couldn't tell if it was Rahlise's appearance, or something else bothering him.

The noodles inside were surprisingly delicious, after they'd steeped, and small spurts of conversation came back to our group as the day wore on. Guffey was still unusually quiet in his seat, though. I waited until Kindred left for the lavatory, then turned my seat around to face him.

"Not even going to try to give me an engineering lesson today, huh?"

He smiled, but there was no joy in his eyes. "Not today, girl."

From any other man, being called *girl* would probably send me off the edge. But Guffey was so . . . harmless. Kind, and ebullient. The complete antithesis of any man I'd met in the desert, who would have said it as an insult. He just said it as fact. Like I was his granddaughter.

"Do you want to talk about what's bothering you?" I didn't bother beating around the bush.

He blinked a few times, eyebrows scrunching down behind his glasses' rims. "You are quite direct for a woman. I like that about you."

"Uh, thanks?" I tried to hold back a snort. Something I found myself doing often, with Guffey.

To my surprise, he leaned forward, lowering his voice and speaking directly into my ear. "I tested the suits myself. Every single one passed a thorough inspection before being delivered to the base camp."

He leaned back, eyes troubled as he looked out our shared window. I sat back, letting this new bit of information sink in. That meant that in the span of a day, roughly, someone had intentionally damaged the suit, as we'd suspected.

I leaned forward and tapped him on the knee to get his attention.

"What would it take to damage a suit to failure, like that? Could it have been a legitimate product of the environment? Or would it *have* to be . . ."

He was already shaking his head before I finished the question. "The only thing in this tunnel that could damage *that* fabric is the diamond-tipped drill bit on the front of the mole. The *only* thing."

I bit my lip, nodding as I pulled back.

"You two look awfully cozy," Kindred said as he took his seat opposite us.

"Just discussing the many perils of a journey like this," Guffey said, an undercurrent of steel in his tone I'd not heard before.

Kindred snorted, the sound oddly delicate. "At least down here no one's shooting at you, like in space."

"Shooting at you?" River spun his seat around, suddenly all ears and looking eagerly at Kindred for details.

"*Yeah.*" Kindred's tone was dry. "Space isn't all it's cracked up to be."

"Why *are* you guys here? We've always been told space was the great escape." I asked, keeping tabs on Guffey's expressions from the corner of my eye. He was a sweet, sincere man, and he had absolutely *no* trader face. It was quite helpful if you were paying attention.

He sighed, draping an arm over the back of his seat. "Do you know what spaceships are? They're vehicles. Just like this." He gestured at the mole's interior. "Would you want to live inside this mole every day of the rest of your life?"

"Oh, heck no," River said, shaking his head. "I'd go stir crazy."

"Yeah, well most of us don't have a choice. You can't even step outside for the weird group dinner. If you're not one of the founding families of Mars, your options are very limited. Terraformed land costs more than most spacefarers make in a lifetime. You could buy the red rock, but frankly, building a hab's not cheap either."

"A hab?" River asked, keenly curious about all things space. Chace was just the same, though he'd be disappointed to hear it wasn't all it was cracked up to be.

"Habitat. You have to have your own oxygenation system, among many other things, to make it livable outside the main city. But for most of us schmucks, that's a pipe dream. We spend our whole lives contained in an ever-rusting bucket of bolts. So, it might be crappy down here, but at least you can breathe the air for free."

"That's . . . wow." River leaned forward, propping his elbows on his knees to continue questioning Kindred about space life now that he'd opened up. I turned back to Guffey, more interested in what he thought had happened to River's suit than the vagaries of a life in space. But their enthusiastic exchange would provide a distraction, so we could speak a little more freely.

"So, who delivered the suits? Someone from your group, or from the city?" I asked quietly.

"We handed them off at the mouth of the cave for distribution." His mouth pressed into a grim line. "A decision I now regret."

As I suspected, it was someone closer to us. Besides the captain, who seemed unhinged, I didn't know enough about any of the other spacefarers to determine if they were more of a threat than anyone else. And I couldn't have made an enemy of them, without even meeting them.

But if they were interested in coming back to earth, surely they'd want us to fix the water supply, if that was possible.

It was nice to have my suspicions confirmed, but still troubling. Commandant Kieran was worried about his reputation with Captain Jacira; so why would he try to separate me and River in a way that was so noticeable to her people? It didn't make sense.

A low rumble rocked through our mole, and I froze in my seat.

"Did you hear—"

Another, louder rumble cut me off, causing the mole to shudder under our feet. An alarm blared, red lights flashing from the control panels up front.

"Seismic activity detected! Brace yourselves!" Fletcher's shout was the last thing I heard before the sound of falling rock drowned everything out.

Sixteen

Collapse

"Frack, frack, frack, frack—" I squeezed my eyes shut and gripped the arm rests of my seat so hard my nails indented the plush upholstery. The mole continued shaking beneath us for several minutes until suddenly, it all stopped.

I didn't move, barely breathed, as Fletcher cautiously rose from his seat and turned off the alarm on the control panel. He was pushing buttons and reading things, Jameson standing at his shoulder and murmuring things occasionally.

The comm beeped, and he picked it up. "Yes, we're all clear. Undamaged, uninjured . . . Okay. Copy."

He dropped the comm receiver back into its cradle and turned back to us. "That was the commandant, checking our status to continue the mission. Seismic activity is normal and expected from time to time, and we are completely undamaged. I know it's frightening, but you can all try to relax—the likelihood of additional quakes today is relatively slim, and—"

A loud creaking noise from overhead froze him mid-sentence. We all looked up, even though we could only see the roof of the mole. The creaking turned into a deafening crack, and the mole seemed to buck before settling back to the ground.

Fletcher dropped a string of swears that would make a Sidewinder proud as alarms began blaring from the control panel again.

One of our overhead lights began to flicker, then shorted out with a buzz. I stared at it in frozen terror, half listening to the angry arguments from up front, when a soft touch on my arm jolted me.

It was River, his long, tanned fingers wrapping gently around my wrist. "Just breathe. We're going to be fine."

"You don't know that," I argued out of habit, but there was no fire behind it. I hoped to any God who'd listen that he was right. I did *not* want to die buried under a pile of rubble, deep underground, while I slowly boiled to death from the ever-increasing heat.

I let go of the arm rest and clutched his fingers instead, the regular thrum of his pulse steadying me slightly. I scanned the rest of the mole, and besides the one errant light, everything appeared to be in working order. Kindred looked bored, River was attentively listening to Fletcher and Jameson's argument, as I should be, and Guffey's eyes were closed, face white as a sheet as he mouthed a silent prayer.

Nanette stormed up the aisle. "Enough!" she snapped, and the two younger soldiers instantly fell silent under her censure. "Officer, this is an emergency, and I'm going to have to ask you to remain—" Fletcher held up a hand, but Nanette was having none of it. "*Move.*" Her order brooked no argument, and the two of them stepped to the side, angry scowls painted on their faces. She lifted the comm, and began rapidly but silently flipping switches, only pausing to check readouts.

The ground shuddered once more underneath us, and I would swear the creaking I heard this time was River's bones in my grip. It stopped in under a minute, but my heart was pounding in my chest. My palms were slick with sweat, despite the pleasantly cool temperature and my suit's best regulating efforts.

I never thought I'd miss the open sprawl of sand that was the Wastes, but in that moment, I'd have given just about anything to kiss the empty, open sand under that wide blue sky. I was vibrating with tension, and everything in me screamed to *run*, but there wasn't anywhere to run to.

Nor would it be safe to leave the mole with rock shearing off and falling from the top of the tunnel.

The internal alarms finally quit, and Nanette studied a tablet while rattling off stats that meant nothing to me into the phone. She was quiet for a moment, and then her attention shifted back toward us. "Engineer Guffey! You're needed."

His eyes snapped open, and his hands shook as he unbuckled his harness. He made his way slowly to the front, and accepted the tablet from Nanette.

Guffey talked to himself under his breath for several tense moments, until he finally looked up. "We've got damage to the fuel cells. It can be repaired, but it's not something I'd willingly work on while the mole is inhabited. If anything goes wrong . . ."

"I understand. I'll put out some comms, find out what our best options are. You can return to your seat for now." Nanette turned her back on him, no longer concerned with his opinion now that she had a course of action.

Low, tense conversations broke out inside the mole, sounding like static to my ears behind the frantic beat of my own heart.

"Nyx, look at me." River shook my hand gently, breaking through the fog.

"What is it?" My words were hoarse, so I cleared my throat and tried again. "Are you all right?"

He smiled softly. "I'm fine, and so are you. There are plenty of other moles, some of them undamaged. If Guffey can't fix mole three, they'll shuffle us all around and put us in another. Okay?"

"Okay," I whispered, searching his icy blue eyes for any signs of doubt, but finding none. Something inside my chest loosened, and I could breathe normally again. I don't know when or how it happened, but, while I wasn't looking, River had become my anchor—my safety in the storm.

His ease brought me ease, his calm found mine. No matter how dire the situation, if he was still smiling, it was probably going to be okay. I squeezed his fingers for a second before letting him go, and unbuckling my harness. The thing felt like it was strangling me all of a sudden.

After a good standing stretch, I turned to face Guffey. "So, how bad off are we?"

His eyes were tight at the corners, and he reached up, running his fingers through his hair and pulling slightly at the ends. It must have been a nervous habit, because I hadn't seen anything throughout the trip except scientific curiosity until now.

So we were deep in it, even if he didn't want to say it.

"Are the other moles functional, at least?" I asked, and to my surprise, he turned questioning eyes on Kindred.

Kindred rolled his eyes, but slipped a half-sized tablet from his compartment, and in a few swipes he hummed. "Only two show damage, but ours is the most critical. One of the fuel cells has been pierced and is leaking. In theory it can be patched, but that kind of damage means that it could explode if the metalwork repair causes sparks, and that wouldn't be good for anyone in a . . . thirty foot radius, give or take. Would you agree, Guff?"

Guffey nodded, face pale. Kindred's answering smile was more a baring of teeth, and it reminded me oddly of King.

A shiver rocked through me, but I pushed it aside.

"Okay everybody, listen up. We're being moved to mole five. Gather your personal belongings, we leave in five minutes. Most of their party is being moved back, but we're gaining two of their members."

I glanced around the close interior, noting that we already filled every single available seat, which also reclined for sleep. Where were we supposed to put two more people?

"Guffey, we need you to apply a patch sufficient to move this mole into one of the bypass tunnels, but nothing long term. We can tow it out on the return trip."

"Yes, officer," he agreed, pulling his satchel over his shoulder with a determined look.

"Is that safe for you, Bernard?" I stopped him with a hand on his arm.

He paused, taking a beat before meeting my eyes. "I know how to handle it, Nyx."

"Okay. See you soon."

He nodded, but was uncharacteristically silent as he made his way down the aisle to the front of the mole.

Nanette was unconcerned, intent on seeing her orders carried out. "Engineer Snell from mole six is here to assist you. The fuel cells are located at the rear of the mole, hatch—"

"Twenty-nine," Guffey interjected. "Yes, I've loaded the schematics. Is there sufficient patch material on board for a gouge this size?"

"There should be, but if not we can also access the repair kit from seven," Kutsuki said.

"Let's get this show on the road, then." Guffey stood and put on his helmet, ready and waiting for the stairs to be lowered again.

Nanette nodded, signaling Fletcher with a finger-wave to come take over the disembarkation so she could gather her own things.

Fletcher resumed his spot with his spine straight, a disgruntled tilt to his lips. He didn't say a word as he opened the hatch, steps lowering gracefully, as if nothing had happened. The slight hitch at the end before it settled to the ground was the only sign of damage.

"Single file, please, in order of seating. Kutsuki and I will remain here to pilot once the patch has been applied, and join you in mole five once the tunnels are clear."

That meant I was first. With my little collection of personal items in my hands, I stepped up to the front. River was hot on my heels when a scuffle broke out behind me.

"I will accompany Ms. Brandt."

The voice was foreign, but I knew even before I turned who it belonged to. Rahlise had his arm blocking River's chest, pressed into the muscle there like an iron band, refusing to let him pass.

"What's the problem, Nightblood?" Kutsuki took a menacing step forward. "You heard Lieutenant Grenkel. In seating order. You're *last*."

"I will accompany Ms. Brandt," he repeated, dark eyes boring into the second-chair, asking him to argue.

"Grenkel, you have any problem with *Rahlise* here going second?" The question was a slow, insulting drawl from Kutsuki's lips.

Fletcher sighed, and I once again wondered why I knew his last name. It was niggling at the back of my mind, something I knew was significant but couldn't place.

Grenkel, Grenkel.

"It's fine. We're all going to the same place, just keep it single file. The tunnels are narrow here."

He waved us forward with impatience, and I took the first step onto the stairs.

"Nyx—" Fletcher called, and I looked back at him over my shoulder. He looked familiar, too. "Watch the rubble. We don't need any broken ankles today."

I nodded, and continued down the stairs. That's when it hit me. The Grenkels were the elderly couple who had been exiled to make space for River and me. The pain hit me all over again, like a fresh wound. I would tell him I was sorry, tonight at dinner. He probably wouldn't care, but he deserved to know we hadn't meant to hurt his family. They had to be related; grandparents, maybe, or perhaps an elderly aunt and uncle. The resemblance was too strong, and everything about his attitude made so much more sense.

When the sole of my boot touched the tunnel floor, it was like stepping onto a purring cat.

I'd only seen one in my entire life. One of the kept women had a kitten when I was a kid. She used to walk around with it curled around her neck, like a live tabby-patterned scarf. It purred when she stopped to let us pet its belly, and that was exactly what the earth did beneath my feet. I froze, the strangeness of it gluing me to the spot. Something popped over my head, the ground jerking at the same time. I looked up, horror dousing me when the ceiling moved, a huge chunk of rock shearing away.

I couldn't move, couldn't think, couldn't *blink*—it was like I was rooted to the spot.

Run!

The thought spurred me into motion, but I knew it was too little, too late. The rock was huge, and no matter how much time had slowed, it wasn't enough for me to get out from under it. One stride, that was all I got.

And then something huge and heavy hit me from behind, throwing me forward to the rough, uneven ground, knocking the wind out of me and sending my ears ringing.

A second, maybe two later, the pain hit. Searing hot agony, like a knife was embedded in my thigh, radiated from the site, and the rest of my body felt detached in its wake. Screams bounced off the tunnel walls, and in my detachment it took a beleaguered second for me to realize the screams were mine.

Seventeen

Powder Keg

Chace

T he guards were acting twitchy today around the rim of the gathering place. They were always unpleasant bastards—probably got it stuck in their craw that I got an early release from the laborer class—but something had changed. I'd been keeping my head low and my ears open since they took my sister, but information came in frustratingly slow drips. Right now I was behind a group of half drunk soldiers.

This time of the afternoon they were off duty, and I'd heard a few things slip. Things like, the commandant's control on the city wasn't as complete as he portrayed it. Apparently, there were *three* factions inside Bastion City. His loyal sycophants were a large group, but there was a resistance brewing after his most recent exile, and *apparently* he'd also pissed off the group that helped get him elected in the first place. Promises had gone unfulfilled, he'd turned to the masses, and they were out for blood.

Not that it helped me any currently, but it was still interesting to see the cracks in the civility they worked so hard to enforce.

None of the city soldiers trusted me, and the spacers that had stayed behind with us didn't talk to anyone not wearing a metallic space suit.

Today, I was going to try again to catch one of the serving girls and see if she'd talk. A redhead had been making eyes at me, even though she was *way* too young for the kind of looks she'd been giving me. Although sometimes I forgot I didn't look as old as I felt.

Because, God, I felt ancient.

Trying to keep me and Nyx alive had been enough work, but getting dropped into Bastion City nearly ended me. With her gone, I had no one to protect, nothing to live for.

I'd never have told Nyx, but if it had taken her a month or two longer, I'd have been a broken bag of bones on the floor. I couldn't think about that now, though, or about the nightmares that I woke up from with every muscle of my body locked in terror.

I scrubbed a hand over my face, but it couldn't wipe away the memories, the pain.

Nothing could, but action helped. Staying busy. Watching our backs, even if my sister got manipulated into leaving me behind.

She wouldn't admit it, but I knew they had done something. It hadn't been her idea; there was no way. But her eyes had begged me to go along with it, so what else could I have done?

I could track down a feisty little redhead and get some details, that's what.

Wandering away from the group of drunk soldiers I'd been eavesdropping behind, I made sure to look bored, kicking the occasional rock and meandering, so my guards on the rim wouldn't pay any more attention to me. A quick glance over my shoulder confirmed that they were deep in conversation with another soldier, so I kept it up, slowly making my way to the back of the cavern. A cluster of laborers were back there, including the woman I was looking for.

Though really, any of them could help me, if they were so inclined. My sister had asked me to find a 'Morgan,' or somebody who knew her. Surely one of these workers did—the city was only so big, after all.

I stopped a few feet away, pretending to be very interested in a brightly-colored section of rock embedded in the flat walls.

"So we meet again, handsome. Did you wander all the way over here for little ol' me?"

I repressed a grin. *The redhead.*

"Maybe, is that a crime?"

She snorted indelicately. "Not yet, but give the commandant six months. It will be."

"Is that so? What a shame. What's your name?"

"Sandy, and don't laugh." The petulant poke of her bottom lip told me everything I needed to know about her. Way too young, and not my type. I didn't want to lead her on, so I'd have to tread lightly.

"I wouldn't *dream* of laughing at you, Sandy, especially not when you're the only one around this place that's willing to talk to me. I am curious, though. You know a girl named Morgan? About your age—I hear she's friends with my baby sister. She asked me to look her up."

That bottom lip disappeared between her teeth so fast, I could have blinked and missed it.

"Morgan? She's *trouble*. My parents specifically told me to stay away from her because she's into some sketchy stuff." Sandy shot me a suspicious look, as if by mentioning the name in her presence, I'd sullied her with said sketchy stuff.

Who knew freedom was sketchy these days?

"Well, I wouldn't dream of getting you in trouble. Just wanted to pass along a friendly hello from my sister. I'll let you get back to your conversation." I gave her a polite nod, but before I took a second step away from her, there was a hand on my bicep. I looked down, surprised to see rich ebony skin, nothing like Sandy's pale porcelain. When I turned back around, there was a young black man looking nervously from side to side.

"You asking about Morgan?" he whispered, casting an anxious look over his shoulder at the gossiping young women and shoving back his thick raven hair. A wave of giggles came from the huddle, and his eyes went wide. I nodded to the side, and he followed, eager to get a little space from them.

When we were a good twenty feet away, I stopped. "So, you know her?"

"Maybe. She really friends with your sister? I don't recognize you."

"Yeah, really. What's your name, man?" I offered a friendly, no-pressure smile, hoping to put him at ease.

He didn't look relieved, and I had yet more proof that I sucked at talking to people. Nyx was the talker; I was the brute force. But she wasn't here, so I'd have to make do.

"Lyle. I'm on the cleaning crew. Got five more years before I can apply for an excursion team position."

"Nice. I just got out of the laborer camp myself, so I don't even have an assignment yet."

That grabbed his attention.

"So, you know how it is."

"Little bit." I shrugged. I hadn't been here my whole life, like he had, so it didn't feel right to claim some great understanding of his struggles. The tip of the sand dune was more than enough to show me I didn't want this life.

"Morgan's a nice girl. She's assigned to the command building, because her uncle's on the leadership panel."

"Think you could wrangle me a meeting with her? Nyx wanted me to pass along her regards, check on her after the brouhaha up top." I didn't bother forcing a smile, this time. Lyle and I seemed to connect better without all the forced pleasantries.

"Yeah, man, that was wild. She should have a break in an hour. Where do you stay down here?"

"I'm in tent eighty-seven, but our lunch is in an hour, also. Which is good, because it'll be easier to slip my guard."

"Guard? I thought you were out of the laborer camp."

"Psh. Yeah, in theory. But my sister's too high profile. I'm leverage now."

"Bad rap. Okay, I'll come find you at lunch."

We exchanged a hand-slap, and then he jogged off to finish up whatever task I'd interrupted.

"Psst," the low call stopped me mid-bite of my stew. I calmly placed the bite in my mouth and stretched, casting a glance over my shoulder.

There was Lyle, at the edge of the crowd. Right on time. A good quality that was hard to find out in the Wastes.

"Hey, I need to hit the head," I called to my guards, but they were deep in conversation, and the nearest one waved for me to go.

They still watched me, but now that Nyx was well and truly gone, and I had no access to leave the cavern except on foot, they'd all but given up on following me minute to minute. Where could I go?

I stood from the table and strolled lazily towards the big wall of bathrooms, before making a hard right at the edge of the lunch crowd and circling around to meet Lyle.

"We gotta run, man. But she is waiting for us."

He took off, not waiting for me to agree or checking that I followed, so I stayed tight on his heels. Thankfully we were running *away* from my guards, and not right past them, or they'd have gotten curious.

He dipped and dodged around people, UTVs, and tents until we found ourselves back behind the low command building. It was cast in deep shadows, and I didn't see anyone waiting. The hairs on the back of my neck stood up, and that "you've been played, sucker" feeling wouldn't die down. And then a diminutive brunette stepped out of a door, and quickly crossed the stone to stand before us. She had freckles and a snub nose, and she was cute in that little sister kind of way.

Not that I needed another one of *those* to look after.

"Lyle," she greeted him with a nod. "And Chace. I have to say, I didn't expect to ever actually meet you. Your sister went through a lot of camel crap to get you back." She looked me pointedly up and down, as if she didn't see what all the fuss was about.

"Yeah, well, we're close. She wanted me to check on you, make sure you didn't get into trouble after the mess up top, and see where the plans stood."

She worried her bottom lip between her teeth, and Lyle interrupted. "What plans? You got another crazy scheme going, Morg? Your uncle's gonna be pissed."

"It's not crazy, okay? Shut up." She shoved his shoulder and widened her eyes at me threateningly. "This guy and his sister are *actual survival experts*. They came from the Wastes, and they've got a truck on the outside. That *works*."

Lyle's jaw dropped and he turned to me. "For real?"

"For real." I shuffled my feet, still uneasy about our out-of-the-way location, though so far it was still quiet.

"Yeah, well, now everyone's worried that Nyx is going to back out. We had *big* plans, and to have them fall apart like that . . . it was a blow."

"My sister is too stubborn to go back on her word, so you can guarantee anybody who needs it that when she's back on the surface, she'll keep her promises. And now she's got me, and I'll help."

"That's what I like to hear!" Morgan clapped, underlining how young our liaison was. "Okay, so, things up top aren't great. The lifeside is all rumbling about how to still carry out our plans with martial law enacted, but the parkside is pure panic. Everybody put their whole belief into the commandant, and he gunned one of their own down. Then he made it worse by allying with the spacers without telling a soul. And I *know* he didn't tell a soul, because my uncle was furious."

"Your uncle?"

"He's on the Leadership Panel. They're supposed to co-lead the city."

"Ah," I murmured, even though I had no idea what she was talking about. "Pandemonium can be good for getting out of Dodge, if we can use it to our advantage."

"Oh yeah? Well how's this for a pandemonium: the commandant's been lying to everybody. Our water source is almost dry. When that word gets out? It's going to be a free-for-all."

Lyle's eyebrows shot up so high, they disappeared under his shaggy black fringe.

"Hold up, how do you know that?"

"Cyndia cleans the control room. They act like she's not there, and two of the water techs were talking about how we were at less than ten percent total reserve remaining."

"Holy shi—"

Morgan elbowed Lyle in the ribs, stopping him mid-swear.

"We're all sitting on a big ol' powder keg," Morgan finished with a flourish.

"Yeah, well, if anybody knows how to light a match, it's my sister. I'll let her know."

Eighteen

GRIT

Day Three

My eyes were gritty, and they didn't want to open. I wanted to wipe them clear, but my hand was stuck, something heavy holding it down. I tried again, and the thing on my hand moved.

"Nyx? Are you awake? Please be awake. I've been staring at you for nearly twenty hours straight, and I'm starting to think you're not going to wake up. You have to wake up, Nyx. I haven't gotten to tell you I love you, yet, and your eyes really need to be open for that. Plus, if I come back without you, Chace is going to kill me, bring me back to life, kill me again, and then take out every single person inside Bastion City."

River.

His voice dropped low, and his hand stroked my hair when he whispered the next bit into my ear. "I gave him the detonator for the T-4 at the gate. He really will take out the city if you don't come back. Please, Nyx. I know you don't want that, and I don't want to be without you. Please. I'm here. You're okay. Just open your eyes, please. *Please.*"

I tried, I really did, but the darkness was just so heavy.

Nineteen

Cut Off

Day ?

"I don't care what you have to do. I don't care if you have limited resources. *Fix her.*"

"Mr. Zeer, I assure you we've done everything in our power to wake her. The nanites in her blood seem to be speeding the healing process somehow—it's quite fascinating—ahh, nevermind. But she's been gravely wounded. Lost a lot of blood. And with the communications down, we can't call back for medical supplies, nor could they get here until the tunnels are once again clear. There's nothing left to do but wait."

A rattling thud and a sharp exhale followed the statement, and I willed my eyes to open. A tiny spear of light made it through, and I squinched it closed again immediately. Light *hurt*.

"Set the doctor down, boy. If you hurt him, there's no one else to attend to her." I didn't recognize the voice, but I did recognize the thud of boots landing back on the ground when River obeyed.

"Riv—" I tried, but no sound came out. I wanted to clear my throat, but it was so dry.

"River," I rasped again. And this time, warm, callused palms encased my cheeks.

"Nyx? You're awake!" His forehead dropped to mine, and his hands shook where they held my face.

"Yes. Thirsty."

"On it. She needs water." His words weren't quite a shout, but they weren't calm, either.

"Yes, of course."

Shuffling sounds had me trying to turn my head, but River held me still. "Shh, Nyx. You've been through a lot, and you're going to be weak. Your body needs you to stay still a little longer.

"Here you are." The doctor's voice again, closer this time.

A straw prodded my lips, which I opened, sucking down the cool water greedily. I nearly choked myself, but I couldn't stop. It was so good, so sweet and so cool, that I never wanted anything else. My stomach rumbled.

Okay, so, a meal bar wouldn't hurt. But nothing could top cold water.

"Can you open your eyes?" he asked gently after I drained the entire water cup.

"No, they're stuck. Also, the light is too bright."

"I'll get the lights," the mystery voice said.

"I'll get a warm rag and see if we can't unstick you. Just hang on." He blew out a breath, then added. "I'm so glad you're awake. You scared us to death, Nyx." One last squeeze of my hands, and then he vanished for a minute.

When he came back, he gently worked over my eyelids with a warm wash cloth until I could open my eyes freely.

His face was the first thing to come into focus. He was pale, and there were lines at the corners of his mouth that I didn't remember.

"What is it?" I asked, searching his eyes for an answer. "I'm okay, you can stop looking so worried now." I tried to smile, but that hurt, too, so I stopped.

"Take it easy. You're all bruised up from the fall, and probably pretty sore."

"Too bruised to sit up?"

"No, we can help you sit up, if you're up for that."

"We?"

"We." The mystery voice crystallized as Rahlise stood from a chair by the door. He crossed the room and tucked a hand under my other armpit without compunction, helping River sit me up in the bed. Even with their painstaking movements, most of my body hurt. The worst was my left leg, though. It felt searing where everything else felt dull and achy. I moaned, the sound low and deep as pressure on the area had me questioning my decision to sit up.

"I know, I'm so sorry. We can ask the doctor about stronger pain meds, if you want. He said it could make you off-balance, though, and it would be better if you can be up and moving soon so we can get you out of med bay."

"Are we at the water generator? How long have I been out?" River winced at the question.

"No memory loss from the head injury. Good." Rahlise nodded approvingly, then crossed back to his chair and sat down.

"We're not there, no. We actually haven't moved since you were injured. The rock fall that took you out also blocked the tunnels." River gripped my hand, and I did my best not to hyperventilate at the news.

"Behind us or in front of us?"

"Both," Rahlise answered, ever succinct.

"Both," I repeated, my voice growing higher. We were stuck. *Stuck.* Underground. In little moles, with— "Don't these things have drills on the front? Why are we still stuck?"

"They do, yes. And they are working on clearing the tunnels, but it's slow. These tunnels were made with much bigger machines, and the tunnels are only wide enough here for one mole to work at a time. So they've been working in round-the-clock shifts, and in another day or two we should be back on the road. Err, trail?" he stammered, trying for levity even while his eyes held mine apologetically.

"Okay, a day or two. So, how long was I out?"

"Two days. You got knocked on the head pretty hard when you landed, but Rahlise saved your life. That rock was heading straight for your head, and he knocked you out of the way. Your leg . . . it's going to be okay. A piece of the rock sheared off and pierced your suit. We extracted it, cleared out the debris, and stitched you up. You lost a lot of blood while they were trying to get you out from under the rocks. The doctor said you'll probably be weak for a while, and you need to take it as easy as you can, until we arrive."

"How thoughtful," I groused. Even grievously injured, my value to them was still painfully clear. But that was no surprise.

"Yeah. Oh, and your . . . *Hema* is upset. Rahlise would probably be better to tell you about that." River looked to him expectantly, but he remained pointedly silent.

"Or not. Look, Hema wants you transferred into the mole with only Nightbloods. Apparently they've got two, at the back of the caravan that are theirs alone. He doesn't trust that attacks won't keep happening—"

"Attacks? The literal tunnel collapsed. It was a freak accident." I rubbed my forehead with a shaky hand. My head was pounding the longer I sat, and I didn't see how my bad luck constituted an attack. Or anything that would have been solved by being in a different mole.

"He's not convinced. They haven't found proof, but Nyx . . . I think I agree with him. It was too much of a coincidence. Our mole was the *only* one damaged. We were the only ones who had to evacuate. You were made to walk out first, and then the rocks fell. It's one too many things to line up."

I shook my head, until the pain stopped me. *Surely not. Someone tried to collapse a freaking tunnel on my head?*

"Why? Who gains from killing me, River? It makes no sense. I get if they try to take me out after, but if I'm really the only one who can fix the water generator, why would anyone try to stop that? We all die without water. Every last one of us."

Frustration rose in my chest so fast, it almost choked me. The only reason I didn't fight against being here was so we could possibly fix the water situation. We all needed it. We should all *want* it fixed.

But who wouldn't?

It was a question that had been nagging at me, ever since Chace's warning about them trying to isolate me. Who did it benefit if the water generator wasn't repaired?

"I don't know, Nyx. I'm not like you, I can't read people's minds from their facial expressions. That's the other reason you need to rest, so you can get well and help me figure this out." I dropped my hand from my head back to my lap, and exhaustion had me tilting to the side.

Rahlise steadied me, concern knitting his eyebrows together. "You must lie back down." He commanded.

I wanted to rebel against anyone bossing me around, but I swayed again as soon as he removed his hand from my shoulder, and realized it was pointless.

"One more glass of water, first," River said, jogging across the small space to a pitcher, and poured another cup of the cool, perfect water. As soon as I drained it, they helped me get horizontal in the bed again. The last thing I remembered were the steady, smooth strokes of River's fingers over my forearm.

Twenty

Legacy

When I next floated up from the blackness, a different face loomed over me. The eyes were kind and worried behind his face covering. *Hema.*

"Παιδί μου, you scared me half into the grave. Never again." The gentle chiding had me trying to shake my head, and this time it was a touch easier. No immediate pounding, at least.

He tsked. "Stay still, daughter. It is only I, and your lover. You are safe."

Some part of the back of my brain wondered if I should be embarrassed at my father calling River my lover, but I dismissed it. There were bigger dunes to climb.

"Water?" I asked, unsure how to address the fatherly concern. I'd never had any, and now it felt like an ill-fitting pair of favorite pants.

They should have fit, but for some reason just wouldn't button.

Hema snapped, and River pressed a cup into his hand. He held the straw to my lips tenderly, and I flashed back to the cave. He'd nursed me with single-minded intention, and suddenly, everything made more sense. He'd suspected, even then. But would he have stopped for any stranger? Or would I have been a dried up husk in the Wastes, if we didn't share the same nose?

I'd never know, and that bothered me.

I wanted to believe him to be a good man, at his core. The man who'd saved me. Who cared for me. But he ran a gang who did bad things. Who murdered innocents. Who stole young boys from their families.

The dichotomy was enough to torment me on a good day, and today wasn't one of those.

"Am I allowed to eat?" I asked, once I'd drained the cup of water.

"A little. The doctor doesn't want you throwing up." River appeared at my other side, and stroked my hair back from my face.

"Anything," I murmured, searching his face for signs of what was going on. I was glad Hema was well, but at the same time, I didn't know how to be around him.

River turned away and rummaged through a cupboard, before bringing back some options.

"There's this . . . jiggly stuff." He shook a clear container full of green goo toward me, and it did, in fact, jiggle strangely. "Or instant . . . scrambled eggs?" He held up a vacuum sealed foil pouch, and my stomach turned over at the prospect.

"Not that."

He cracked a grin, that dimple popping for a brief instant before he continued listing my options.

"Date paste, a meal bar, or cactus juice."

"Meal bar."

He rolled his eyes, but put the green goo and the dehydrated food away, pulling out the familiar, roller-pressed rectangle and unwrapping it for me.

I took a bite slowly, savoring the familiar flavor. "Berry delight," I murmured, taking another bite with a little more vigor.

"Easy, παιδί μου. Your stomach has been empty for days. You don't want to overtax your system with this cardboard."

I nodded, chewing slowly as the awkwardness returned.

"I must ask you some questions, Nyx, and I apologize if they are uncomfortable. The doctor here has shared with me that you have special nanites in your blood. These were not present when I took your blood sample the first time, nor, according to River, do you know when you received them. Is it possible that the people of the city performed an experiment on you during your time with them?"

I blinked a few times, surprised both by the directness and the line of questioning. I hadn't had the nanites when he took my blood in the desert.

That was new information.

"But the nanites came from your side of the family. I'd just assumed you had them, too. That I'd always had them."

He took a step back from my bedside, staggering as if I'd hit him.

"Apparently not, Nyx. Chace doesn't have them, and neither does Hema. Jaen . . . well, there's no way of knowing, but since Chace doesn't have them, we can only assume that they're not, in fact, inherited."

If I wasn't already lying in bed, I probably would have fallen over. How could it be? Then something clicked.

"They tested both of our blood, River, so that means you don't have them either, right?"

"No, I'm nanite-free."

"The decontamination room. Everyone who comes into the city gets decontaminated. You were fine, River, but I passed out. What if whatever they sprayed on us—"

"I, too, went through this decontamination shower." Hema's voice was quieter this time.

"Did it knock you out?" I was scared to hear his answer, as much as I needed it like my next breath.

"No, none of my men suffered any ill effects."

"That doesn't mean it couldn't contain the nanites. The commandant could be keeping secrets about exactly what happens when you're brought into the city." River was angry, tension radiating off him in waves.

"We don't know that, River. Let's find out before we strangle the man." I placed a hand on his forearm and he settled slightly. "I've been all over the desert. There's no telling where I picked them up." I briefly considered the locket powder, but perhaps the nanites were why I survived, when nobody else did? There was no way to find out without exposing someone else to the powder, which could kill them.

"True. I just don't trust him." River squeezed my fingers lightly, but the anger was gone, for now at least.

"That is wise. Someone is trying to kill my daughter before she can complete this mission, and everyone is suspect."

"Not *everyone*. You two aren't. Rahlise saved my life, from the sounds of it. Is he okay, by the way?"

"Rahlise is fine, apart from some bruising which he was honored to bear for you. He has made a blood oath to me and my line, as have all of the men I brought with me on this journey. To harm a hair on your head is to forfeit their next breath."

"Uhm." I didn't know what to say to that. His eyes were intense, his posture was stiff. Everything about him was a lot. "Why would they do that? They don't know me."

"They know what you mean to me. That is enough. You are my legacy, παιδί μου, one I never dared dream to have." He ran his hand over my hair, and gently over my cheek. "You are my own daughter, my own blood. Nothing is more important than you."

I didn't know what to say, so I said nothing. My throat was clogged, anyway. I'd probably sound like a prepubescent boy if I tried to answer.

"When I am gone, you will rule over them. They know this, and will protect you with the same fervor they protect me."

"I'm sorry, did you just say she was going to rule over *the Nightbloods* when you're gone?" River cut in, incredulity coating every word.

"Yes. She is my sole heir. And her children will rule after her. Though . . . it would be more desirable if she chose a *loyal* man of the blood to carry on her line." His words cut through the tension in the air like a lightning bolt streaking through the afternoon sky.

He knew who River was. And he was not happy.

"Loyal? To the men who murdered my parents? Never." River's snarl caught me off guard, and I shoved up on my elbows. The two of them leaned menacingly over me, as if they wanted to tear each other's throats out.

"Mind your tongue, boy, or I shall cut it out. Perhaps she will tire of you, then, and make a better choice of bed companions."

"Try me." River was seething.

I placed a palm on each of their chests.

"Could you not fight? River is loyal. *To me*. And if you hurt him, I won't be happy with *you*." I stared Hema down, hoping he understood the depth of my sincerity. "And River, I know you've got bad history with the Nightbloods. I know, and I hate it. But he's my father." My voice shook. Something felt *weighty* about the admission. Something better left unexamined. "He's the only parent I have left. And I need you to try to get along. For me."

"I'm sorry, Nyx." River was the first to cede the staring contest, brushing the back of his knuckles over my cheekbone. There was real contrition in his eyes, and a knot loosened behind my breastbone. Hema, however, wasn't so quickly swayed.

"I'll not tolerate insubordination. Not from anyone, under my protection, or no." He finally dropped his gaze to mine, frustration still evident despite the shrouds of black fabric that hid him from me. "You need to think long and hard about where your loyalties lie. I cannot protect you from those you hold onto against my wishes."

With that he turned on his heel, and left.

The knot behind my breastbone turned to a stone, cold and bitter, its metallic taste coating the back of my tongue.

"What does he want from me? We're practically strangers!" I threw the half empty cup of water at the door, and it hit with a satisfying thud. Water droplets arced through the air, and horror at what I'd done washed over me, drowning out the brief satisfaction. "Oh, frack. Frack, frack, frack! I just threw water." My breaths came in great, heaving gulps that made my ribs hurt.

"Nyx, settle down. It was only a little."

"River! We could *die* down here if we run out of water! How could I be so wasteful?" I buried my head in my hands, and fought back angry tears. That would only waste *more* water.

His arms came around my shoulders, gently at first, and then more firmly when I didn't wince or pull away.

"He'll be back, Nyx. I'd bet my last water credit that *nobody* has ever stood up to him before you. Everyone else was too afraid. But you're not, and you shouldn't be. If he meant what he said, he'll be back." He rubbed my back in slow, repetitive circles.

And all the while, one thought plagued me.

But what if he doesn't come back?

Twenty-One

WOBBLY

Day Six

"That's it, Nyx. Take it slow."

All my breath hissed out between my teeth. "Fraaaaaack. Oh, that sucks. My leg burns."

"That's quite normal after the level of injury you've sustained. Frankly, it's nigh unto miraculous that you're alive at all, let alone upright a few days later."

I ground my back teeth together, locking in the belligerent words that wanted to fly at the curious doctor.

Miraculous. If it were *miraculous* it wouldn't feel like shards of glass shredding my flesh. Right?

"That's enough. I need to sit," I panted as River and the doctor helped me settle back onto the edge of the bed.

"I think you're well enough for the brace. It gives compression to the wounded area, and also support so that it's not under such strain. You still need to take it easy for a week or two, but it will get you out of med bay, and back to your team. Presuming, of course, that you *wish* to go back to your team?" He adjusted the small collection of already-tidy medical tools on the side table, and politely skirted the issue of Hema making a stink about where I would go for the rest of the journey.

"Let's try the brace, first." I gestured for him to hand it over, and he did.

It looked uncomfortable, but anything had to be better than the ground glass sensation I currently got when putting any weight on my bad leg. The hard composite rods would encircle and protect the injury, while the *smart fabric* molded itself to me. It was the same color blue as the suit, so at least it wouldn't be obvious to everyone at first glance that I was still busted.

The weakness felt like something to hide, not flaunt. Too many years of scrabbling to stay alive made you cautious, and the back of my neck prickled every time I thought about leaving this protected space with a big, red flag proclaiming me *damaged*.

Blissfully unaware of my negative thoughts, River helped me shimmy it up to my left thigh, then let go once I could maneuver the top. I tugged it into place over the still-sore wound, and as soon as I released it, the fabric began to shrink down, molding itself to my wounded thigh.

The sensation was strange, at first. Then panic-inducing. It gripped me like it was going to cut off my circulation, but then slowly eased as the fabric reformed, lengthening to encase the entire area from knee to groin. Once it was still, the doctor clapped his hands.

"Okay, time to try the standing test again. Nyx, if you're ready . . ." He held up a hand for me to take, and River did the same on my other side.

I wasn't ready, but I *was* sick of people looming over me like an invalid. Sucking in a deep breath, I grabbed both of their hands and slid off the bed. This time, with the brace compressing my entire thigh, I was able to stand with only a slight twinge of pain.

"That's . . . incredible. No more glass." I met River's eyes with a grin, and he grinned right back, showing off that dimple.

"Glass? What do you mean?"

"Ah, nothing. Just that it's barely a pinch compared to before."

"Excellent, excellent. However, This is not an invitation to overdo it. We have several more days of travel ahead, and you are to rest. This will help you get to and from the lavatory, but your meals should be brought in, and you should remain reclined to keep weight off the area as much as possible. Are we clear? If you rip open the stitches, you'll have to be brought back here to the med bay, and we try to keep the sickbed open whenever possible. If we weren't on a mission, you'd be stuck in the clinic for a few weeks, yet."

I found myself suddenly grateful to be underground, miles and miles from the clinic.

"I'll keep a close eye on her, doc."

"I believe you will. You're lucky to have a man like this, Ms. Brandt."

River shook his head lightly, running his thumb along the side of my neck. "I'm lucky to have her, doc." His words were barely above a whisper, but I heard them all the same.

"What's that?" The doctor turned back around, adjusting his glasses.

"Nothing. We're just ready to get out of here." I shoved down my concerns about looking weak and forced a smile, so he'd believe me.

"All right then, you're dismissed. If you have any bleeding or pulled stitches, you know where to find me."

I had to lean on River's shoulder, but my leg was mostly weight-bearing. When the hatch opened, the sight in front of us made my jaw drop.

"What the frack?" I asked under my breath, but nobody heard me. They were all too busy arguing.

"You've proven your inefficacy. She was gravely injured, nigh unto death. Were it not for her enhancements, she would be gone, and this mission would be lost!" Hema didn't yell—never yelled, in my limited experience with him—but he had a serious angry voice going on.

"And if the mission is lost . . . you'll find your allies not so willing to support you." Jacira wasn't visibly angry, but the threat of her knife was unmistakable. Sure, she was only cleaning under her nails with it.

Until she sliced off one of your body parts.

I wanted to step back from the threat, but River's arm around my shoulders was a bolster, and a shackle. Which, let's be honest, probably stopped me from falling bass-ackwards onto the med-bay stairs.

"What's going on?" I asked the obvious question, hoping to get them to stop focusing so much on each other.

When every head swiveled toward me, I regretted it.

"You'll be finishing the journey with the Nightbloods," Hema stated flatly, as if there was no question about the outcome.

"She will be finishing the journey in mole five, as per the new seating arrangements." The commandant's voice was cold, and he and Hema resumed staring at each other. But there was a small smile playing at the corner of Jacira's lips that I didn't like, not in the least.

"Why would where I sit matter?"

"Because he has failed to ensure your safety," Hema spat, real vitriol behind the words.

"And we all know that you are the linchpin keeping this mission worthwhile," Jacira's smile was half feral, and I wanted to burrow into the ground to keep her from aiming it at me. I kept my trader mask in place, though, and tried to look at this critically. Something more was going on here. I just had to tease out the threads.

Carefully.

"The Nightbloods are trying to isolate you. I won't stand for it." Commandant Kieran lifted one eyebrow at me, reminding me of his leverage, before continuing. "I assume that you don't want to be separated from your companion?"

River stiffened at my side, but didn't say a word. He was learning.

"No, I do not."

"We'll make room for two, if we must." Rahlise spoke, the words a challenge.

"The life support systems on the moles are only rated for ten. You're already at capacity, and none of the other moles are keen on the idea of a passenger swap."

"So you're not in control of your own people? That's a shame." Jacira twirled the knife idly. "My people wouldn't dare defy my wishes. Would they, Alix?" she purred, running the blunt handle of the knife down the man's chest.

"Never, Captain." His bored tone couldn't hide the way his body responded. She was tracing his clavicle with the handle, and the whites of his eyes showed even though he didn't dare flinch away. He only relaxed marginally when she snapped it back, and pointed it at the commandant instead. "If you can't run this ship, I will."

"I can and *am* running this mission. Anyone who's not willing to follow my guidance—"

"Captain, Commandant!" Guffey, out of breath and still running, called out, stopping the commandant mid-threat.

"We've had a breakthrough. One of the side tunnels was able to be reached. This one connects back to the main track, far enough along that we can bypass the remainder of the collapse. As soon as we're all reloaded, we can resume the journey." He dropped his hands to his knees, and stayed doubled over as he sucked in great lungfuls of air.

"Good work, engineer." Jacira's sultry voice had him bolting upright, oxygen deprivation or no.

"Any update on the communications, engineer?"

The commandant's question confused me. What had happened to the comms? I had a vague memory of someone mentioning it, but my time in the sick bay was a haze.

"No, sir. Unfortunately our replacement of the damaged node did not restore the communications signal from base camp. It would take extensive troubleshooting—" He swallowed hard, shooting a nervous glance at Jacira. The motion was so fast, I nearly missed it.

But something in my head clicked. *Jacira wanted the mission to fall apart.* Was she also behind the lapse in communications?

Why would she want to cut us off, when she was down here, too? Her people and ship were still on the surface. I didn't know what she stood to gain by isolating us, but would she also gain from killing me?

I stared long and hard at Guffey as he continued rattling off the technical details about how they'd tried to restore the communications, but he never once looked my way.

Something was off.

"Excellent troubleshooting, engineer. I think we're all in agreement that no further delays are needed, even if communications with base camp can't be restored?" Jacira practically dared the other two leaders to protest, but neither of them did.

"We can proceed without communications, as soon as everyone returns to their designated vehicles. The comms from mole to mole are still functional."

"Nyx—" Rahlise began to argue, but I cut him off with a raised hand.

"I don't want to cause trouble for the mission. This is important for all of us. I'll return to mole five, but I have doctor's orders to stay inside, and rest. Perhaps the Nightbloods would be willing to bring me my dinner, and spend the evenings with me, while my crew is out?"

It was a stretch, but I held Rahlise's gaze, before turning to Hema. I could see his many questions, but he nodded.

"We accept your proposal."

"Excellent, now—"

"One more thing, Commandant. If I could make a request?" I kept my voice calm, pleasant.

"What is it?" His jaw ticked, the tiny muscle movement the only indication of annoyance he'd allow.

"Maybe we could appease everyone, if we evened up the numbers in mole five. If we swapped out one of the Bastion City soldiers with another member of the Nightbloods, we'd have two from each party represented. The Nightbloods, the city, the spacefarers, and River and I representing the rest of the Wastes. That should also give everyone an equal chance to ensure my safety." I smiled, the action not at all taunting, and tilted my head slightly to the side.

The picture of innocence, or at least I hoped. Nobody was innocent these days.

Not even me.

Twenty-Two

Red Handed

Chace

"Come in, Red Riders, come in."

Nothing, yet again. I'd put out the call every night since Nyx left, but all I ever got back was silence.

I lay on my back, staring up at the thin canvas of my tent. My guards were gone for the night, both having turned in to sleep at the same time. A week in, they were certain I wasn't a flight risk anymore. It probably helped that I'd been pretending to snore for nearly an hour.

I spoke into the tiny clawed device burrowed into the side of my water meter again. "Red riders, this is Chace Brandt. Red riders, are you out there?"

I dropped my wrist back to my cot and let out a frustrated sigh. Nyx had seemed so sure

189

of these people, but I couldn't help but feel like her trust was misplaced. If they were such good allies, where had they been the last seven days?

Maybe it was pointless. Surely between the Nightbloods, her friends on the surface, and the three of us we could figure out a plan.

Assuming the Nightbloods stood with us. Though I still wasn't sure I trusted that alliance, either. The idea of them being *on our side*, even if Hema was Nyx's sperm donor, was far-fetched. Where had he been when Jaen threw her on the streets to thirst to death when she was seven?

Or when she was twelve, and got her period, which I, at fifteen, had no fracking clue how to help her handle. Not to mention when she got assaulted, and I beat the man to death with my bare knuckles and then she didn't speak for a month.

Where was he then?

My old man was dead, and I never missed him. What was the point? The dirt bag gave me my first black eye, and I was better off with him a bag of bones.

A crackle from my water meter broke the thick cloud of dark thoughts. I lifted it close to my ear, waiting.

"Brandt brother, this is King Louie of the Red Riders. Do you copy?"

Holy hell. She was right, after all.

"Copy, King Louie. My sister sends her regards."

"The Night Goddess has our regards, as always. What can we do for you?"

"How do you feel about a road trip?" My blood pressure spiked as the question left my lips.

"Our wheels are her wheels. What do you need?"

Twenty-Three

High Tension, Low Depth

Day Seven

Officer Kutsuki was booted from the second chair of mole five, under great protest. Nanette moved up to the second seat, and Rahlise gained a buddy. He introduced himself as Leon, and then joined Rahlise's silent vigil in the back row.

I was nervous when the annoyingly endless rumble started back up under our feet, but it quickly faded to background noise as we moved into the clear side tunnels.

It was good to put the scene of the accident behind us, even if the pressure was mounting higher by the minute.

After my first hobble to the lav, I almost fell over when I looked up and saw River waiting inside the bathroom door with his arms crossed over his chest.

"Whoa, easy now." He leapt forward and steadied me on my feet with gentle hands. "Sorry. Didn't mean to scare you. I just feel like I missed something out front, and wanted to steal a quiet moment."

With a sigh, I freed myself from his grip and hobbled under my own power to the sink to wash my hands. "Guffey knows something, and I want to know what it is."

"Uhm, he knows a lot of things, Nyx. He's an engineer. He spent nearly twelve hours discussing *sediment*. Asking him anything is dangerous." River barely concealed his shudder. He was more a man of action than words.

One of the many things which I appreciated about him.

"Yeah, but he wouldn't make eye contact. The man who's been acting grandfatherly to me is now giving mc a wide berth, and I want to know why."

"Have you considered that he could feel guilty that you got hurt?"

I froze mid-dry of my hands.

"Why would he feel guilty? He didn't make the ceiling fall."

"No, probably not. But he could have survivor's guilt. He walked out first, and you're the one that got creamed. Maybe he feels like it should have been him."

"Well, I guess we'll see." I threw the towel into the mini reclaimer and waved for River to open the door.

Lunch came and went with Guffey still avoiding not only talking to me but acknowledging my existence. He definitely knew something.

When our mole stopped for dinner that night, I waited for Nanette and Fletcher to disembark, stood up as if to follow, and then turned right around to face Guffey.

"I think we need to talk."

He swallowed hard and adjusted the collar of his suit.

"Nyx, I don't know—"

"Yes you do. You're avoiding me, Bernard. I thought we were friends."

"Of course, Nyx. We are friends." He dropped his eyes to my knees and refused to look up.

"Friends confide in each other. Has something happened?"

"Lay off the old man, night goddess. It's me you should be talking to."

You could have knocked me on my butt with a single finger. Kindred stood from his seat and squeezed Guffey's shoulder before patting him on the back like they were close friends. He ignored my shock, though, and addressed the two Nightbloods, instead.

"Can we have a few minutes while you procure her dinner?" Kindred asked respectfully.

"We have been personally entrusted with her security," Leon argued, but Rahlise looked to me for approval.

I nodded. "I'd like to speak with them. You won't be far, and River's here if I need backup."

"Yes, αγαπημένη. We will return in ten minutes."

Rahlise gestured for Leon to lead, and the two of them exited the mole without looking back.

"We want to hear whatever you've got to say, Kindred, but Nyx needs to sit back down, first." River leveled a no-nonsense look on me, so I sank back down into my chair. I bit back the sigh, though. He wasn't trying to point out my weaknesses, he was trying to care for me. But the two of us had very different definitions of risk.

I'd have to ask him to stop next time we were alone, and he wouldn't like that.

Once I was off my bad leg, I cranked my chair around to face the two space travelers.

Guffey ran his hands through his hair, sending the tufts in a new direction. "This is dangerous, Kindred. I'm not sure I'm comfortable with you taking this risk."

Apparently Guffey didn't care about revealing weaknesses. He really was an open book, and it was going to get him killed if he stayed in the commandant's stratosphere.

River held up a placating hand. "Why don't we start by letting Kindred say whatever it is he thinks we want to know."

"The external comms aren't really broken."

"Kindred!" Guffey groaned and dropped his head into his hands.

"And your captain is just lying to the commandant about it? Shouldn't he have tech people who can tell?" River asked.

"Maybe, but no. We've got better technology than they do. On the surface it just appears dead, but actually I've encrypted it. Guffey, being annoyingly superior to most everyone—"

"Kindred, *please*," Guffey pleaded, but the man was unstoppable.

"Figured it out, decrypted it, and also found the directive from Captain Jacira to keep the comms down for the remainder of the mission, or until she ordered otherwise."

"Kin! As your superior officer, I command you to *stop talking*." Guffey was all exasperation and no heat, a fact Kindred seemed to know as well as I did.

He just shrugged, completely unapologetic.

"You absolutely cannot share this *privileged* information with anyone," Guffey tried commanding me this time. I cocked an eyebrow at him and focused back on Kindred.

"If he's your superior officer, why did Jacira order *you* to close the comms instead of him?"

Kindred kicked back in his chair with a wry look on his face. "Straight to the heart of it. I knew you were smart."

"Thanks, but I'd rather you save the compliment and answer the question."

"I'm sure." He looked at Guffey, who threw up his hands.

"You may as well toss the bathwater out after the baby. We're already dead if she finds out you told them."

"Guffey's too easy to read. Not to mention, too dedicated to the good of humanity. Me? I'm okay with bending the rules when it suits me."

"Uh-huh." I kept myself perfectly still, waiting for the other shoe.

"But I like you, night goddess, and I feel like you've got potential."

"Why do you keep calling me that?" It was inane, and absolutely not the question I should have been asking. But it was the first thing that popped out of my mouth. *River was rubbing off on me.*

"You don't know what your name means? 'Nyx'—it's from Greek mythology. Old, old earth stuff. She was the 'goddess of night.'" Guffey raked his hands through his hair. "Can we get back to the topic at hand? Nyx, you absolutely cannot share with the commandant that the communications are down on purpose, or Kindred and I will face severe consequences."

"Ahh." Now we were getting to the crux of the matter. I leaned forward in my seat, ignoring the pinch of the stitches in my leg. "Sounds to me like there's more to it than just cutting off communication. Is there?"

Guffey took off his glasses, pinching the bridge of his nose.

Kindred answered, "I'll say it, if he won't. It's treason we're looking at, Nyx, so we can't directly go against her. We've no love lost for the captain, okay? Her cutting off that guy's ear? That's any day of the week back on board. She's making a power play, and the last thing that's good for anyone is *her* getting more power, more resources. Someone needs to work against her, but *we* can't, or she'll kill us."

"Just like Jakan." Guffey paled at the memory.

"Jakan?" I questioned.

"Her brother, the original captain. She slit his throat and showed up on the bridge twirling the knife and wearing nothing but his blood."

"That's more than a little unsettling," River muttered.

"I see. What do you want me to do about it?" I asked, confused. Them tampering with the comms had nothing to do with me, besides Guffey acting squirrelly.

"I don't know if you *can* do anything about it. But someone has to. Because if she takes over? We're all screwed."

"And I thought *we* had it bad," River said, shaking his head.

"The commandant's not much better, though. When you guys showed up, he had just announced martial law, and had one of his citizens shot. Sharing information with him isn't high on our list." It was more than I was usually willing to share, but it felt like we were building a rapport, and that required a degree of trust.

And an in with the spacefarers was worth the risk. We'd need all the help we could get, if we were going to keep the commandant from continuing to terrorize the people of the Wastes.

"Still not as bad as exiling that elderly couple," River interjected. "I'm not sure I can get past that, even if he doesn't play with knives like dolls."

Footfall on the stairs intruded on our moment of sharing, and I quickly wrapped it up. "Thank you for sharing. We'll see if there's anything we can do. And if there is . . . can we trust that the rest of your people have similar thoughts?"

It was a dangerous question, but one I had to ask.

Guffey was already down the aisle, heading out to dinner with a pained smile on his face. But Kindred met my eyes and nodded before following him out of the mole.

Rahlise and Leon were already back inside, and with them was a veritable horde of Nightbloods.

Twenty-Four

BONDING AND BLOODSHED

T wo of them pressed a bowl of stew into River's and my hands, and then they all took up perches around the mole. Once they were all inside, one close to the front shut the door. I swallowed hard, second-guessing my earlier instincts that it was a good idea to lock River and me inside an enclosed vehicle with them.

But instead of laying into me for not agreeing with Hema's requests, they all dropped their face coverings, and wide smiles and warm greetings began to fly our way.

"We're glad to see you up and well, αγαπημένη του αίματος. Hema was concerned for you."

"Thank you, ah . . ." I sort of recognized his face from our visit in the base camp, but I wasn't sure of the man's name.

"Georgios." He proffered a hand, so I shook it. Then he shuffled around so the next man could offer me well-wishes.

The meal wore on with laughter and jokes, and while I felt like an outsider at first, they really did endeavor to pull me into the conversation. River too, though there was more hesitancy from the men where he was concerned, each greeted him after passing me.

After yet another man called me the Greek endearment, and introduced himself, I put a hand on his arm, stopping him from continuing the Ferris wheel of greetings.

"Sax, what does that mean?"

"What?" He looked genuinely confused. He would be easy to remember as, so far, he was the only red-haired Nightblood I'd met. Freckles dusted his nose and forehead, so even with his coverings on, I'd be able to spot him from here on out.

"Oh." He blushed. "Beloved of the blood."

"Okay. Why 'beloved of the blood?'" Watching his embarrassment made warmth bloom in my chest, and I fought down a ridiculous blush.

"I don't think you understand, Nyx. When Hema found out about you, he threw a week-long celebration. You mean something to us."

"You're right, I *don't* understand."

He celebrated me? Just for existing?

"Doesn't he have other children?"

Sax shook his head. "No, you're the only one. I guess his line is not particularly . . . fertile?" He shrugged.

I squeezed his arm and released him. "Thank you for telling me. It's Greek, right?"

"Right."

He stepped past me and paused in front of River, studying his face.

"River," he nodded.

"Sax, you look well," River returned.

"As do you. It's been a while."

That caught my attention, and I cut my gaze to the right, to watch the interaction closely. *They knew each other from before?* It was bound to happen eventually, but it was strange to see it play out, regardless. River cut a sideways look at me, and I quickly stuffed a bite of stew into my mouth.

"It has been a while. How is your family?"

"Well, well. Sina got married."

"What? Little Sina, already?"

"She's as tall as me now, man." Sax held up his hand at eye level.

River shook his head. "It's hard to believe. Who's the lucky guy?"

"Julian."

"Ah, I'm glad to hear that. He'll take good care of her." River's smile was genuine, and he offered Sax a fist bump.

"Yeah, they're happy. My parents will be glad to hear you're well."

"Better than ever." River wrapped his arm around my shoulders, and pulled me into his side.

"I'm glad, truly." Sax bobbed his head, and continued moving down the line.

"You're a *terrible* eavesdropper," River whispered into my ear, and I almost snorted my stew up the back of my nose.

"Sorry. Shameless, I know. But that's the first person you've recognized since all of this started. Color me curious."

"I get it. I'd be curious if you had an old friend pop up. Or an old boyfriend." He gave me a long look, to which I shook my head.

"None of those, sorry. Although I suppose I never asked if you had any old girlfriends hanging about . . ."

"I—"

A pounding on the mole's hatch saved him from answering, and the jovial atmosphere in the room evaporated faster than a drip of water on a hot stone.

"Get out here, quick! The captain's challenged Kennet to a fight!" someone hollered through the door.

Curses echoed around the room as the hatch lowered painfully slowly.

"Who's Kennet?" I asked.

Sax looked worried when he said, "One of us, and he usually keeps to himself. I can't imagine why she'd challenge him."

Bowls of stew were abandoned on nearly every surface, and as soon as the hatch was halfway down, Nightbloods started vaulting over it to the tunnel floor below.

I took a hasty step forward and wobbled, but Sax grabbed my arm to steady me. He sent a pained look between River and me. "Perhaps you should stay here, Nyx. This could get ugly."

"No, I absolutely will not stay here."

"Nyx, be reasonable—the doctor wants you off your leg," River argued, stepping into the aisle in front of me.

"The doctor doesn't understand my life, River. I'll rest when there's time. I've rested all day. But if my father's men are getting into a fight with the captain, I'm going to be there to try to keep things from escalating. *Somebody* has to."

"Allow me to go for you, αγαπημένη." Sax bent low, bowing from the waist, and I nearly toppled backwards at the blatant display of respect.

"No. I'm sorry, but *no*. Let's go, before things get out of hand." I made a shooing motion, and their hesitation nearly sent me over the edge.

"Get out of my way. That wasn't a request." I tried to keep the bitterness out of my words, but must have failed, because River recoiled as if I'd slapped him. Sax just stepped aside, but he wouldn't meet my eyes.

I hobble-strode as quickly as I could out of the mole, and then followed the sounds of jeering down the tunnels. There was a ring of people inside the dinner bubble, mixed from all three opposing groups. Some cheered, some whispered behind palms. But all had their eyes trained inward, where the space captain and one of the Nightbloods I'd not yet met circled.

His eyes were stone cold, unblinking, his movements steady. He reminded me of the low-hunched wolf, poised to spring.

She giggled like a young girl, and *skipped* like this was a game of jacks. Both of them held blades in hand.

I elbowed my way to the front of the crowd, not backing down when the man whose ribs I'd just bruised swore crudely at me. *Get in line, buddy.*

River stood stiffly at my shoulder, and Sax melted into the crowd of anonymous black fabric.

"What happened?" I asked the man on my other side, without taking my eyes off the bizarre scene unfolding inside the circle.

"The captain took a slight as a chance to remind everyone of her supremacy with a blade. If you ask me, we've been sitting still too long, and she was just bored."

Rather than censure, excitement filled his tone, and it made me sick to my stomach. Hadn't we all had enough of death and maiming? Survival was hard when we *didn't* pit ourselves against each other senselessly.

"This is fracking ridiculous," I grumbled under my breath. But nobody cared, or nobody agreed, because the two continued circling, until the captain stopped mid-twirl and bolted toward her opponent.

He blocked her with a grunt, bracing his feet for the headlong assault. She spun away just as quickly, light on her feet and moving fast. They flew together and flung back apart, each time coming away unbloodied. The captain changed her angles, her speed, but still the man was ready. Her strange giggle turned to frustrated screeches as she continued.

A thudding stomp started up around the circle, the strange rhythm coming from the Nightbloods. I let my eyes roam around the circle, noting the differences between our groups. While everyone else was raucous, the Nightbloods were intent, focused. Some on the combatants, but nearly as many on the people making up the circle. Always wary. The soldiers of Bastion City cheered, looking bloodthirsty and ready for violence. The spacefarers were mixed. Some intent, some anxious, some bored. There were more drawn faces than not.

I tried to gauge who was on Jacira's side, but few were so easy to read when I didn't know them. Kindred wasn't even watching. He was propped a few feet behind the back of the circle, against a wall doing something intently on his tablet.

All the while, the man in the ring remained calm and steady, pacing the circle opposite her, parrying her would-be blows.

"Do you know Kennet?" I asked over my shoulder.

"Yes. He's our second-best at hand to hand combat," Sax supplied helpfully.

"Second best?"

"Rahlise is undefeated in all of our practiced combat forms."

River snorted. "All of them? Come on. Everybody's got a weakness."

"It's said that his only weakness is his loyalty to the blood," Sax's words were subdued, and when I looked over his shoulder, he was studying me carefully.

I had no doubt that Hema could hold his own in combat, or else he wouldn't have lasted so long as leader. So that left . . . me? I was the weakness for this massive gang organization? That wasn't possible.

A shrill shriek pulled my attention back to the fight.

Finally giving up on her in-and-out approach, Captain Jacira ran at him with the knife raised high overhead, as if she was going to bring it down on his neck. The straight blade looked wickedly sharp in the mottled lighting, and I held my breath as she charged Kennet.

And then he moved. When he broke his steadfast track, it was to meet her in the middle of the ring. Three things happened so fast, it seemed simultaneous.

His knife hand connected with her wrist, sending her blade spinning through the air up over their heads in a deadly arc. The sound of her knife clattering to the floor a scant two feet away made me wince.

Kennet's other hand jabbed forward, connecting with the base of her throat. While her head lunged forward on reflex, he grabbed her hair, dropped into a crouch, and his curved blade disappeared. The captain coughed and sputtered and grabbed at her neck, a thin trickle of blood trailing down from her wrist over the metallic suit. Nobody moved, nobody breathed, and Kennet stayed in his crouch. She wheezed as she stood in front of him, looking like she was barely keeping her feet under her.

"He's got a killing blow," the Bastion soldier next to me said, sounding gleeful.

"What?" I asked, confused. He stepped back, pointing, and I moved over so I could see. Kennet's curved blade was piercing the groin of her suit, poised over the femoral artery. One slash, and she'd bleed out on the floor.

When she realized it, the screeching started again.

Hema stepped forward, hands raised in placation. "You have fought bravely to first blood, and Kennet has disarmed you. Do you concede defeat in this challenge, or will you forfeit your life?"

Kennet still held the crouch, unwavering in his readiness to end the captain. Her eyes were feral, rolling back and forth in disbelief, watching the blood drip from her fingertips into the dry stone under our feet.

"No, this isn't possible. I never lose."

"There is no shame in being bested by a superior foe. Kennet, rise. We want no animosity between our peoples."

Kennet stood with fluid grace, and at Hema's nod, he and Kennet turned their backs on the crazed captain in the middle of the ring. The stomping returned at a much faster beat, cheers going up around the crowd. But I watched Jacira. She was muttering something, over and over under her breath.

She picked up her knife, cradling it briefly like a baby and watching her own blood coat the blade, while Hema and Kennet stopped at the edge of the ring, shaking hands and accepting congratulations.

"I *never* lose." She sounded hysterical, her volume rising as she repeated it to herself, again and again.

And then she snapped.

She hurtled across the ring, arrowing at Kennet's back. This time there were no dance moves, no giggles. Only malice.

"Hema!" I screamed, the sound ripped from my throat. They didn't hear me. They didn't hear anything.

Kennet didn't realize the danger until it was too late. Her knife sank into the back of his arm, dragging down the back of his triceps.

He let out a howl of pain and rage as he spun, backhanding the captain across the face in the process. She clutched her blade tightly even as she flew backwards.

Kennet charged, knife clutched in his fist as he quickly incapacitated her. Within seconds, he was behind her, a nut-brown fist clenched into frosty blonde hair, head cocked back so she stared at the ceiling.

His black, curved blade rested over her carotid, just the tip indenting the skin.

A deranged laugh broke free from her lips, and a hush fell over the crowd.

"Stop! What is the meaning of this!" The commandant pushed his way through the crowd. Hema stepped up beside Kennet, staring Kieran down.

"The space captain has broken the rules of combat, and as such, her life is forfeit." Hema's words were stone cold, daring the commandant to defy him.

"That is absolutely not going to happen. She is the co-leader of this mission. Whatever *insult* your men have suffered—"

Every Nightblood in the tunnel reacted at that. They seemed to flow like water, converging in a tight, inner ring around the three leaders and Kennet before anyone else realized what was happening. Hema held up a hand, and they stopped in a loose circle, leaving about five feet free around the foursome. I could just see the drama unfold between the cracks.

"You think you can threaten me? My people outnumber yours two to one."

"And they too bore witness to this crime. We will be recompensed, or your blood can spill alongside hers. We may be outnumbered, but they will not reach you before your lifeless body falls if you resist."

Hema pulled his own black blade from his waistband, flipping it lightly in the air and catching it smoothly.

"An eye for an eye."

Everyone looked at Jacira, still hanging limply from Kennet's grip. A worrisome puddle of blood was forming under his right arm from the deep gash she'd dragged through it.

I couldn't look at it, or I felt faint on my feet. Breathing through my nose, I gripped River's hand tightly in mine. He was pressed right against my back, and I was grateful. My pulse was pounding in my wound, as well as behind my temples.

"Alix! Come to me," Jacira called, her voice hard, all signs of joviality gone.

The man wove through the crowd, stopping at the ring of Nightbloods. Hema gestured for him to be let through, and he stepped up to the leaders.

"Turn around." Alix's face paled, as if he knew what was coming, but he turned his back to his captain, offering himself to her, and sickness churned in my gut.

"My man will stand in my stead for punishment." The tension was high, thrumming in the tunnel like a living, breathing thing. But nobody spoke up for the innocent man. Not one space soldier made a cry of protest.

I searched the crowd now, looking for Guffey, for Kindred. Guffey's head was turned away, eyes closed and face white. But Kindred? He burned with rage.

He hated the captain, hated that she held their lives so lightly. If I had wondered before why he would share information with me, I didn't anymore. It was a sentiment I saw echoed on many faces in the crowd.

"Jacira . . ." Commandant Kieran looked from her to Hema, who stood unmoved, and then to the soldier, who was pale, but silent. "Do as you must."

He turned like the coward he was, and left the ring, gesturing for his people to follow. Some reluctantly began to exit the dome, but many lingered to watch the horrible scene play out.

"Kennet, do you accept this offering?" Hema's words carried.

"I will not raise my blade to an unarmed man." He swayed a little on his feet but held his own. The pool of blood beneath him was growing alarmingly large. He needed medical care, and quickly. I tried to step forward, but River held me tight, an arm banding around my upper chest.

"I'll do it. Release me," Jacira said.

My jaw dropped. Surely not. Surely she wouldn't carve up her own soldier?

Hema nodded, and Kennet released her, dropping back into a defensive stance, knife raised in his left hand.

Jacira walked lightly to her own blade, dusted it off on the leg of her suit, and then approached Alix's unguarded back. Without hesitation, she raised the knife, and dragged it down the back of his arm, in the same blow she'd inflicted on Kennet.

He wasn't so stoic, though. Alix cried out, and I clenched my eyes shut. I heard the twin thuds of his knees meeting the stone, followed by his retches of pain.

"Are we even?" The captain's voice held no remorse, no care for her own crimes, and I knew then that she was truly a sociopath.

The commandant might have been a conniving bastard who used people for his own power. But Jacira?

Jacira would light us all on fire, just to watch us burn.

They both had to be stopped.

Twenty-Five

Changing Tides

Day Eight

M ole five was unnervingly quiet the next day. Not from tension, as one might expect. A brooding air had consumed us, and no one, from any of the four factions, had any joviality left. Lunch was quiet, and dinner brought the exodus of all except River, me, and the two Nightbloods. When the others arrived with dinner, the mood finally perked up a little. They first ones in grabbed seats, and then the rest settled for leaning against every available surface when those were full.

To my surprise, Hema was among the group this time. He took up a casual position leaning against the side of my chair.

He pressed a bowl of warm stew into my hands, which I accepted with a nod. As much as I enjoyed my meal bars, stew was starting to grow on me. And my hydration meter was happy with my consistent water supply; it hadn't dipped below ninety-two percent since the journey had started.

Though now, I had to wonder if the physiological changes I'd seen in myself were from the nanites in my blood. Rapid healing, lower levels of dehydration. That alone made the little techno-bugs miraculous. I was still stumped on when I'd picked them up, but a theory was forming that I had no way to test, or prove myself right or wrong about.

"How's Kennet?" I asked around a mouthful of stew.

Hema smiled, and it struck me as odd, actually being able to see it. The Nightbloods only lowered their face coverings behind closed doors, and the change in them as a group was still jarring to me, even though I'd seen it a few times. They were lighter, freer.

"He is strong—he will recover. I'm pleased that you've taken an interest in my men's welfare."

I shrugged, ignoring the uncomfortable itch between my shoulder blades at the praise. A quick glance at River across the way showed that he wouldn't save me from my own awkwardness. He was engrossed in a conversation with two other men, hands gesturing wildly as they swapped stories.

Nope, I was on my own with my father and his praise.

It probably said something about me that it made me more uncomfortable to be praised than it did to be criticized, but I wouldn't turn over that particular cactus pad. I already knew I was messed up, so there was no point getting my fingers pricked questioning it.

"I don't want to see anyone needlessly harmed."

There. That was true, and neutral. Not condemning the stupid fight, nor supporting it.

"Yes, I've noticed this about you. It makes me worry for your future. Sometimes, hard decisions must be made. I won't be able to shield you forever."

"I know how to make hard decisions, Hema. Otherwise, I wouldn't be here standing in front of you."

He smiled again, fondly this time, and raised a hand in a peacemaking gesture. "I have no doubts, beautiful παιδί μου. You are my child, therefore you must be strong and capable. But still, sometimes necessity drives us to do things we must, not what we wish. I sense that moment coming for you, and I know you are up to the challenge."

The words brought back Chace's confession, and my gut twisted uncomfortably.

I was barely ten when I had to kill the first one who thought he could take her, and I was lucky if three or four months passed before the next one showed up thinking he was bad enough to do what the ones before him had failed to do, and I'd have to get my hands bloody again.

Was it true? I wanted to deny it, deny that men had killed to see me safe. I prided myself on being independent, a survivor. Smart enough and strong enough to make it on my own. I'd stayed alive after Chace was taken, after all.

But I couldn't deny that the Sidewinders had nearly ended me, on more than one occasion. That Nagesh, if not for River's intervention, might have assaulted me. The memory of being the weak one burned and made me feel ashamed. So, I shoved it down—pretended it hadn't happened.

Was the day really coming that I couldn't hide anymore, not even from the memories?

I let my eyes roam over the men gathered here, laughing and sharing a meal as if we were all one big family. A concept I knew nothing of. Hema did, though. He'd built this, though I hated his methods.

"Why do you do it?" I asked, unable to pretend anymore.

"Do what, παιδί μου?"

"Kill people and steal them from their families."

He grew still, his spoon poised over the bowl as if time had stopped. He slowly set it down and gripped the bowl with both hands. His eyes were grave when he answered me.

"There was a time, Nyx, when there was unrest in the Wastes. There was nowhere safe, nowhere free. You could not trust your neighbor, because you did not have one. Going to a well was a death sentence, or your own hands were bloodied. This is the world I was born into, and I will not apologize for who it made me. But I have worked to change things. There is still unrest, but not among the Nightbloods. We are safe, and we are free. And if that means that our hands are sullied with the blood of others, so be it. Fear is a tool, and I have learned to wield it well."

He picked up his spoon and began eating again. I couldn't, though. My mind was racing. I needed time to process.

From my perspective, it was easy to judge. But I didn't have the responsibility for all the people he did. I didn't have the same experiences he did.

I'd never had to make the choice to kill or be killed. Sure, it had come close. But could I really judge him? I'd taken sick satisfaction from Nagesh's end, after what he'd done to Jaen. I'd been the cause of two elders from Bastion City being exiled to their deaths. And apparently, Chace had been killing people for years to ensure my safety, even though I never knew.

My hands might not have been bloody directly, but I felt the weight of those choices, those lives, on my soul, just the same.

"Are the external comms still down? I'd love to speak with Chace, if it's possible."

Hema cocked an eyebrow at my subject change, but didn't call me on it. "They are, but my men are working on it."

"I might know someone that could help, if you were both willing to get along and work together."

"If it's one of the city soldiers, I wouldn't waste your breath. To a man, they seem wholly blinded to their Commandant's corruption," he said, words tinged with bitterness.

"It's not."

"Are you certain you can trust this person?"

After yesterday? Absolutely. "Yes."

He nodded and waved over one of the men at the end of the mole. "Nikolaos, this is my daughter, Nyx."

"Well met, Nyx, θεά σε σάρκα." He was close to my age, and handsome. He had dark hair much like mine, but his eyes were forest green with gold flecks.

He extended his hand, so I shook it. I wouldn't normally give my dominant hand to a stranger, but with my father standing next to us and River across the aisle, I was safe enough for social niceties.

"She would like to introduce you to a contact who will aid us in restoring communications with the surface. You two should talk. I think you'd get along nicely." The look on Hema's face was strangely smug, but I didn't have time to overthink it.

"You've made a friend amongst the enemy, huh?" Nikolaos's tone was light and teasing, and it left me on the back foot.

"More an acquaintance, with similar ideals."

"Very diplomatic. Your father must be proud."

"My father . . . is a complicated man."

"And you're a simple woman?" He smiled, showing off straight, white teeth. "I doubt that sincerely."

Was this man flirting with me? Did he not know about River and me? I shot a quick glance at River, whose arms were crossed over his chest as he kept an eye on Niko. He looked neither light nor teasing. He was ticked, and he had the jaw muscle twitch to prove it. But was it at me, or something that had come up in his conversation?

I bit my lip and realized that Nikolaos was waiting for a response. "No. I guess not."

"So, you're still stuck in the mole until your leg heals up. Do you want me to switch with Leon, so you can make introductions?"

"It might be difficult to arrange, but I don't know of a better way."

"Consider it done." He grinned at me again, and I returned my best facsimile of a smile, but there was no heart to it. Flirts were dangerous. They'd smile to your face and then try to drag you behind a tent as soon as you got comfortable with them.

It had happened to me once when I was fifteen.

Chace had beaten the man with his bare knuckles until both of them bled and I ran away, leaving them to the fight. It was a memory I'd squashed before now, pressed down in the recesses of my mind. But now, it bubbled to the surface, refusing to be denied its time in the sun. I'd never seen the man again; and the question plaguing me was whether that was because he left, or because my brother had killed him?

"Nyx, did I lose you?"

"What? I'm sorry." I looked back up at the expectant Nikolaos, and found that he'd stepped forward into my personal space. I took a pointed step back, wobbling a little on my sore leg. River's warm hand encased the back of my arm, steadying me.

"Easy there, Nyx. Everything okay over here?" River's voice was as uncharacteristically tight as his stance, and I placed my hand over his.

"We're good. Thank you for catching me."

He dropped his gaze to mine, and I resisted the urge to run my fingertips over the tight line between his eyebrows. "Always."

"I'll just go let Leon know about the swap." Nikolaos left us, and River's posture loosened a fraction.

"Are *you* okay?" I asked the question quietly.

"Fine." He rubbed his hand over the back of his neck, his surefire tell for agitation.

"Uh-huh. Try again."

"*Niko* is your father's favorite. Or, he was, until he found you."

"His favorite . . . what?"

"Soldier, next-in-line. He was grooming him to take the lead after his time was done. Now, it looks like you're the one who will take the lead, so he wants to push the two of you together."

"He knows I'm with you, River."

His lips flattened into a hard line, but he didn't respond.

"River, I'm going to say this as many times as you need to hear it. I choose you. What anybody outside the two of us wants does not matter to me. Have you changed your mind about me?"

"Of course not, Nyx. Don't even say that."

"Well, neither have I. Our lives are changing in ways neither of us ever expected. But I'm the same. I'm still the same skeptic who made you ride on the back of the Bronco for a week, sure you were going to rob me blind or murder me if I let you ride shotgun."

He reached up and cupped the back of my head, threading his fingers into my hair, a barely suppressed smile on his lips. "I remember you more as the spectacular woman who saved my sorry hide, even when I was a homeless runaway with nothing to offer."

"Six of one, half dozen of another." I smiled, and this time, River's return smile held all the sunshine I loved to bask in.

"Nyx? Well met. I'm Stephano. I just wanted to introduce myself."

I slowly turned and greeted the new man—another Nightblood that had joined us for our meal. But this time, River's chest stayed pressed into my back, our fingers tangled together at my side.

Twenty-Six

PATCHED

Day Nine

The comm up front went off just before our usual lunch time, and Fletcher rose to answer it. A few terse words later, he turned to face us all.

"Lunch is going to be pushed later but will be the communal meal today. We're close to the aquifer, and there won't be a suitable spot to stretch our legs this evening. From here on out we'll be driving straight through."

A groan went up around the mole, but nobody protested outright.

"Not my decision. It won't be too much longer," Fletcher promised and re-took his seat.

"Frack. I'm starving. I used to go a long time without meals, but we've been on their strict schedule for more than a week now, and my belly expects a tribute." River cranked his chair around toward the aisle, kicking his long legs out into the space to stretch.

Kindred surprised us both by speaking up, and turning into the aisle as well. He was tall, too, and executed a move similar to River's. "You should be glad. The temperature is really climbing, and it's nearly a hundred forty outside the moles right now. By dinner, even in the temp-controlled suit you'll be sweating."

Nerves danced in my belly at the reminder. My suit was new, replaced after the original was pierced with falling rock, and was untested except for a few minutes outside when I'd watched the fight between the captain and Kennet. But when we arrived, I'd be expected to head out with Guffey, and figure out how to fix the water generator. The one that I had absolutely *no idea* how to work.

"Don't scare them now, Kin. The suits do their jobs," Guffey groused, but with affection.

"Doesn't make it comfortable. Humans weren't meant to exist at these temperatures, and it only gets hotter from here. And I thought the *Wastes* were bad."

River snorted and the two of them launched into a playful conversation about their new favorite topic: surface vs. space.

I picked at the arm of my chair, a single loose thread drawing my attention.

"It's going to be fine, Nyx." Guffey's soothing tone did nothing for me. I didn't know how to be soothed, how to not take my own future into my hands.

"I don't know how to fix a water generator, Guffey. You're a brilliant engineer. Why do they need me? Why does it matter that I'm descended from the creator of the machine?"

"I don't know, Nyx. But we have to trust that we'll figure it out." He squeezed my shoulder gently.

I studied his face intently, then decided to ask the unspoken question. "Why do you all follow the captain, if everybody hates her?"

He pursed his lips, casting a long glance around the confined space, but everyone else was lost in conversation—except the Night-bloods, who sat stoically in the back, as usual, ignoring us.

"Fear is a powerful motivator to those who feel powerless."

I nodded, understanding that game well. The Sidewinders ran Coyote Springs much the same way. But something stuck out.

"Who *feel* powerless, or who *are* powerless? You have to be some of the brightest, most talented people. Surely you can take control from one woman?"

He shook his head slowly. "It's not so simple. Creating a power vacuum isn't the answer.

Whoever takes out the captain will be expected to lead in her stead, and the ship hasn't been in good financial standing for some time. That's why we're here. We've run out of resources, and out of options. The ship is in need of major repairs, with no way to complete them. Establishing a connection with earth again, finding a new source to glean from, was our only option."

That was more complicated than I'd hoped, and frustration rose in me at the fact that there never seemed to be any good answers. Why couldn't any of us do better?

Bastion City was corrupted by power.

The Wastes were run by violence.

Even space was no escape, like we'd all thought. So what was left? What was our hope, if that was all there was? Someone had to stand up and stop all of this, and I was sick of waiting for someone else to do it.

They wanted someone to take control, someone to lead? Resolve replaced frustration, a cool assurance that I'd continue landing on my feet.

I'd figure out how.

The mole lurched to a stop for our lunch break, and I had a decision to make.

Everyone stood, queueing up to leave the mole while the stairs descended slowly. I stood too, making eye contact with River and holding it. He shot me a questioning look in return, but

I waited until Fletcher and Nanette had already descended before making my move.

I stepped out, blocking Kin and Guffey in the aisle.

"I need your help."

Guffey's face paled, but Kin just grinned, the smile stretching wide across his sharp features as he spoke.

"Do tell."

"I need you to stay here for lunch, so I can introduce you to someone."

"And why would I do that, little night goddess?"

"Because we have a mutually beneficial task to complete."

"All right, then." Kin plopped back down into his chair, though it was hardly ungraceful. He pulled his tablet from its compartment and looked up expectantly.

Guffey looked back and forth between us nervously, before shaking his head and continuing out of the mole without comment.

Turning to Rahlise, I asked, "Can you cover for their absence from the lunch? I need uninterrupted time with Niko and Kindred."

"Consider it done, αγαπημένη." Rahlise bowed formally, and then skirted past us up the aisle.

"Niko, this is Kindred. Kindred, Niko."

"Well met." Nikolaos gave Kindred a slightly less formal bow, and then turned to face me. "I'm always happy to be of service, θεά σε σάρκα."

Kindred eyed him curiously but didn't translate the Greek for me.

"What is it you need exactly, Nyx?" Kindred's question was a slow drawl.

"I need you two to fix the long-distance comms long enough for me to talk to my brother."

"Now why would I do that, and put myself in the captain's crosshairs?"

"Because I think that if you put your heads together, you can do it in a way she won't notice. I don't want *everyone*'s comms restored. Just one, so we can communicate with the surface."

"Your brother isn't on the surface, Nyx."

"No, but *he* has a direct line to allies who are."

You could have heard a moth's wings flutter, so still were the next few heartbeats.

"You're trouble, but I like that about you." Kin's lips quirked up at the corners, but a squeeze on my shoulder distracted me from the technical conversation which followed.

"I'm going to get you food, and be right back." River pressed a chaste kiss to my cheek, but lingered there next to my ear. His next words were whispered. "Don't take any risks, Nyx."

And then he was gone, out the door at an easy jog, helmet clicking into place as he disappeared down the stairs.

"—I'm annoyed I didn't think of that myself," Niko muttered under his breath, but was working across the aisle on his own tablet. "So how do we restore pinpoint comms with that system?"

"We don't. The main channel has to stay down."

"New channel?"

"New channel."

I sank back into my own seat gratefully, my leg still twinging a bit at the pulling motion, though it had improved the last couple of days. A few minutes later, River returned with our lunches, and waved the door closed. The two of us sipped down our meals quietly as Kin and Niko worked together.

"Okay, I think I've isolated his signature," Niko announced some time later.

"Time for a test, then. Night goddess, you're up." Kin tapped a few final times on his tablet, and then my water meter blinked, green light flashing. Camel-sized butterflies stampeded in my stomach when I spoke.

"Chace?"

A heartbeat of silence, then another.

"Give me one second."

Relief washed over me at the familiar clipped tone of my brother's voice. He was still alive and breathing, at the least.

The rustle of tent fabric preceded his words. "I'm here, Nyx. I was told all communications were down, something about a broken node?"

"Let's just say that anything is possible if you're determined enough. I'm short on time, and I need an update. How are things on the surface?"

"Not good. The Riders are at least two days out, the Nightbloods have the city surrounded, and tensions inside the city are high. Morgan says hello, and that there's a rumor going around up here that the water is almost gone."

A knot of tension beneath my sternum released. She was still alive, still okay.

But was it true? Was the city's water nearly gone?

It couldn't float. The delicate ecosystem it supported wasn't able to be picked up and carted off like so much luggage.

"'Hi' back at her. Things down here aren't so good. We're still not to the aquifer, but we're close."

"Are you safe?"

"I am, but there have been . . . accidents."

Silence was his only response, but I could almost see him tense in my mind's eye, a move he'd made so many times in our lives.

"I'm being targeted, and the captain is a loose cannon. We're going to need to act as soon as this is over."

"I'll see that we're ready. But if you can stall . . ."

The stairs began to lower, and our time was up.

"I'll do my best. Love you, big brother."

"Love you, baby sister."

Kindred tapped again and the light went off, the connection severed. I felt hollow, but also hopeful. I had no idea how we'd take control when we were back on the surface, but if anyone was going to negotiate a change, it had to be me. The only question was whether Hema was right, and my negotiations would turn into insurrection.

Twenty-Seven

DROPS

Day Ten

Something was different. My eyes opened in the dim interior of the mole, but everyone else was still and asleep. I was still groggy, so it took me a moment to realize that the constant droning grind of the tracks was now accompanied by . . . sloshing?

I lunged upright, not bothering to move my seat, and pressed my face against the glass. It was dark in the tunnels, the exterior lights practically non-existent during our sleep cycle. I couldn't see the ground, but sure enough, clinging to the windows were tiny droplets of moisture.

Water.

"River," I whispered, poking him in the arm.

He sat bolt upright, eyes wide as he looked for a non-existent threat.

I made a calming gesture then jerked my head toward the window. He rose slowly and followed me to my side of the mole. I pointed out some of the bigger drops, but stayed quiet to keep from waking anyone else.

"We're close," he murmured, squeezing my shoulder.

"Yeah, we are." I pulled his arm around me, wrapped myself in his strength. He was my anchor as we stared at the tiny rivulets of condensation that formed and ran down the outside of our vehicle. It was insular, like we two were alone in a foreign world.

"I don't know how to fix it." The admission cost me, but I had to say it.

"The water generator? You'll figure it out, with Guffey." He chafed my arm lightly, comfortingly.

"No, not the water generator. I mean, I don't know how to fix that, either. But I mean . . . all the rest. The fighting, the killing, the hatred. Is this all that's left of humanity? We're going to pick each other apart until there's no one left?"

He was silent for a few long heartbeats.

"Some problems aren't ours to fix, Nyx. And I worry that following that path . . . it might take you from me."

I froze in his arms, trying to process. I didn't want to dismiss his concern, but I also didn't know how to fix it. "I don't want that to happen, River."

"I know. But I see you, Nyx. I see you stepping up, putting yourself forward, risking yourself even when you don't realize it. You can't be anyone else, and I know that. But a part of me wants to steal you away from here and keep you safe somewhere far away."

He wanted to tuck me away, like a doll on a shelf. Like every other man with a kept woman. I turned in his arms, unable to have this conversation without seeing his face.

"That won't work, River. Because *nowhere* is safe."

He gave me a sad smile, but it didn't reach his eyes. "But I still wish there was somewhere I could protect you."

Wishes were for children. I hadn't had any in so long, I didn't know what to say.

"Nothing's changed, Nyx. Not between us, at least. It's just a passing dream. And in the morning, it will be gone." He stroked my cheek, the touch as light as his whispered words.

I saw the truth in his eyes. And so I turned back, nestled myself against his chest, and together, we watched the drops grow fat and heavy, before sliding down, only to disappear.

Twenty-Eight

AQUIFER

W hen the mole rolled to a stop, water sloshed against the sides. The exterior lights were up, and I could see that we were inside some sort of cavern. But rather than the naturally formed one that the base camp was in, this was a near-perfect sphere, aside from the flattened ground. The walls were also strange, filled with holes as if we were inside a giant rock sponge. But the longer I looked, the more I saw the cracks and crags that interspersed the holes. This wasn't machine-made perfection; this was a chunk scooped out of raw nature.

"Okay, the first round of people out of the mole will be the science team, who will be testing for structural safety and seismic activity. Next up will be the engineering team, who will go straight to the generator apparatus. Everyone else will be assigned a shift, so that you each get a few minutes outside, but it's going to be limited, so prepare yourselves. The heat is intense, and there is an uneven surface beneath the water. If you feel faint at any time, return to mole five immediately, and drink at least sixteen ounces of water. Any questions?"

We all stayed silent, Fletcher's words slowly sinking in. First up was safety, then it was time for me to go. I looked back, checking on Guffey, but he was too busy looking out the windows and muttering to himself about shale and limestone inconsistencies.

"You ready, Guffey?" I asked, and his eyebrows shot up.

"Oh, yes, of course." He reached up and adjusted his round-lensed glasses. "I was calculating the likelihood of a cave-in due to the vibrations caused by the moles."

"Ah. And what did you determine?"

"We shouldn't linger any longer than necessary."

"Great." I dropped back into my seat with a huff, trying to squelch the nervous energy swarming me. My knee jiggled, and I resisted the urge to drum my fingers on my thigh.

I watched as Guffey packed his hip bag, moving things back and forth, back and forth until Fletcher stood to answer another comm.

"Okay, Engineering team is up next. You four ready?" Fletcher pointed at me, Guffey, River, and Kindred.

"Six," Rahlise rose, Niko mirroring the action. "We are here to protect her, and we can't do that from inside."

"She's got an assigned guard. They will remain at the entrance to the temperature-controlled area at all times while her team is working." Fletcher's eyes cut to Nanette, who stood with her arms crossed over her chest, considering.

"It's not going to hurt anything, but you won't be on rotation with the rest of your people. No extra time—Commandant's orders."

Rahlise nodded, not arguing the point.

Fletcher nodded tightly and punched something into the system at the front. "Okay, helmets on before the gate's lowered. The heat down here is no joke."

"Why is it hot down here when it was cold in the base camp?" River asked, snapping his helmet on with a grumble.

Guffey's spine straightened at the invitation to expound. "We've burrowed ourselves quite a ways further down towards the earth's center, which is heated. Much further than this, and even our suits wouldn't be sufficient to protect us, and we would have to remain suited *and* inside heat shielded vehicles. It was excellent planning to put the generator here, at the very edge of both safety and effectiveness. Truly, brilliant." He smiled, seeming excited to be here, now that he'd finished calculating his cave-in probabilities.

He pushed to the front of the mole, and I happily let him go first. My own enthusiasm was nonexistent, and the enormity of what we were trying to do weighed on me heavily. Once we were all ready, Fletcher waved to lower the door.

Stepping off the stairs into water was a strange sensation. The suit was already molded to my body, but the water pressure seemed to push the air up to the top of the suit.

It splashed around my ankles, dragging against my feet and making me clumsy as I followed the exuberant Guffey. He might have been older, but the man didn't waste time when he was excited about a project.

My gaze wandered past his rapidly moving form to a big, clear bubble butted up against one of the pockmarked walls. Half a dozen pipes bigger around than my thigh jutted up and disappeared into the rock ceiling. River caught up to my side, and Niko took the other.

"Is this the most water you've ever seen, or what?" River had a crazy grin on his face when he looked at me, the humidity in the air already coating his faceplate with mist.

"It is a lot," I agreed as my foot bobbled on something loose under the water. Two hands shot out and steadied me, from both River and Niko. I pretended I didn't notice them eyeing each other over my head after I steadied myself and kept walking.

Guffey waited impatiently at the entrance—a rectangular transparent door, made of the same plasticky material as the rest of the bubble, and with a thin black frame inside it. As soon as we caught up to Guffey, one of the guards waiting inside opened it up. Rahlise sealed it back behind us, and then our group fanned out, giving me my first clear view of the water generator. The annoying slosh of water under my feet became background noise as I took it in.

One of the stony-faced guards put a hand out to stop the Nightbloods from following us to the machine.

"You two can stay right here, with the rest of the guards."

Rahlise looked at me for direction, and I nodded discreetly. No need to make waves; he was still in shouting distance. With that settled, we headed for the machine.

It was massive, made of some kind of matte black metal. The thing was taller than I was by at least half, and the length of one of the moles. The pipes I'd seen going up ran through the machine on one side and then somehow passed through the bubble, which sealed perfectly around them. It wasn't until I was standing this close that I realized another six ran *down*, deep into the earth underneath. They had no labels or markings on them, so there was no telling what they did. Guffey was already crossing the space, ripping off his gloves, now that we were inside the bubble, and pulling out tools.

I trailed after him, feeling like a lost kid, as he began to circle the machine.

"This is fascinating. The fact that it's stood up to the constant load and damp conditions for so long . . . it's a marvel. The maintenance records state that it only needs attention once every fifty years, and that a member of Chrysanthe's family must be present to complete the maintenance."

He spoke offhandedly, but it was all news to me.

"How long has it been since one of her descendants was able to service the machine?"

"There's nothing in the official records that states that," Guffey answered, but Kindred chuckled behind us.

Looking over my shoulder, he'd also taken his gloves off and was tapping away at his tablet, the same one he used to *disable* the external comms for the whole party. Hopefully whatever he was doing, it wouldn't disable the generator, or any of our life support systems.

"None of her direct descendants have been inside Bastion city for a hundred fifty years. So, three maintenance cycles have passed." Kin arched his eyebrows at me and drummed his fingers over the side of the tablet.

"No wonder they've been looking so hard for you," River said, placing a hand possessively on my lower back.

"Enough chatter. Let's divide and conquer, and if anyone spots anything that appears to have stopped the machine, call it out." Guffey's words were jovial but there was no question that they were also a demand. We scattered around the machine.

I walked around the back, following River. The back side was covered with panels, each tidily battened down with latches. River walked up to one and popped it open as if he did this every day of his life.

Ironically, for all that I had the necessary ancestry, he was far more qualified to assist Guffey with this particular task than I would ever be. I knew how to artfully break things and barter like my life depended on it. Fixing things was above my pay grade. Still, though, I watched as he opened each panel down the line, touching various tubes and switches, but changing nothing. Nothing jumped out at me, and I didn't recognize anything that looked like it was causing a problem. Yet as we reached the end of the line, we found the rest of our engineering party dismayed as they stared at a massive pipe, bigger than all the rest and poking out the back of the temperature-controlled bubble. It didn't lead anywhere, simply stopped a couple of feet away from the machine. If I was so inclined, I could have climbed right into it.

"What is it?" I asked. "Is it supposed to be open like that?"

"Yeah, it's supposed to be open. It dumps into the aquifer, and there are pumps around the cavern that direct the flow once it's over a certain depth, so that a larger area receives water. See how big that pipe is?"

"Yeah, it's taller than me."

"Exactly. Seems like it should be able to handle a *lot* more volume than it's outputting, don't you think?"

At that, I looked down at the bottom of the pipe. A bare trickle of water ran out the very bottom, the stream no larger than my thumb as it poured out into the porous rock that made up the aquifer.

"Engineering team, please return to your moles, your time is up." I jumped at the harsh bark from the guards by the door. River placed a steadying hand on my shoulder, and then we lined up to return to the mole.

I'd known it wasn't going to be easy, but as I cast a last glance over my shoulder at the hulking black machine, I couldn't help but think I'd bitten off way more than we could chew. And I'd dragged my boyfriend right into the deep end with me.

Twenty-Nine

H20

Day Twelve

Two days. It had been *two days* of constant six-hour rotations, in and out of the mole to poke and prod the slumbering generator. One hour out, five hours in, on repeat. The small dribble of water flowing out of it never faltered, but nothing we tried increased it, either. My dread grew each time we climbed back up the mole's steps no closer to an answer.

Kindred was growing more frustrated by the hour, Guffey seemed lost in thought every waking moment, and River had a near-permanent concentration line etched between his eyebrows. Me? I was bored. Bored *stiff*.

The worry about the endless tons of rock overhead had faded, now that we'd been underground nearly two weeks, and all I had left

247

was restlessness. I was envious of the people who got to use their time outside the mole for exercise. There was always someone splashing around in the water in the main part of the cavern, and I wanted to be out there stretching and moving more than almost anything at this point.

Instead, I found myself mapping the interior of the tunnel while the others worked, noting that there were four tunnels bored into the walls, in addition to the one we'd traveled down to reach the machine. Small pumps sat in the mouths of each tunnel, and other teams from the remaining moles were servicing those. Apparently they were all simple, if sturdy, machinery and required no special bloodline to adjust.

Not that anyone had figured out what I was supposed to do yet. Special nanites or no, I had no clue what I was supposed to do to this machine. They didn't come with an instruction manual.

"Okay, helmets up." Fletcher's monotone call would haunt me, if we ever made it out of this hellhole. I'd heard it so much I could probably parrot it back with alarming accuracy. Unfortunately, that didn't help move us any closer to our end goal. Water.

We trudged back toward the generator, water splashing with every step. At least I didn't trip; the few fallen hunks of rock that had tripped us on the first day had been removed, leaving a wide path clear to the work site.

When we walked past the cluster of armed guards, I nodded at each of them, before pausing at the end. Officer Kutsuki had replaced the fifth guard who'd been on duty with our group each time before now.

"Kutsuki." Nanette nodded at him as she joined the group standing watch.

"Officer." He returned the nod, staying at attention.

The rest of us continued to the generator, swapping sides from our last hour, so everyone got a fresh perspective, according to Guffey. My only perspective was that the giant black spider was taunting us, withholding life-sustaining water for no fracking reason. River picked a panel and started poking, feeling along the seams inside the cabinet, now that they'd thoroughly ruled out any leaks or problems with the parts themselves.

Frustrated with the whole business, I splashed down into the water, plopping onto my butt. I rested against the metal, observing the back wall of the cavern instead of following River like I had been.

"Really? Just going to give up?" He sounded amused rather than irritated as he continued his methodical work.

"You already know I'm useless. What's the point in looking busy, when I'm no help?"

"Hey, you're not no help. Eventually we'll figure out what you need to do. Then you'll be the most important one down here."

"Right, sure." I grumbled. He went back to work, and I swished my hands back and forth under the water. It was a strange feeling, to be submerged yet dry. Eventually I let my hands wander on the ground, as I stared up at the rock. It was ugly, frankly. All dimpled and cracked. There was no art to it, no sweeping highs or dramatic lows.

My eyes glazed over as I stared at nothing, and in that moment, when my vision blurred to abstract, I saw it. I froze, my hands going still against the rock as I studied it, the faint etchings on the wall. There was a rectangular shape, with the vague shape of pipes sticking out the top. But there was only one other detail, a black square, at ground level, dead center of the shape. It was so small, I would have missed it if the perfect square didn't stand out against all the other random, natural shapes. I stood slowly, not wanting to draw attention to myself until I figured out if it was significant. For all I knew, the little square could be one of the endless panels they'd all patiently checked over.

It was low, so I crouched down, eyes right at the water line as I walked down the machine.

I didn't see anything the first time, and I brushed past River without speaking as I made the return pass.

There.

The bottom of the little box shape was marred by the ripples of the water, but it was a perfect square, in the middle of the machine.

"River." I said it quietly, nerves spiking at the discovery. "Have you already checked this?" I pointed to the tiny box-shaped indent that was smaller than my palm.

"No, actually. Good eye, Nyx." He smiled warmly and dropped into an easy squat. When he touched the panel, the door retracted up into the machine, blue-green light spilling forth from the square interior and reflecting up off the water.

Please insert the key.

The pleasant feminine voice brought tears to my eyes. Because it wasn't a robot. It was a recording of Chrysanthe's voice. The very same one I'd heard in the recording from the locket.

When we didn't stick anything into the hole, the light slowly dimmed, and the door clicked softly back down into place.

"Do you know what the key is?" River asked me.

"No, I have no idea. Probably something square, right? Maybe there's something in the documentation Kindred found."

"Hey, Kin, Guffey!" River called, and they came sloshing around to the back side.

"Everything good?"

"Yeah, is there one of these on your side?" River asked, poking the box.

The light shone again, and the voice repeated its message.

Please insert the key.

Guffey's eyes lit. "This is the breakthrough we've been looking for. Kindred, what can you tell me about a key?"

But he was already shaking his head. "Nothing. There's nothing in any of the printed materials about a key."

"That's okay. We can keep digging, trying things. We did find some loose components in the bins that would fit in that box. We'll try them all."

With nods, the three men moved, each going to grab whatever bits they'd found, but I just poked the box again, making the panel retract and the message play.

Please insert the key.

No one else seemed to realize whose voice that was; and how would they? They'd never heard Chrysanthe speak, unless she was recorded somewhere in the archives that I hadn't been told about. River had heard the message, too, but even he didn't seem to catch the significance. Was that a message for me, her descendant? Or was it merely a coincidence of the fact that she was the creator?

I stared up at the ceiling. The dim night-cycle lighting inside the mole didn't illuminate much, only enough for me to barely see thin lines between the panels overhead. Soft sounds of breathing and a few errant snores filled the air, but still, I lay awake. I couldn't sleep, because every time I closed my eyes, I saw that thin trickle of water sputtering to a stop, and I'd jolt right back awake.

My mind spun with possibilities, as well as confusion. We'd tried all the loose bits and bobs that had been found poking through the machine. Only a few actually fit inside the square, and of those none of them had been accepted.

The shining light and message played on repeat, unchanged by anything we'd tried. But I couldn't let go of the fact that it was Chrysanthe's voice. What would she have wanted? I cast a more careful glance around the mole, but nobody stirred. I thought of the old, handwritten journal I'd found at Chrysanthe's home and turned over onto my side.

The pages were yellowed and brittle, and I wished desperately I had it with me now, so I could review it. I wasn't sure what I was look-

ing for, but maybe if I understood my ancestor better, it would help me figure out the
key. But I didn't have it, and all I could do
was comb through my memories, in case I remembered something that would help. Chace's
words hung over me like Damocles's sword,
urging me faster and faster.

*There's a rumor going around up here that the
water is almost gone.*

The thin, anemic trickle from the enormous
pipe was all I saw when I closed my eyes, so I
didn't.

Thirty

No Cigar

Day Thirteen

"We would've been back today," Guffey muttered, slinging a sweat-drenched rag with frustration into a compartment. He dropped his head to his forearm for a second before turning to stare over at me, where I sat in the water with my back propped up staring at the barely-there diagram on the wall. He'd taken to working without his gloves and helmet, which wasn't *advisable*, but at this point we all trusted the temperature-controlled enclosure.

"How do you figure?" I asked, breaking my gaze to look back at him. Staring didn't actually do anything, other than free my mind to think.

"It was supposed to be a seven-day journey, but I happen to know that those puppies can make the trip in five, with a clear tunnel and under full power. Seven days down, one day to fix this heap, and five days back. We were supposed to be in base camp right now."

"Ah. And that bothers you?"

He chuckled; the sound oddly dark for the jovial engineer. "What do you think happens if we *don't* fix it, Nyx?"

I went still, my heart hammering against my ribs the only movement. "We *will* fix it."

"Yeah, kid, keep telling yourself that. Your great-great-great grandma was brilliant, but a real piece of work."

"Why do you say that?" It shouldn't have amused me to see him so disgruntled, but it did.

"Because, instead of choosing just to save humanity, she chose to put *strings* on it."

"No use griping about it now, old man. All we can do is figure it out," Kindred said. He grew more cheerful the worse the situation got, and at times it felt as if I was watching him and Guffey slowly change personalities. But then Kindred would look over at the soldiers sparring, and the cold glint in his eyes would remind me that he was a deeper well than he appeared.

He continued, "Could be worse—she could have never built the thing. You and I'd have come down to bare, dead rock." He slapped Guffey on the shoulder, then wandered back around to the other side where he and River were putting their heads together.

Guffey went back to re-checking fittings, but my mind was spinning. For all he'd meant it as an insult, Bernard was right. Chrysanthe *had* put strings on her gift to humanity. But the difference was, I knew she'd had a very good reason—fear for her family's safety. *My* safety.

And those fears had been well founded. Despite the promises made, none of her descendants lived inside the city she'd helped build and sustain.

So what key could ensure that we were always present?

The locket.

It held the directions to the city, a personal message. It only opened when I'd bled on it, and I had special nanites in my blood that only her descendants had.

I stood, water sloughing off me with a great slurping splash as I fumbled for my helmet. "Guffey, help me get this off!"

"What's wrong? River!" he hollered, a red flush rising in his cheeks as he splash-stomped to my side and helped me unhook the helmet from my suit.

"Nothing, I've just got an idea."

River came skidding around the corner of the machine as my helmet popped free, and nearly tumbled head over feet, the water dragging at him and changing his center of gravity. Kindred missed running into him by a matter of inches when he stopped.

"Guys, chill out. I just had an idea of something else we can try." I waved at them to stand down, and carefully unclasped the locket from around my neck, nervous anticipation thrumming through me like dry lightning.

"What does your jewelry have to do with anything, young lady?" Guffey looked disappointed when I gathered it into my palm.

"I don't know, but I intend to find out." Before I took a step forward, splashing steps heralded the arrival of two of our guards.

"Everything okay back here?" Lieutenant Kutsuki asked, a line of concern etched between his eyebrows.

"We're fine," Kindred answered, his eyes trained on me as I crossed to the little door and pressed to open the compartment. The light shone.

Please insert the key.

I blew out a shaky breath and placed the locket inside. The door snapped shut, and a whirring sound hummed out from the compartment.

River gasped, gripping my shoulder as we all stared intently. It had never *closed* over anything we'd tried before, and I dug my fingernails into my palm as it purred.

Three sharp beeps emitted from the machine, and the door popped back open.

Key invalid. Critical mode activated.

Frack. Disappointment tasted sour on the back of my tongue as I gently scooped out the locket and placed it back around my neck. What else could it be?

"Uh, should we be worried about critical mode?" River asked, fidgeting with his gloves nervously.

"No, it's been on critical mode. That's what the trickle means. It is programmed to never shut off, best as I can tell," Guffey said, scratching at his head but hitting helmet.

Kutsuki shook his head and muttered under his breath as he sloshed back to his position inside the entrance of the enclosure, leaving the four of us to stew over it alone.

"Do you want to tell us why you thought your necklace would work?" Guffey's words were kind, his grandfatherly patience back in full force.

"It was Chrysanthe's, and I'm the only person allowed to touch it."

"I'm sorry, it's jewelry. How can anyone else not be *allowed* to touch it?" His fingertips reached out as if tempted to test it himself, but River's hand came up lightning fast and slapped it away.

"Dude, not a good plan. That thing kills anyone that's not her—I've seen it with my own eyes."

Kin's mouth flopped open for a second as if to argue, then snapped shut again without a word.

"That's time!" Kutsuki called from his post, and we let out a collective sigh. Another day, and we were still no closer to finding the solution.

Maybe Guffey was right, and we *should* be worried about what would happen if we couldn't fix the machine. I carefully screwed my helmet back into place and traded a dour grin with River. He squeezed my shoulder again.

"It was a good idea, Nyx. It at least did *something*, so that's progress. It's ignored everything else we've put inside it."

"Yeah, it felt right," I admitted as we passed the guards.

"Chin up, Nyx." Kutsuki surprised me by smiling at me. "I'm sure you guys will figure it out. Maybe the answer is closer than you think. Besides, if you don't, well, we're all dead anyways." He shrugged, as if it was no big deal either way.

But it was, and the growing pit in my stomach insisted that time was running out.

The mole's stairs had barely closed behind us when the comm light began flashing. Fletcher picked it up.

"Yes, sir. Yes. I understand—immediately, sir." He dropped the comm back into its cradle.

"Don't strip down yet—the commandant wants us all in mole one."

River groaned, rubbing his sweaty hair. He'd popped off the helmet already and glared at it where it lay on the seat as if it had personally offended him, rather than having kept his skin from blistering on his face.

"Not happy about it either, Zeer. But get that helmet back on, he wants us all."

"That's going to be a tight squeeze," Nanette surprised me by grousing. "Are the captain and her people still there?"

"He didn't say."

"Goody." Her sour expression matched my feelings perfectly.

We all filed back out and slogged through the muddy water up to the lead mole.

The steps were already lowered, and we filed inside quietly. I had been on edge ever since Jacira's name was mentioned, and my eyes roamed over every detail of the mole, and how it differed from ours. It was about six feet longer, and the interior held bunk beds on the back walls, with a conference seating area at the front. Captain Jacira reclined in one of the over-sized seats, while the commandant stood casually, hands clasped over his elbows.

"Make yourselves comfortable." The commandant gestured vaguely in our direction, so we all started slowly removing helmets and gloves.

The stairs slowly rose behind us, ratcheting up my nerves another notch with every inch the gap closed. When the soft click of them sealing off reached me, I swallowed hard, not taking my eyes off the two volatile leaders.

"We need a status update on your progress with the water generator," the commandant said.

There was a beat of silence, then another, before Guffey stepped forward, chin high. "All of the basic parts in the diagram are accounted for and in good repair. The supply pipes providing hydrogen and oxygen are also sound."

"And?" he prodded, one eyebrow raised.

"And it still won't run. There is an unlabeled compartment which we found, that when opened asks for a key to be inserted."

"A key? Is there any documentation on a key?" His gaze flicked to Nanette, who shook her head.

"There are no markings on the machine indicating what it might be?" Jacira asked, drumming her fingers impatiently on her crossed thigh.

"No, Captain."

"I see. And why haven't we been able to interface with the machine and read the specs on this key? Surely we can hack it and override it, if nothing else." She turned the question on Kindred, completely ignoring Guffey.

"The machine remains completely unresponsive. The records indicate that it hasn't been serviced properly in over a century—"

"And why is that?" The tapping stopped as she eyed the commandant. "Surely your people *understood* the importance of this generator."

His eyes were cold when he stared back at her. "The records are incorrect. It has been serviced every fifty years, as per the instructions."

She swiveled in the chair, leaning both elbows onto her knees. A delicate blush heated her porcelain cheeks, but I'd have bet my last water credit it was sparked by pure fury, not any sense of embarrassment.

"Why did you say it wasn't properly serviced?" She directed the ice-cold demand to Kindred, and still it took everything in me not to take a wary step back. She was psycho, and I could practically *feel* the threat floating in the air around her.

Why did I let myself be trapped in a sealed vehicle with this woman? Oh yeah, I didn't get a choice.

"The full records state that a simple service isn't sufficient; a member of Chrysanthe's own

263

family *must* be present for the machine to run at optimal levels. It has been more than a hundred fifty years since the last time that occurred, and the machine is running in emergency mode."

"Emergency mode?" She leaned back in the chair again, considering.

"Yes. Kind of a lowest possible level of generation, which it can maintain for a longer period. There is no documentation on why a relative must be present—or about this key—or how long the machine can remain in emergency mode."

"So you think it's going to stop altogether." It wasn't a question, and Kindred stiffened under her critical gaze.

"I didn't say that."

"You didn't *have to*, Kindred. I'm not an imbecile, and I can read between the lines."

"There's no need to catastrophize, here." Commandant Kieran made to step forward, but Jacira shot to her feet, staring him down.

"You can run your own operation as badly as you wish, per the terms of our truce. But you will *not* interfere with the handling of my own people, *Commandant*." She spat the title like a curse word, and the commandant stepped back, averting his eyes.

When she rounded on Kindred, he didn't cower. The knife was in her hand and scraping along the ridge of his cheekbone before I saw her move.

"You're of no use to me if you can't *use* this brain to solve this problem for me, Kindred. I don't like waiting, and I don't like rooming with a narcissistic peon. You have twenty-four hours, Kindred, before I'll take something you can't replace."

"Yes, Captain."

"For now, a simple reminder will do." Her smile was sickly. *Deranged.*

"What?" He blinked, surprised at the sudden change of tack.

I registered the threat on a subconscious level, and everything happened at once—the knife slicing down through the air, the unholy gleam in her eye.

"Kin!" I rammed into his shoulder, not thinking it through beyond *Get him away from the psycho with the knife.*

He grunted and took a staggered step to the side, knocking into the captain's shoulder as the knife made contact with his flailing hand, then clattered to the ground. She shrieked and guards I hadn't known were inside the back of the mole swarmed forward.

River's hands were around my waist in an instant, snatching me back from the captain and Kindred, and putting himself between me and the guards. But they ignored the two of us, forming up around the commandant.

Kindred stood frozen, staring in shock down at his hand and the blood streaming from his flayed-open palm.

The captain was likewise still, but she held her own hand in front of her face. She stared mesmerized at her hand, where blood coated her palm and wrist. I bit back a sickened groan when I realized half of her pinky finger was gone, the source of all the blood.

"Ma'am, you need medical attention." Nanette was the first in motion, waving at Fletcher to open the mole doors.

"The knife slipped," she said, her voice wondrous, instead of angry or pained. Bile rose up the back of my throat making my nose burn, and I knew that I would puke all over the once-pristine interior of this mole if I didn't look away.

I felt like a coward when I leaned my forehead against River's back, but I needed a second to compose myself. The gate lowered, and then everyone was in motion. River snatched the helmet on over my head, mouth pinched and eyes tight as he tugged my gloves on a bit more softly. I started moving again, albeit woodenly, and finished putting my own gloves on so we could get the frack out of this mole.

Nanette slapped a helmet on the captain and ushered her out, shooting me a look over her shoulder that said I was in deep, deep camel dung.

"Come on, Nyx. We've got to get Kin bandaged up and keep you out of the captain's sight."

He tugged me toward the stairs, but I froze at the blood spattered all over the white floor. There were already footsteps in it, smearing it into a grisly mess.

"Nyx!" His tone was sharp, and I ripped myself away from the horror, and put one foot in front of the other. But one thing played on repeat in my head.

Twenty-four hours.

We only had a few chances left, and then the captain wouldn't aim for Kindred's hand. And something told me that I would be on the chopping block right next to him as soon as she snapped out of her stupor.

Thirty-One

Key to My Heart

Day Fourteen

One shift passed, and then a second. We had two left, Kindred was a hand down, and panic dogged my every step towards the enclosure.

We were *missing* something. But what was it? I'd finished the entire journal, and there was nothing at all that led me toward a possible key inside. It was all fear and anger and scientific distance. Nothing concrete, nothing I could use.

An idea struck me, as I watched them unzip the door for us. I elbowed River in the ribs and then darted around the outside of the enclosure. Niko appeared at my side as if by magic, his steps splashing in almost perfect time with mine.

"What are you doing, Nyx?"

"Testing a theory." My faceplate fogged with my breath, and shouts and splashes echoed behind us as I ignored them all and darted for the pockmarked wall. The engraving was out of reach, over my head. How could I get up there?

"You couldn't test this theory without causing a ruckus?"

"Probably not," I grunted, lunging upward—I was over a foot too short. I spun around. River and Rahlise were only a step behind, and the older man must have read my mind, because he didn't wait for anyone else. He scooped me up at the thighs and lifted me straight overhead.

It took me a second to reorient to the new height, but then I spotted it. The perfect square recess in the wall, cleverly hidden in plain sight. I leaned forward but didn't see anything out of the ordinary. I shoved my hand into the hole, feeling carefully. At first I thought it was empty, but then something shifted, loose.

I pulled it out and clutched it in two hands, careful not to drop it into the water below.

"I got it, put me down!"

"Got what? What the frack, Nyx?" River's exasperation was underlaid with curiosity. I opened my hands, revealing a smooth black stone, nothing like the red-striated rock of the tunnels, or the flat sheets of pockmarked rock making up the walls. Into the rock was carved a single flower, nothing else. It was the same carving on her gold compact, the one I'd kept for the pretty inscription from her husband.

But I *knew*, and I smiled even as the guards surrounded us and ushered us back towards the front of the enclosure. They shoved us gracelessly inside and sealed up the door. The angry city soldiers formed up around Rahlise and Niko, as if they could keep them under better control that way.

Kutsuki was seething as he addressed us. "We're all under strict orders not to touch the surrounding stone! Are you trying to bring the whole damn place down on our heads?"

I darted straight for the generator, ignoring Kutsuki and the expletives he yelled at my back. I had to know if my hunch was right, or if I'd brought even more trouble down on us for nothing. I skidded to a stop at the key port, tapped it open and didn't wait for the message before I shoved the rock inside.

It clicked closed and the humming sound returned. A few seconds later, it popped back open.

Key incomplete. Critical mode activated.

What the frack?

I hauled off and slapped the side of the machine, frustration and inadequacy bubbling behind my sternum like acid.

What was I missing? The locket didn't work. I'd figured out the rock—the single bloom, Chrysanthe's signature from her husband. Surely only one of her descendants would know that. So, what was I missing?

And then it hit me. Incomplete. Not invalid, *incomplete*.

"Does anybody have a knife?" I whirled around, ripping off my helmet and then pulling my fingers out of the gloves as my team shook their heads.

"Nyx, what are you doing? This is madness." Guffey's eyes were full of concern, but I ignored him. I had to be right. I *had* to. There was nothing else left.

I jog-slogged around the machine towards the guards. "I need a knife!" A few of them startled at the proclamation, but nobody offered one. "Anything sharp, come on, I know you've got something!"

One of the soldiers pulled a multi-tool from his suit pocket, pulling out an inch-and-a-half blade that looked dull. It would have to do.

"Thank you!" I snatched it and splashed back, my breath coming in short gasps in the warm, humid bubble.

I pulled the rock back out of the key port, and it snapped closed, extinguishing the light.

"Nyx, why do you have a knife?" Kindred's wary tone made me sad, but I ignored him. I snapped the pocketknife back open, and before one of them could stop me, pierced the tip of my thumb. It burned as I widened the cut, smearing fat drops of my blood over the small carving, until the whole rock was damp and sticky. I shoved it back into the port, squeezing out another drop or two before pulling my thumb back.

The door snapped shut once more, and I squeezed my thumb into my other palm to staunch the bleeding as we all waited. River plucked the multi-tool from my hand with a frown and slid it into his pocket.

The resonant hum increased in intensity, and lights began to flicker and turn on around the machine, leaking from the edges of closed panels as well as highlighting some that had been sealed before. And then, I heard it. The beautiful, glorious sound of water gushing from the massive output pipe. Euphoria rushed through me.

I *did it.*

Thirty-Two

Thicker than Water

S houts and cheers rang out, both from the men surrounding me and from those out in the cavern. River's arms came around me and squeezed, lifting my feet off the ground.

"You did it, Nyx," he said with a laugh, holding me close. "You saved us all."

"Murder and Mercury." Kindred whistled low and whipped out his tablet, already checking to see what he could find out about the newly awakened generator.

But I wasn't listening, wasn't joining in on the cheers. I squeezed River back and patted him on the chest to put me down. He did, and the blood rushed in my ears as I sloshed around to the back of the machine to stare at the huge spray of water flowing out of the pipe. The constant rush was forceful and magnificent as it crashed to the ground outside our bubble, and warmth bloomed in my chest at the sight.

It was real. *It was real.*

We were all going to be okay.

I walked back around to the machine to find Guffey and Kindred heads-down over the tablet, checking output readings. Since they were occupied, I tapped the key panel and removed the carved rock. All traces of my blood were gone, as if it had been sucked dry by the generator. A little part of me worried that it would turn back off, but apparently all it required was proof that I was alive, well, and carrying Chrysanthe's DNA—or nanites—in my blood.

I put the stone in my pocket, until I could safely return it back to its resting place up in the wall. When I looked up, River was watching me with an awed expression.

"Shouldn't you be helping those two assess the machinery?"

He shook his head. "The water generator is fine. The problem was the missing key, not anything inside the machine."

"You sound awfully confident for someone who's never seen a water generator until this week."

He shrugged, the lopsided grin on his face making his dimple pop. "When you know, you know. How do you feel?"

How did I feel? I had no idea. Relieved, sure. Anxious to get back on the earth's surface, definitely. But just because we'd fixed the water generator didn't mean things up top were going to resolve themselves, and no matter how much water this thing put out, it had a *long* way to go before we'd see much difference in other parts of the desert.

The euphoria was already leaving, replaced by a mountain of worry about securing freedom and safety for all desert dwellers, not just from Bastion City, but also the captain. The more time I spent around her, the less I was sure she'd actually trade with us and leave.

"Nyx, come here, you've got to see this." Guffey's excitement was contagious, and after a shared smile with River, we both walked over to peer at the offered tablet. It was a strange, dotty and multi-colored map. A red beacon showed where we stood, and no less than twenty other blue beacons dotted what looked like all of North America, but instead of the familiar outlines, the shapes and colors made up strange watery patterns.

"What is this?" I asked, confused.

"An aquifer map of North America. Nyx, this isn't the only generator."

"Holy frack," River said, expressing my thoughts exactly.

"That has to be at least twenty or thirty more." I looked over toward the end of the machine where I could just see the halo of mist coming off the water billowing out of the pipe, and then back at Guffey and Kindred. "That would be *huge*."

"Even if we estimate half don't work or can't be accessed without structural repairs to the access tunnels, this amount of ground water creation could have enormous impact on the surface."

"Can you send me that?" I pointed to the map on the tablet, and Kindred grinned.

"I can do you one better." Both of mine and River's hydration meters beeped, and I looked down at my wrist.

Update requested. I tapped to accept, and a little progress bar popped up.

"You've now got this map, the generator schematics, every bit of anything I could dig up on these, and a big comm update. I don't know what the captain will do once we make it to the surface, and if I trust anyone to do the right thing with the information, it's you two." His gaze flicked quickly to my thumb and then away.

"So, it's not readily available?"

"Not . . . quite. I'm guessing the commandant has access, but how many people below him? Couldn't say."

I nodded, immediately catching what he didn't say. It wasn't in Commandant Kieran's best interest to restore water to the whole continent. He just wanted *his* city to stay strong and in control. The rest of us, he would happily leave to die in the Wastes.

Was that why he took my blood? To ensure he had a backup if needed, or to take charge of every other water generator without needing me?

The idea of a world where there were no more Wastes—or no more risk of dehydration, even if the sand stayed—was beyond my comprehension. But somehow, I didn't see the commandant being that charitable.

My water meter vibrated on my wrist. When I looked down, a happy little *Update complete!* message displayed.

When I tapped it, a hologram projected in the cight inches above the device, showing a menu.

"What the— How did you do that?" I jumped, and the hologram disappeared as soon as my arm moved.

Kin laughed. "Who do you think has the technology to run the water credit system and create all the hydration meters?"

"I honestly never questioned it. It seemed like a holdover from old times."

"It might have started that way, but most of the tech came down from the people that left. There are humanitarian organizations on Mars that still keep things running."

I just stared at him, so shocked by this information I wasn't even sure what to ask, though I was sure later I'd have a million questions. Like, why the frack didn't they come *get us* instead of just maintaining our infrastructure?

"Everybody, time's up! They're cutting it short, since the machine is running, and we don't know how long we have left until we get stuck in the tunnels." Kutsuki hollered, and I pulled my gloves back on as we started moving towards the door. Rahlise met my eyes from his position at the entrance and gave me a deep bow.

"You've done it, αγαπημένη. Your— *Hema* would like to congratulate you." He nodded off to the middle of the cavern, where a group of Nightbloods stood, staring our direction. I was sure Hema was in there somewhere, so I lifted a hand in a wave. None of them waved back, but I got quite a few head-bobs of acknowledgement.

"I'd love to see him." I smiled up at Rahlise, and over at Niko, too. If I couldn't spare a smile today, when we'd solved the immediate water crisis *and* found out that there were more generators all over the world, when could I?

"Let's go, let's go, everybody keep it moving—" One of the guards barked at us, and we fell into line. This time, they didn't waste time sealing the enclosure back up behind us. They started dismantling it, so it could be packed away into one of the moles for travel.

We branched off from the stream of people to veer towards the cluster of Nightbloods. One man stepped forward from the group, arms open wide, as if for a hug.

I was practically floating as I closed the distance between us. He clasped both of my hands in his, drawing me close and pressing his covered cheek against mine.

"Well done, παιδί μου. Well done."

"Thank you." I smiled warmly at him, and he let his thumb graze my cheekbone. It was an oddly intimate gesture, for two people standing in the middle of a hectic underground cavern.

"Nyx, let's move!" Nanette's barked order made me jump back from my father. She waited impatiently there with Fletcher, hand on her hip.

"See you soon?" I asked.

He nodded. "As soon as we are once again allowed to stop for nightly dinners."

"Good." He squeezed my hand, and then let go, sending me off with my guards.

I tried not to analyze the warm glow in my chest at his approval and just enjoyed the rare moment, instead.

Thirty-Three

Sacrifices and Second Guesses

Day Seventeen

The days in the mole escaping the rising water were like existing in a surreal bubble. We only stopped once in the three days, and I wasn't allowed out except for a quick visit to the doctor at the back of the convoy. He cleared me to remove my brace ten days after the injury had occurred, a fact which he wondered at. Apparently, puncture wounds of that size typically take a month or more to heal and are prone to infection. According to the doctor, the nanites in my blood were working overtime to improve my health. Even the stitches came out cleanly, and I had almost no scar.

I had mixed feelings about it, and was once again awake during the night cycle, nothing but the dim glow of the running lights to keep me company amidst the even breaths and soft snores of my companions. A tablet screen flickering on suddenly made me jerk in my seat.

"Sorry," Kindred whispered. "I was going to read."

"It's okay. I was already awake."

"That good, huh? Want to talk about whatever's bothering you?"

Did I? I hadn't even mentioned it to River. He'd been so *happy*; I didn't want to burst his bubble with questions we'd probably never find the answers to. But Kindred was offering, and everyone else was asleep.

"The commandant took several big vials of my blood ahead of this mission, and I don't know why or what he did with it. I assumed it was for the water generator, but now . . ."

He tapped lightly on the rim of his tablet, eyebrows drawn down low. "Do you want me to do some digging?"

"I— Can you? Will you get into trouble?"

He snorted lightly, barely an exhalation. "Can I? Yes. Will I get into trouble? Who cares." He winked at me and began tapping away on his tablet.

We fell silent again. Nervous energy zipped through me like dry lightning, and I found myself considering retracting the request. Did I want to know? Would it really change anything?

"Oh, wow."

I sat bolt upright, dropping all pretense of being asleep. "What is it?"

"Come here," he gestured me forward, so I crossed the little aisle and crouched next to his chair, so I could see the proffered tablet. It was a chart, with a rapid decline at the end, until it met the baseline.

"What is it?"

"It's the number of nanites remaining in your blood sample over time. They took a larger sample of your blood to test the nanites, see if they could be recreated. But they've apparently all self-destructed within forty-eight hours of being removed from your body." He jabbed his finger into the little part of the chart where the number of remaining nanites dropped to zero. Forty-seven point five hours.

"Uhh—what does that mean, do you think?"

"It means that whoever gave you those nanites is smarter than we gave them credit for. They enhance you, but they also don't stick around when they've been taken away from you."

I just stared, confused. "But why? I don't see the point of having such helpful technology destroy itself. Those nanites have helped me heal and reduced my sensitivity to dehydration. Shouldn't whoever invented them *want* them to last, so they can help more people?"

"I have never met someone so innocent. Honestly, how you survived out there in the desert is a wonder."

I bristled at the criticism. "I survived just fine, thanks. I don't see why that makes me innocent, to care about the rest of humanity." I turned to storm back to my seat, but he put a hand on my forearm, stopping me before I took the second step.

"Nyx, come on. Don't be like that. It's not an insult. I just . . . I've never met anyone in my life who wants the good of humanity more than their own power, or wealth. It's refreshing. But my point is, it was Chrysanthe. It *had* to be. She's the only one who's thought far enough ahead, in all of this."

"What?" Confusion and annoyance tangled up like tent lines in my chest. *Was there anything she didn't have a hand in? And why am I the only one who didn't see it?*

"She made it so that her descendant had to be alive. If the blood is outside the host, the nanites die. After seeing this, I'd bet my last water credit that she knew people like the commandant would come along, and try to get rid of her line. She was too smart, and paranoid as frack. So what did she do? Made it so the tech couldn't be removed from the host. You have to stay alive, or none of the water generators stay working."

"So if I die without having a child . . . the water generator stops again in fifty years. And these nanites ensure that they can't just save my blood for a rainy day."

"Looks that way."

"Holy frack. But why couldn't they just insert my blood into someone else; give them the nanites before the forty-eight hours were up?"

"I don't know. They may have tried over the years—it doesn't say here. But if I had to guess, she thought of that too."

"I don't even know how I got the nanites. Neither of my parents have them."

"Interesting. Well, maybe it is purely DNA. But over the generations, the amount of shared DNA with her would wane. I would bet these nanites are the true key, however you got them. Either that, or one of your parents isn't *really* your biological parent." He shrugged, as if that meant nothing, but the mere suggestion had me recoiling.

"Surely not. Neither of them had any reason to lie."

"Well, you picked them up somewhere. Maybe how isn't so important. You knew your blood was the key, and that's all that matters in the end." He smiled and clicked off the tablet with a yawn.

I took the hint and stepped back over to my seat, sinking into the soft cushions with my mind whirring. I knew I should sleep, but my thoughts were so tangled I stared out the window watching the rock tunnel walls roll by long into the night instead.

I woke when the mole stopped. My head was pounding; lack of sleep and a few midnight tears led to one heck of a next-day headache.

"We're stopping for lunch today, and we're finally high enough up that the temp has dropped and we can actually stretch our legs. About two more days of hard travel, and we'll be back to base camp."

Fletcher's proclamation was met with a cheer. I winced, and River squatted by my seat.

"You okay, Nyx? I know you hate being cooped up almost as much as I do, but you don't look happy."

"Yeah, just a headache. It'll pass."

"Ahh. Lunch should help. And you finally get to stretch your new bionic leg." He waggled his eyebrows at me, making me chuckle.

"It got stitches, but I'm not sure that qualifies it as *bionic*."

"Apparently you're already full of super-cool nanites. Surely the stitches make up the difference." He smiled, the dimple popping in his cheek, and I returned it, though I knew it was a watered-down smile. His eyes were full of concern as he watched my face.

"Are you sure that's all?" His question was quieter, low so as not to be overheard in the mole.

"I'm sure." I squeezed his hand, and then the hatch was lowered so we could all file out. River and I walked hand in hand to the lunch table, accepting our bowls of travel stew gratefully.

We found a spot to stand off to the side, propped against the rough, cool stone of the tunnel wall.

Happy chatter and little bursts of roughhousing filled the space, the overwhelming sense of relief making everyone lighter, freer than on the way down. I wasn't, though. Too many questions, too many uncertainties about what would happen next seemed to be riding on my shoulders.

I ate my stew quietly, while River talked to onc of the Nightbloods who'd found us. Not Niko—those two seemed to be like oil and water. It was hard to tell with the face coverings up, but based on the few freckles I could see around his eyes I guessed it was Sax.

I placed a hand on River's arm. "I think I'm going to head back to the mole, try to get some rest while it's still quiet."

"Of course, let me walk you." He looked around for a place to turn his half-full bowl in.

"No, finish your lunch. I'm going straight to the mole, and then straight to my seat to lie down. Seriously, you two keep catching up." I forced a better smile this time, and his shoulders relaxed.

"Okay, if you're sure. But grab Rahlise before you go back, please."

"I will." I squeezed his forearm gently before letting go, leaving him to his chat. I walked slowly through the Nightbloods, looking for Rahlise. Before I found him, though, I found Hema.

"Παιδί μου! There you are. Where is your male companion?"

He still refused to call River my boyfriend, or anything warmer than *male companion*, but I ignored it. "Chatting with Sax, I think."

He nodded. "Yes, those two knew each other before. I'm still surprised he's left your side." *Surprised* looked a lot more like *displeased*, but Hema was never particularly pleased about anything to do with River.

"I told him to. I was looking for Rahlise, actually, so I could go and lie down. Headache."

"Come, I can walk you, myself."

"Okay, thank you."

We walked out of the ring of lights into the dimmer tunnels, skirting along the wall in relative silence. It was comfortable enough, and I didn't feel the need to fill it with empty words.

"Our time draws short, παιδί μου, before we will return to the surface. My men and I have spoken at length, and we will support your bid for change on the surface."

I stopped dead, searching his dark, serious eyes over the thin strip of fabric that blocked his expression from me.

"I don't know what that looks like, yet."

"I trust that you will figure it out." His eyes crinkled at the corners, and I knew he was smiling, even if I couldn't see the twist of his lips.

A loud clang off to our left caught our attention and we both froze, taking in the shadowy opposite wall of the tunnel, on the far side of the moles. The sounds of a scuffle broke out, and we exchanged a glance as grunts of pain and thudding ensued, as if someone was being rammed into the side of the mole.

"Let me go!"

I didn't think twice, didn't stop to consider. The voice was young and afraid, and my own personal demons came roaring to the front. I leapt between two parked moles, charging straight into the ruckus. When I rounded the corner, three men in blue temp-control suits were huddled, the smallest one's shoulders pinned painfully against the back of the mole.

"Let him go!" I demanded, Hema hot on my heels as I rushed the closest attacker. He was a good foot taller than me, but I didn't let that stop me. I dropped my shoulder and rammed it into his stomach. He managed to get his arm down, diverting some of the blow so he kept his feet, but at least I'd evened the odds for a second. The third man stayed cowered at the back of the mole, letting us duke it out without him.

"Nightbloods, to me," Hema hissed into his comm before drawing a curved black blade from his waistband. I didn't have time to worry about what he intended to do with it, though, as a sledgehammer-sized fist was barreling towards my face.

I ducked and jumped back, slamming my own back against the tunnel wall so hard that I nearly winded myself. The giant of a man was quick to follow, closing the distance in a matter of heartbeats. He swung again, and this time there was no room behind me, nowhere to run. I threw up my forearm, swearing under my breath as the impact rattled through my whole body and wrenched my arm painfully against the carved rock wall.

And then a hand was closing around my throat, squeezing, tighter and tighter until black spots crowded into the edges of my vision. Scrabbling for grip against the rock wall wasn't working, I couldn't buck him off of me, and panic had well and truly set in. I wedged the toe of my left foot into the crevice where wall met floor, the rock rough enough there to catch the toe of my boot. The tiny bit of leverage allowed me to whip my right knee up and nail him in the groin.

He grunted as his grip loosened, and I sucked in greedy gulps of air past my bruised throat. And then, Hema's hand flashed up and my attacker was gone. I stumbled forward into the space he used to occupy, wildly looking around for the next threat. But he was running, clutching the side of his neck as a red waterfall trickled down his blue suit.

Hema stepped into my personal space, his black blade slicked with the giant's blood as he gripped my shoulder with his other hand.

"Παιδί μου, are you okay?"

I tried to speak, to answer, to say *something*, but all that came out was a wheeze, followed by a tight cough.

He spoke rapid-fire Greek into his communications device, squeezing my shoulder again briefly in support.

The third man in white, the one who'd been pushed against the mole, approached and said, "You two saved me. Thank you so much. Are you okay?" A face bobbed into my still-narrowed vision, and after two blinks it came into focus. Kutsuki.

The worried frown on his face struck me as strange. He reached out for me as if to help me sit, but Hema batted him away with the hand still holding the knife.

"Do not touch her."

"Easy, man. I was just trying to return the favor." He dropped his hands to his hips, the frown deepening as he looked back and forth between me and Hema. "She really looks like she should sit down."

I was still clutching my throat, cupping the bruised airway as if that would make it suddenly work better.

Hema whirled on him, and I would love to say I didn't stagger when he let go of my shoulder, but that would be a lie. I folded forward, bracing myself on my knees. My arms shook like limp canvas caught in a breeze, and the world was still a very, very small place. I could see Hema's back, his feet spread in a fighting stance.

Kutsuki stepped forward. "You're being ridiculous! Just let me help her sit down. Rogers nearly strangled the life out of her." His finger pointed incredulously at me. I waved, trying to tell him to lay off. I was going to be fine. Air, cool and damp and earthy, was slowly starting to ease the angry swelling in my windpipe. If I concentrated on shallow breaths, just enough to keep the panic at bay, the muscles loosened by a fraction.

"I tried, old man. It didn't have to be like this." Kutsuki's voice went cold, and I snapped my head up to look.

It would be the regret of my life, that I couldn't scream, couldn't jump up in time to change the trajectory of his gunshot. Everything slowed to molasses around me. My heartbeat and the sharp percussion of the bullet being ejected from the chamber blocked everything else out. There was no tunnel, no moles, no surface, no other people than the three of us, locked into this awful time warp where I watched Lieutenant Kutsuki shoot my father at point blank range.

Hema staggered back a step, jostling me as I tried to grab him with hands that felt too numb, too clumsy.

Kutsuki swiveled; the barrel pointed directly at me over Hema's shoulder, who was sinking down, down to the ground, and pulling me with him under his weight.

"Hema, no. Hema!" I whisper-screamed, trying to haul him back to his feet, but his head was lolling, and even if I got him back up, there was no way I was getting either of us out of Kutsuki's line of fire. That deadly weapon tracked us with unerring certainty, and I squinched my eyes shut as I heard the weapon click as he cocked the hammer back. We were on the ground, Hema's head and shoulders in my lap, the hard stone floor a terrible reminder of where we were, alone and buried underground.

But the second shot never came. Instead, the solid thud of bodies colliding jolted my eyes back open. A whirl of black fabric had smashed into Kutsuki, and I realized with a start that it was Niko, his hood swept back as he grappled with the soldier, the glinting weapon forced high overhead. A second thud heralded River's arrival, slamming right into the two of them and knocking them both back a few feet from where I held Hema. The gun flew free from Kutsuki's grip, arcing overhead before disappearing into the gloom with a clatter.

Within another heartbeat, Rahlise was crouched in front of me, holding his fingertips to Hema's neck, checking for a pulse.

There was so much blood. So much blood. I knew it was bad. His eyes were glassy, his body limp over me.

"Nyx, stop shaking him. Nyx!" My entire body froze under his censure. I didn't realize I'd been shaking him, through some deep desire to wake him, jostle him to awareness that I knew was quickly slipping between my fingers.

"He won't wake up," I was hysterical. I could hear it in my own voice; the squeaky screech of words felt like knives in my throat, but they were imperative. Rahlise had to do something. He had to, he had to.

I couldn't lose another parent, not like this, not when I barely had him.

But Rahlise rested a gentle hand on his leader's shoulder, before reaching up to remove Hema's face covering. Hema was pale, so pale. I'd only seen him uncovered a few times, but there had been a bright vitality to his face. And now, he was waxy, waning.

Rahlise rested his hand on his cheek, the small touch leaving red streaks on his olive skin. "Να μπεις στην επόμενη ζωή ειρηνικά, φίλε μου."

"You need to do something, Rahlise! What are you doing! Get the doctor!" I shoved his hand off Hema's cheek, so he let it drop into his lap.

"He is gone, αγαπημένη του αίματος. He has flown free unto the next life."

"No! You're wrong, his heart's still beating, do something!" I screamed now, the words torn from me like daggers rending my flesh.

"I'm sorry, Aíma. I'm sorry. Long live the blood, long live the night." And then he bowed, even though we were seated. He bowed to me, as I cradled Hema's lifeless body to my chest and sobbed.

Thirty-Four

LIT MATCH

Chace

Alarms blared overhead. Red lights strobed, people scurried, and chaos replaced the typical staid order of the camp.

I darted for the back of the stone bowl, taking the opportunity to gain some distance from my guards. There was no group of workers today, but I spotted Lyle, his hair bouncing as he jogged across the back pathway, sweat shimmering on his dark skin under the flashing lights.

"Lyle! What's happening?" I risked a low call, and he swung his gaze towards me without breaking stride.

"There's been a revolt on the surface. A bunch of gang members from the desert showed up with trade goods, but when they opened the front gates to send out Excursion Team Three, soldiers we didn't know about started pouring out of the ship, attacking the excursion teams left on the surface. All hands are being called up to support, apparently."

"Gang members? You mean the Nightbloods?"

"No, they're staying back, honoring the terms of their agreement while we've got their leaders. Of course, they're not going to stick their necks out and *help*, either. These guys all wear snake tatts and most of them have shaved heads."

"Sidewinders," I spat the word like the curse it was.

"You know 'em?" he asked as I cast a wary look over my shoulder. My guards were gone from the rim of the bowl, but were they looking for me, or called away?

"Yeah, they ran Coyote Springs, where I'm from. Real bad news. The leader, King, is a piece of work."

"Great. Well, they've all retreated inside the city, but the spacers followed them in. We were already under martial law, but they're roaming the streets, shooting anyone they see. Apparently the Sidewinders have taken over one of the entryways in the skirmish."

"Frack. Where are you going?"

"There's a protocol for when the city's under attack, even down here. I'm responsible for locking up all the storage rooms, and then I have to report back to my team leader."

"I'll help." I surprised myself with the offer, but something told me that I needed to stay on the move, keep out of my guards' sight so they forgot about me.

We locked up at least a dozen little rooms tucked into the mouths of tunnels I'd never been in, and then headed for the command building. Lyle paused, tugging at the collar of his suit. "It's probably better if my team lead doesn't see you. Can you go around back and wait where we met Morgan last time?"

"Yeah, see you there." I slapped him on the shoulder as we parted ways.

"Come in, Brandt Brother, come in." The crackle from my wrist startled me, and even though my location behind the command building was deserted, I still cast a reflexive glance around in case it was overheard.

"I'm here, Red Riders. Are you in position?"

"Affirmative. But it seems the party has started without us. Our scouts are reporting scuffles coming from inside the city, as well as unexpected activity on the outskirts." There was a long pause, and then in a more serious tone he added, "You should know, we don't have the numbers to stand against the Nightbloods."

"I know, Louie. You don't need to, this time. Actually . . . I don't want you near the city at all. Can you fall back to a cave nearby? We're still underground, and I'd rather have you close while the city's in turmoil."

"Affirmative. Do you have coordinates?"

"Uh, let me get back to you on that. I know it's due west of the city, and it's big."

"We'll swing that way and wait for instructions."

"Thanks," I finished, but he didn't answer. King Louie was a man of few words.

The back door of the command building burst open and I swiveled to face it.

"There you are." Morgan's face was grim as she waved me forward. "I've got a hookup with a radio, and we're sneaking you in. Just keep your head down, and if anyone asks, you're new on janitorial team C."

"Okay." I didn't bother arguing, just slipped through the door behind her and made sure it closed silently behind us.

The inside of the building was all white walls and harsh overhead lights that made my eyes hurt after the dim cavern we'd been in for so long. We were in a narrow hallway, and passed three doors before Morgan rapped a special pattern on the door.

"Is that *really* necessary?" Lyle groused when he pulled open the door. "We all knew it was you."

"Let me have my fun, Lyle, sheesh." She winked at me before ducking inside.

There was a huddle of older teens inside the dingy break room. Half the furniture appeared broken, and the bright white paint was covered in scribbles and swear words, but they were all quietly focused on a silver radio.

"Lifeside is refusing to open the gates. Do we force an override?" Gasps rang out around the group as they huddled tightly around the radio.

"Camel crap. They shut the gate?" Morgan tossed a worried look at me as we joined the back of the group. "The gate between the lifeside and parkside hasn't been locked down . . . well, *ever*."

"Pipe down, Morgan," an older boy snapped. She stuck her tongue out at him, but stayed quiet.

We stared at the radio as if we could see who was talking when it crackled back to life.

"No, for now it's probably best if the intruders have no access to the lifeside. They could do a lot more damage over there."

"Than to the park? Are you kidding?"

"No, I'm not kidding. They won't damage the park if they have any brains left in their oxygen-deprived skulls. Who would hurt a real live tree?"

Lyle whispered, "That's Officer Kutsuki, I recognize his voice. He's running the city while the commandant is down here."

"Running it into the ground, you mean," Morgan whispered back.

The radio conversation continued, "They don't have any problem *shooting* in the park, so yes, they could damage the fig tree."

"Well, get the excursion teams together and deal with it!" Kutsuki snapped.

"Two is with you, One is underground, and Three is non-responsive."

"Were they taken out in the attack?"

There was a long pause.

"Report, Queens!" Kutsuki snapped.

"No, sir. They weren't, they're just non-responsive. I'm getting word . . . I'm getting word that there's a rebellion, Officer."

"From inside the city? While we're under attack?"

"Yes, Officer. Word got out about the critical water stores. The commandant's been lying for a long time, to a lot of people, and they aren't taking it well."

Kutsuki's curses rang off the dingy walls, even over the radio. "Anyone who thinks now is a good time to rebel deserves to be put down. See to it."

"But, Akio—" Queens protested wearily.

"No buts, Queens."

The silence was so loud, I didn't want to breathe. A full-on rebellion, while we were trapped underground and separated.

Things couldn't get any worse.

Thirty-Five

Egress

Nyx

"**F**rack, frack, frack. Nyx!"

River's frantic words barely reached me because I was a shredded pulp of a woman.

"Nyx, I know you're upset, you have every right to be. But the moles are moving and we have to get out of the way and figure out what's going on."

The moles were moving? What?

I looked up from Hema's still chest, and realized River was right. The moles were pulling away, and we weren't on them. Rahlise still crouched, waiting for me to say something, but I had no words left. None. I was hollow inside, like someone had scraped out all my guts and left me empty of any emotion except grief and bitterness.

It was senseless, Hema's death, and nothing would ever put it to rights. Except . . .

"Where's Kutsuki?"

"Nikolaos has him in hand. Would you like to participate in his questioning?" As soon as I nodded, Rahlise surged to his feet and held out his arms. "Let me take him, αγαπημένη . Your man is right, we must move now or risk being crushed."

I clung tighter to Hema's body for a moment longer, and then nodded. Sitting around like an idiot and letting the commandant crush us wouldn't bring him back.

Nothing would.

River pulled me to my feet as soon as Hema was in Rahlise's arms.

"Come on, Nyx." River kept my hand clasped tight in his, and my legs moved woodenly.

And then something made me stop. "Hang on," I knelt down reverently, and picked up his curved, black blade. It had fallen from his fingers while I held him, and I couldn't bear to leave any piece of him behind. I clutched it in my free hand, and then let River lead me away.

The numbness began to leak away as we moved, and fury swelled in its place as we dodged between the rolling moles, back around to the side where the doors were.

Was any of this an accident? Because as we watched the moles steadily leaving, it felt intentional. We caught up to our mole, and River risked getting close to the slow-grinding tracks to bang on the hatch.

"Hey! We're still out here!" He hollered at the top of his lungs, and we saw Guffey's face press against the long window. He turned and started shouting, presumably at Fletcher and Nanette, before pressing his face back against the glass and gesturing frantically.

I couldn't tell what he was trying to mime, between the fog of his breath on the glass, and the bumps in the road jostling the mole.

"What the hell? They're not stopping. Here, let's back up and regroup." He dragged me off to the very edge of the tunnel, and the nearly dozen Nightbloods who'd come to Hema's call clustered around us, some facing out in case of further attack, but the tunnel was still except for the sonorous crunch of the moles' tracks grinding over the rocky tunnel floor.

My water meter beeped.

Incoming comm request.

I tapped to accept it, and a holo-message floated above the tiny screen.

Nyx,

We're locked inside. The commandant has somehow overridden all individual controls. Fletcher and Nanette are attempting an override, but I don't think it will work.

I've been locked out, as well, and can no longer raise the captain to report the issue. If anything changes, we'll come back for you.

Kindred, out.

River cursed, reading over my shoulder.

"Why would he leave you here? What the frack is he hoping to accomplish by killing your father and dumping you in the tunnels?"

My palms were sweaty, despite my temperature-controlled suit's best efforts to keep me cool. We had no food, no water, and no transportation. According to best estimates, we were two full days of hard driving from the base camp, let alone from the surface. If I had my guess, the commandant intended to let me rot down here so I couldn't interfere with any of his politics back in the city. But was I meant to die, or just be delayed?

I cast a sorrowful glance over at Hema's still form, then quickly looked away. There was one man who knew more than we did.

As the last of the moles pulled around the corner of the tunnel and out of sight, I pushed my way through the Nightbloods until I found the ones holding Kutsuki.

His wrists were bound, and they had him backed against the tunnel wall, flanked by three guards.

"Let me through," I demanded. They parted like sand under the Bronco's tires, and then I was standing before my father's killer.

"Why did you do it?"

He stared sullenly down his nose at me but didn't say a word.

"If you have *any* sense of self-preservation whatsoever, you'll talk. We're on foot now, with no food or water, and I'm sure every single one of these men would rather slit your throat than waste energy hauling you back to the base camp."

He swallowed hard, and his eyes darted through the cluster of black-clad men glaring back at him, before landing back on me.

"He wasn't supposed to die, he just got in the way."

"In the way of what?"

"You. I was supposed to kill you."

I blinked slowly, letting the information sink in. It wasn't a surprise, not really. River's suit had been sabotaged, and I'd been nearly crushed under falling rocks that incapacitated our original mole.

"Why?"

He shrugged, as if he didn't care. "I don't question the orders, I just execute them."

"Whose orders?" Rahlise's question was deadly quiet, and I watched a bead of sweat roll down

Lieutenant Kutsuki's face as he clenched his jaw shut.

"Seriously? What good does it do you to protect whoever gave you the orders now? They left you down here to rot."

"Aíma, why don't you let me take over the questioning?" Rahlise's voice was a low rumble at my side.

"Knock yourself out." I threw up my hands and stepped back. "Apparently he needs to be more scared of us than he is of them."

Rahlise didn't say a word, but he did throw a punch. Kutsuki's face snapped to the side, and he groaned low and long.

"It was the commandant, okay? She wasn't supposed to make it back alive, or how could he take the credit for fixing everything?" He spat the words bitterly.

The commandant wanted me out of the picture. It wasn't a surprise, not really, even though it was short-sighted. The man had never cared about anyone but himself, and this was the proof, sure as the sun rose every morning.

Rahlise punched him again, this time letting his fist connect with Kutsuki's chin. His head flew back into the wall, and then he went limp between his two guards.

One of them glared at Rahlise. "βλάκας! How will you get information from him when he is unconscious?"

"He'll wake eventually to tell us the rest. For now, we need to get moving. Aíma is correct, we have no supplies down here and a long walk ahead of us still."

He turned to me and bowed his head.

"We follow where you lead, Aíma."

"Why are you calling me Aíma? You know my name, Rahlise."

He stilled, considering, and then dropped a hand to my shoulder and led me out of the group of Nightbloods. River stayed at my side, his presence comforting even in these dire straits.

"Nyx, Aíma is a title, much like Hema."

"What do you mean, it's a title? His name was Hema."

"Hema was his title. He was *the* blood; our pulse, our leader. Now you are. You are the Aíma, and from now on, anyone of the blood will refer to you as such."

I rocked back on my heels, the information like a physical blow when I already felt so weak. I hadn't even known his real name. He was gone, and I barely knew him. And now I had an entire gang I was expected to lead?

"What was his name?"

"Peleus, after a great king of myth. It suited him."

I nodded.

"So what do we do now?" River gripped my hand, running his thumb over my knuckles as he asked the question.

"That is up to Aíma." Rahlise shrugged one shoulder, as if he couldn't care less.

"I want to get the frack out of these tunnels, and deal with the commandant."

"Me, too," River agreed.

Rahlise was all business. "We should start walking, then. It is a long way still to the top."

I lifted my water meter, inspecting it carefully. "Let's start walking, but I've got another idea, too."

"Have I told you lately that I love it when you have ideas?" River quipped, wrapping me in a quick side hug as we started the hike.

Thirty-Six

Melee & Murder

Chace

"Chace? Can you hear me, Chace?"

My sister's voice sent a frisson of relief through my veins.

"I'm here, Nyx." I spoke to my wrist, even as I glanced around and stepped away from the milling teenage workers. They'd all started talking at the same time shortly after the radio went silent, and then talking turned into arguing about what we should do.

Their official orders were to stay inside the building until further notice, but only about a third of them were interested in obeying those orders.

"Things have gone south. The commandant left us down here."

Her voice shook, and I knew it wasn't a faulty connection. Nyx was terrified and trying to hold it together, which meant she was leaving information out of the big brother download that she thought would piss me off.

"What do you mean, he left you? How far down are you?" I kept the words gentle, even though I vowed I was going to tear the commandant's head off with my bare hands the next time he was in grabbing distance.

"Uhm, two days, give or take. We don't have any food or water, so if you could find a way to wrangle some vehicles and drivers, we could really use the lift."

"Who's we?" I needed all the facts if I was going to pull off a rescue with exactly zero resources and no time to plan.

"Me, River, about a dozen Nightbloods, and one Bastion City guard." I cocked an eyebrow at *that* headcount. She was definitely leaving something out.

"Okay, so a ride for thirteen, water, and probably some weapons for self-defense. Anything else I should know?"

"There— There is one more thing . . . Hema's dead. One of the Bastion City soldiers killed him."

"Oh frack," Morgan breathed from my left. I was so entranced with the conversation that I hadn't even noticed her eavesdropping, nor the several teenagers lingering behind her, looking anxious. Hopefully she was as trustworthy as Nyx believed her to be, along with all of her friends.

"Are you safe with the remaining Night-bloods?"

"Yes, they saved me. The hit . . . it was on me."

I closed my eyes, letting my forehead drop against the cold cement wall. It took three deep breaths through my nose before my anger simmered enough that I could talk again.

"I'm on my way, Nyx. Just hold tight and make any progress you can climbing up."

"Uh, not to be a Moody Morgan, but how, exactly, are you going to go retrieve her from the tunnels? There's a guard at the entrance, a whole bunch of moles in the way, *and* oh yeah, you don't have a vehicle. Not even to get yourself down there, let alone get a baker's dozen of people back up."

"I'll steal something if I have to, and the guards will move or get flattened." I turned for the door, not stopping to belabor the conversation. I knew where the UTVs were corralled, and I was strong enough with hand-to-hand that I could disable at least two guards without getting caught.

"Hold up, speedy." Morgan threw her small frame between me and the door with far too much confidence. "Did you stop to think that there might be another way?"

"The fastest way is the best way. You can help by getting me a net full of water orbs, or even better, two."

"Yo, Kimmie, can you handle the water?"

"Yeah, on it." The girl was on her feet and skirting past Morgan and out the door before I could blink.

"Lyle, can you rustle up some meal bars? Maybe some fruit?"

He scrubbed back his hair thoughtfully. "Fruit might be a stretch but I'll see what I can do."

She nodded, and he hustled out the door after Kimmie. I watched in awe as she dispatched three more kids to round up other emergency supplies.

"Now, all that's left is transportation. See? Sometimes you've just got to call in the cavalry to get things done."

The cavalry . . . I wondered if the rest of Nyx's buddies were as capable as the girl in front of me?

I popped my wrist up to my mouth, tapped the tiny burrowing comm device, and waited for the beep.

"Hey, King Louie. You around? The Night Goddess needs backup."

Three hours later, Morgan and I crouched behind a boulder that had been left centrally placed inside the entrance to the main cavern. Apparently, it was too big to move, and too tough to bust.

Or so Morgan had informed me during the last thirty minutes of our wait. The sound of running footsteps had me spinning to face the threat. A taller woman a few years older than Morgan but with the same reddish hair was running straight towards us. She didn't sound any alarms, though, and Morgan looked peeved rather than worried when she slid into our hiding space with us.

"What are you up to, little cousin? I just checked the break room, and you and four of your best troublemaking friends weren't in it." She cast a disgusted glance at me. "And this one is *way* too old for you. Time to go back."

"Uhm, for one, *gross*. He's like, thirty or something. Two, this isn't that kind of mission, Jacie."

Jacie groaned and hung her head. "Morgan, what are you thinking? This is serious! A full-scale lockdown comes with big, fat, *adult* consequences when you break it. Don't you want to make it onto an excursion team? Four more years. You just have to stick it out four more years." She rested a hand on Morgan's shoulder, and I saw a flicker of guilt pass over her freckled face.

"She's been helping me, but you can take her back. I don't want to get Morgan in trouble, just to get my sister out of it." Jacie locked eyes with me, a worry line appearing between her eyebrows.

"Your sister?"

"His sister is down in the tunnels. I just arranged a few rescue supplies. I was *considering* going along with him, but I can't ride a motorcycle."

"Motorcycle? Good grit, Morg. Go back to the break room and keep your head down. I'll see if I can't help—" She gave me a questioning look.

"Chace."

"I'll try to help *Chace* pull his sister out of the stew." She ruffled Morgan's hair which elicited a groan and a shove, but Morgan gave me a dutiful wave then bolted off in the direction of the command building. Jacie rolled her eyes and dropped down to prop her back against the rock next to me. "That girl is going to give me gray hair before I'*m* thirty. Which isn't that far off, and definitely isn't gross, by the way."

"I'm only twenty-seven, for what it's worth. And thanks for sticking around, but I can handle this if you've got somewhere to be." I gave her a tight smile—hopefully that would encourage her to leave and make sure Morgan ended up back where she was supposed to be.

"Really? You've got three backpacks of supplies, but I only see one *you* to carry them. And *for what it's worth*, trying to ride a motorcycle down here is a really stupid idea. There are rocks. Big ones."

"They're dirt bikes, and that's the only option available."

"Yeah, dirt bikes are still a bad idea. It starts getting hot as far down as they went in those tunnels, and if the moles are having a problem? You're not going to have much luck doing what they can't. Those things are basically cylindrical tanks with better life support systems."

"The moles are fine. The problem is that my sister isn't in them. They left her, and I need something small enough to get *past* a mole inside the tunnel. Quickly."

Her jaw dropped, and horror washed over her delicate features. She was pretty, with elfin features and bright green eyes, even though it was a wildly inappropriate time to notice. I'd probably never see her again after today, and that was for the best.

"They left her. And she's still alive, you're sure?"

"Yeah, your commandant is a real piece of work." I looked away, out over the storage crates and extra mining equipment neatly stacked against the side of the cavern. Blaming her for the commandant's crappy behavior wasn't fair, but it was way too easy to paint all the city people with the same brush.

"*My* commandant . . . which means you're not from Bastion City. But you're in one of our suits, which means you must be—" She broke off abruptly and cussed a blue streak under her breath. "Chace Brandt, brother to the head troublemaker in charge, Nyx Brandt. Of *course* Morgan was helping you. I'm going to strangle that girl if we survive this."

That surprised me. "We? I already told you, I've got this covered. Help is on the way, so there's no need to dirty your hands helping me."

"Yeah, that's not how this is going to go down. Morgan's involved, which means I'm involved. If you do something really stupid, it could blow back on my cousin, and I'm not about to skip off and let that happen."

"Look—" My argument was cut short by the sound of revving bikes, echoing off the tunnels.

"Oh, frack. You were serious. Where the hell'd you find dirt bikes? We don't have them in the city, and you've been in the laborer camp for *months*." She pushed to her feet, peeking carefully around the edge of the boulder, while I hurried to gather up my supply packs.

"It's a big, wide world out there, Jacie. And this is where you decide if you're in or out. No pressure, but we're not going to have long when they clear the mouth of the cavern."

"I'm in, jerk. Give me a bag." She glared at me as she shouldered the backpack and clipped the chest clip into place. The sounds of the bikes were getting louder by the second, and I could hear chatter from other parts of the cavern as people took notice.

"They know where we are, and the first two riders are going to peel off for us to jump on. Rider three is taking the extra pack, and the rest of the convoy is going to create a distraction until we're secure. Once we're on, we're driving straight for the tunnel, and we're not stopping no matter what they try to throw at us."

"Oh, good. So, it's a nice reasonable plan, just like I hoped."

"Smartass."

"We all have our talents." She winked at me, not even a little bit put off by my prickly demeanor.

The first bike skidded into view and stopped not three feet from where we stood, with the next two only half seconds apart. I threw the spare bag to the third man, then swung up behind the lead rider. Jacie was already holding her driver around the waist, and the instant my butt hit the leather seat, we were in motion.

Shouts rang out as we skidded back into the melee. Soldiers in white were running toward us, guns raised. The driver punched the gas, and I almost flew off the back of the bike. I gripped him tightly around the waist as he dodged soldiers. Thankfully they were holding their fire, opting to shout at us instead of shooting immediately.

"Halt! This base is on lockdown, under the commandant's orders!" One of the soldiers dove in front of the pack, risking life and limb to keep us from taking the direct route to the tunnel entrance. The first bike fishtailed as he braked to avoid squashing the soldier, but the ones behind him saw the threat in time and swerved, darting into the sea of canvas tents occupying the left front quadrant of the cavern.

"Oh, crap. Most of these are occupied," I warned my rider as we followed suit, taking advantage of the narrow wheels to take a path that was harder to block. The pack of bikes broke into individuals, each dodging and weaving their own path through the tent maze. Terrified screams and angry shouts came from some of the tents as we passed, but the evasive move did throw off the soldiers.

The sound of metal wrenching against stone and the thud of bodies impacting exploded off to our right. One of the riders crashed, flipping over a person trying to flee their tent and taking them both out in the process. I closed my eyes against the grisly scene, unable to do anything while I was clutched like a tick on the back of my driver.

My driver cringed as his friend wiped out. "Damn, that was Adam. We've got to get out of the tents or we're going to lose half the pack before we hit the tunnel, and we need every rider if we're going to get the troops back out. Hang tight—it's time to change things up."

He'd no sooner spoken than he hooked a hard left at the next tent-gap, slinging me like a rag doll with the momentum.

"I said hang on! Use your legs!" He was more amused than pissed, thankfully, and sped up as soon as I was straight again in the seat.

He let out a loud whistle, calling all the other bikes to follow us. When I looked over his shoulder and realized where we were headed, I wished I'd fallen off where I'd had a chance of the tents breaking my fall.

"This is a bad idea!"

He laughed. *Laughed.*

The psycho *cackled*, and we were driving full speed toward the giant bowl at the back of the cavern. I was definitely going to die before I got Nyx out of the tunnels.

The ground dropped away beneath the front tire and my stomach floated into my throat as we fell. My overgrown hair lashed my face, obscuring my vision as we made contact toward the bottom third of the slope. We landed hard, and my vision went double for a second. I swore, but my driver kept control of the bike, and by the time I could see straight we were already speeding towards the far rim.

Oh frack. Frack, frack, frack—

My stomach was busy taking a trip back south when the gunshots started. There was nowhere to hide from the onslaught, and I felt a sharp, hot sting skip across my shoulder blade as we started to freefall through the air. I couldn't worry about that, though, because we were arcing back towards the ground with alarming speed, and headed straight for a line of soldiers barricading the tunnel mouth.

"How are we going to get past them?" I shouted into the back of the driver's helmet.

"They're going to move, trust me."

He landed the bike once again with a hard bounce, but he didn't lose control for more than a second. He shocked me by leaning hard right, starting a circle in the road. More and more riders followed us, until we were a whirling vortex of steel and leather. One rider peeled off, driving straight towards the blockade, and we cut out immediately after him.

The rider in front of us was a mountain of a man, easily three hundred and fifty pounds of muscle, and on his shoulder was the barrel of a grenade launcher.

I didn't have time to process what a bad idea it was to fire one of those *underground* until it was too late. Soldiers dove right and left, but

RPGs flew faster than they could run. It hit one of the UTVs and exploded, launching the vehicle into the air, and suited soldiers with it. We flew through the fiery opening, and hot air and smoke scalded my lungs for a few seconds until we were swallowed by the deep darkness of the tunnels.

Thirty-Seven

Bear Up

Day Eighteen

I was thirsty. It had been so long since I'd been truly thirsty, I almost didn't recognize the sensation at first. That dull ache at the back of my throat, the dryness stretching the skin of my lips. But as time and miles wore on under my boots, my body remembered. I'd lived through much worse, so I set it aside.

The Nightbloods were silent as they walked, no jovial chatter. They were a funeral procession mourning their Hema, carrying him dutifully through the tunnel system. And I was now their figurehead.

It hadn't sunk in, and I wasn't sure it ever would. I hated gangs. I hated what they stood for, how they ran things, how they destroyed everyone who wasn't exactly the way they were.

Now I was supposed to lead one? I barely kept myself alive. So far, Rahlise was quietly suggesting everything, and letting me make the final call. Was that how the rest of my life would be? I could see it like blood splattered over sand. The rest of my life, nothing but me faking a smile and a wave while my people waited at my beck and call, scattered like ants to do my bidding—or Rahlise's, through me.

The smile wouldn't even matter; eventually they'd expect me to cover my face, and the thought made me feel dead inside.

I didn't want it, not any of it. But what *did* I want? My lifelong dream to just go north and live out of this endless wasteland felt childish, and out of reach. Things had been set in motion that I couldn't turn away from. My father was *dead*. The pain and anger had been banked to angry coals behind my breastbone, burning night and day while I put one foot in front of the other. Right now, we had to survive. Get out of this blasted tunnel and get back on the surface; after *that*, I could afford to let the anger and the sadness out.

But then what? As much as I chafed at the idea of running a gang, I couldn't afford to cut the Nightbloods loose. I couldn't turn them away, and still get out of this mess. We needed them, River, Chace, and I.

Because as much as I hated all the fighting and killing, I couldn't deny that there was a fight coming. Definitely for our freedom; most likely for our very survival. The idea crystallized in my mind as we walked, the pieces falling grimly into place.

The commandant had turned on me; I'd done what he needed, saved his precious city's water supply, so I was no longer of value to him. Disposable, like so much chaff. A threat to be removed.

The captain wanted to use me, study me. The way she looked at me made me want to crawl under a rock to get out from under that dead, lifeless gaze. She was a merry butcher, and I would do almost anything to stay out from under her sick blades.

The Lifesiders were expecting me to still get them out of the city, help them get established at Wolf Well.

The Nightbloods expected things from me. River expected things from me—different things, but the expectations were there, just the same. Chace wanted me to still run for it, leave this mess behind.

It was all suffocating. *Suffocating.* My chest was tight, my legs were lead, my eyes burned—whether from dehydration or unshed tears, I'd rather not examine. There was no way forward for me, no way that was free of disappointment and suffering.

All I ever wanted was to be free. To be my own woman, living my own life, out from under everybody's thumb. Away from Coyote Springs, away from the Wastes, away from the gangs who poisoned it.

Yet somehow, the further I got from Coyote Springs, the more tied down I became.

And no matter how far I walked, how tired my muscles became, how much I burned on the inside, I couldn't leave behind the oppressive weight of expectation.

Thirty-Eight

Mad Chace

The pebbles were vibrating under our feet. Just a little, so little that I wouldn't have noticed if we hadn't walked so long in the cadence of steps; of breath; of the smallest exertions.

Soon the vibrations increased, the sound of engines racing toward us growing to a crescendo.

"There's a side tunnel coming up soon. If we hurry, we might be able to hide in it, see who's coming before they see us." River squeezed my arm, pointing to the dark hollow ahead.

I nodded. "Let's go." I picked up the pace, though I wanted nothing more than to curl into a ball on the side of the tunnel, and let them come, whoever they were. My throat was so dry it was trying to stick together as my respiration increased.

We slipped into the side passage and melted into the darkness. Rahlise and Niko took up positions in front of River and me, their dark clothing helping to hide us in plain sight against the tunnel wall.

We didn't have long to wait. The sounds of whoops and engines revving reached us just before the dirt bikes did. The first one who zipped by was massive, a broadly muscled torso wrapped in leather against the cold, riding a patchy red bike. He glanced into our hiding place but didn't pause. The second was much the same, a smaller rider in a red skull-cap style helmet, but he had a man in a blue suit riding on the back. His sandy hair and piercing eyes had me shoving forward.

"Chace!" I shouted his name, but they'd already zipped out of sight by the time I shouldered past my devoted guards.

The entire group surged forward behind me, and somewhere around the fourth rider they slowed, spinning the bikes nimbly to face us.

There were too many to count as they formed up in a semi-circle around us. But I was too busy running to my brother to care.

He hopped off the back of the bike a little stiffly, but his hug was so familiar, so safe, when he folded me into his arms, suddenly, the weight of it all felt a little less heavy.

I sank into him, clutching him back too hard, but he didn't care. He never minded being my rock. My *shield* as he called himself. River stood patiently at my back, not judging the fact that I'd shut him out, pulled into myself, yet so freely threw myself on my brother.

Sometimes, the comfort you needed was family. Though, as I clutched my brother, I realized that River was family now, too. He'd become that for me, over the months of our journey. He'd stuck by me, stayed with me, loved me. I reached out an arm for him, and he stepped into my side, too.

We stayed that way until Chace leaned back, looking down at me. "You ready for a drink, sis?"

The words brought my bodily needs roaring back to the forefront, and my stomach grumbled angrily.

"I'll take that as a yes. Here," he said, peeling off his backpack and pulling out water orbs. He pressed one into my palms and then the next into River's. A woman I didn't recognize sidled up next to Chace, looking nervously over our heads at the cluster of Nightbloods.

"Ah, Chace? You sure about this rescue mission?" She murmured the words, clutching the black straps of her own pack so tightly her knuckles were as white as her suit. Her *Bastion City soldier* suit. I stiffened, taking a step back.

"Easy, Nyx. This is Jacie. Morgan's cousin. And yes, of course I'm sure. She's with us."

"Oh, hell," Jacie said with a groan. "I guess I am 'with you.' What did Morgan get me wrapped up in?"

Chace snorted. "Welcome to my life. Nice to have you aboard." He cocked an eyebrow at her as he started lobbing water orbs to each of the waiting Nightbloods. They didn't drink, though, and wouldn't until they had privacy to remove their face coverings.

Shoot. How was that supposed to work? I glanced around, and pointed them towards the side tunnel. "Go, take a few minutes. We all need to rehydrate for the rest of the trip."

Most of the men filed into the tunnels gratefully, but Niko stubbornly refused to budge.

"I will stay with you. We don't know those people."

"Actually, I think I do. Is that you, Cade?" I called to the giant of a man, who sat quietly off to the side of the circle looking bored with our reunion.

"Yeah," was all he said.

"You're exactly as eloquent as I remember." I turned a pointed look on Niko. "The Red Riders Collective are allies. Go, drink, and come back." I put all the steel I possessed into the words and his eyes tightened at the order, but this time he went.

I turned back to Cade. "How's Vinna?" His little daughter was adorable, and hopefully far, far away from this cluster of disaster.

"Good. Most of the crew's already at the Well." He nodded, acknowledging my help in finding them a safe place to land. Well, safer. There was no true safety in the desert. "Lady named Marl's got a hotel where all the kids are staying until we get established.

My heart clenched with relief. Marl was still alive, well, and protecting innocents. I let my eyes sink closed for a second. "That's good, really good. She'll keep an eye on them."

"She's a mean old bat—I think she will."

Chace laughed, the sound deep and full, bubbling up from his chest.

"What's so funny?" I elbowed him, eliciting a grunt.

"It's just . . . too normal." He lightly tugged the end of my braid, the gesture achingly familiar as I swatted him away.

The driver of Chace's bike popped off his helmet, revealing sweaty russet hair, and a straight, aquiline nose.

"I'd like to get back to that normal, but I'm not sure what the plan is from here on out." He dropped the helmet carelessly on the seat and crossed his arms over his chest. I couldn't place him, though I'd met quite a few of the other riders here.

"And you are . . .?"

"Steve. Sasha's brother. I hear we've met," he said, sarcasm dripping from the words.

"Ahh, the camel's hump!" River remembered quicker than I did. "Which one of the four were you?"

"The only one you couldn't shake off," he said, lifting his chin.

"Well, hopefully you don't hold a grudge. Because we're neck deep in crap at this point."

He rolled his eyes. "Grudges don't hold water in the Wastes."

"Great. So glad you're all one big weirdly happy family. But we've got bigger fish to fry than catching up," Jacie interjected. "There are a whole lot of pissed off people in that cavern, and we've got to go through it to get you all out of here."

"So, you made an impression on your way down?" I directed the question to Chace.

He winked and pressed a meal bar into my hand. "Always, Nyx. I *always* make an impression."

Thirty-Nine

R IS FOR RECON

Day Nineteen

The Collective cut their engines, letting us all roll to a natural stop. The tunnels were quiet; after the deafening roar of the engines for so long, my ears could barely pick up the bare rustle of Cade's leather jacket as I released my grip on him. We'd ridden straight through, with only a few stops for bladder breaks as the hours wore on.

But now we stopped to make a silent approach on foot. From here on out, we'd agreed to roll the bikes so we could scope out our options before roaring back through the main cavern. We had the rest of the Nightbloods to round up, as well as Morgan and any of her people she wanted to drag along for the ride to the top.

Which meant more vehicles to procure, and more complications. So, stealth.

My Nightbloods were already slipping off the bikes and surging ahead, silent and deadly as they raced toward the outlet of the tunnel. The rest of us were meant to wait, getting as close as we dared while remaining out of sight. The riders had passed the moles on the way down, but now they had cleared the tunnels, which meant they must be parked inside the cavern.

There was a curve a few hundred feet ahead where we'd rendezvous with them, so I slid down from the seat and began walking. The Red Riders pushed their bikes, while the rest of us walked in a silent stream. River loped up to my side, a boyish grin on his face despite the tension hanging heavily in the air. He bumped my shoulder playfully before matching my stride. Chace was ahead of us, speaking in low tones with Steve and Jacie.

"I think we should try it. If it comes out at a different part of the cavern, it's probably less guarded than the one they know we went down," Chace stated.

"We don't know that it's guarded at all," Jacie argued. "The moles have been back for at least twelve hours; the commandant knows what's going on overhead. There's *no way* he's still sitting down here in this tunnel with the captain instead of putting a stop to the attack on the city."

Steve groaned. "Guys, we can scout it. We can send three riders down the side tunnel, and if they drive for a couple hours and it hasn't come out anywhere useful, they'll turn around. We could all use a rest before charging out, anyways." He tugged at the front of his hair, leaving it in crazy spikes.

Steve looked tired, with deep purple smudges under his eyes; we were all tired. I wasn't sure how long it had been since we'd slept, only that it was too long.

I checked my water meter and frowned down at the yellow fifty-five percent. We were nearly out of water orbs because Chace and Jacie had been able to steal only so many on short notice. I grabbed River's arm and lifted his water meter. What I saw had me biting my lip. Forty-four.

"Chace, can I get another water orb?"

He reached into his bag and tossed it to me without breaking his conversation. "Splitting up right now is a bad idea. There aren't that many of us. It's risky to get separated before we know the lay of the land."

I cracked open the orb, taking a single sip before passing it to River. He needed it more than I did, and I could go longer without, thanks to my nanites.

"It's risky to sit around on our thumbs knowing we're almost out of supplies. And we have no choice but to go through that cavern, one way or another. We're not going to be able to hold hands and skip our way out of this. Did you forget we blew up their people with a grenade launcher to get your sister back? Because they definitely didn't," Steve snapped, temper rising.

"Okay, lay off, all of you." I raised both hands in a calming gesture. "How far is the side passage?"

"Less than a half hour," Steve supplied.

"On foot?" I asked.

"By bike."

I ran a hand through my wild hair. "Send your three fastest riders. We all need a break, or we're not going to be thinking clearly. We may as well get as much information as we can before we finalize our plan—but tell the scouts to keep it to an hour's ride in. Two and a half hours max, and they should be back here for some rest."

Chacc stiffened, not pleased I'd overridden him, but he didn't argue. Steve nodded, and crossed to the group of bikers who were all stretching and shooting the breeze twenty feet back. Jacie sighed to his retreating form.

Steve and two other riders grabbed helmets, and jumped back on their bikes. Cade was already ambling over to where we stood, ready to take up the leadership role while Steve was gone. I was surprised that Sasha had sent Steve on the rescue mission, given their fighting in the past. Heck, he'd tried to trap us and steal our water before we even made it to the Collective, initially. But now he was here, and he'd helped us, so I wasn't going to argue with her decision-making process.

"Let's all find a spot to get horizontal. Rahlise will wake us when they're done scouting." I tried not to yawn as I gave the order, but I was definitely swaying on my feet.

"There's a good spot over here, come on," River urged, looping his arm around my waist and steering me away from the makeshift leadership meeting. The injury in my thigh complained loudly as I lowered myself to the hard stone of the tunnel floor, then rolled slightly onto my side against the curve where wall met ground. River laid in front of me, resting a hand on my hip as he settled down. I pillowed my head on my arm, and within a few heartbeats, I was asleep.

Chace shook me awake.

"The scouts are all back, sleepyhead. Thought you'd want to hear the reports."

I levered myself up off the cold, hard stone and gently nudged River. He didn't move. Mouth-open, head-lolling, passed-out-level asleep.

"Yeah, I already tried that. Lover boy sleeps hard."

"We'll let him catch a few more minutes, then." I carefully stepped over him, and he blissfully slept through it. Jacie, Steve, Rahlise, Niko, and Cade were waiting a few dozen feet away, at the other side of the tunnel. Most of our people were passed out along the same wall, so we picked our way quietly between them.

Niko's face was grim; Steve had a bored expression; but everyone else just looked resolute.

"So, how do things look?" I directed the question to Rahlise, first.

"Not good, Aíma. The mouth isn't too heavily guarded, but there has been damage to the main command building, several sections of the tent housing are flattened, and the captain appears to have taken control of the cavern."

"Not completely," Steve interrupted. We overheard some of her soldiers on patrol. The commandant is missing, and they are still hunting for him. Apparently, when things went south, he went into hiding, like a true hero." He sneered in disgust at the Collective's long-time tormentor.

"So, can we get the people we need, and get through? Or are we going to have to deal with the captain down here? I'd rather be above ground before confronting any of her people."

"Yes, the full strength of the blood should be behind us before striking, and we must lay Hema to rest," Rahlise agreed.

I swallowed hard at the reminder. The men had wrapped him completely in black cloth that first day, and I was studiously not looking at his body whenever we were stopped. They carried him without complaint, devoted to the bitter end.

"So how did the other tunnel look? You found guards, so it must come out in the main cavern." I forced myself to focus on Steve, not the sharp knife of grief stuck in my ribs.

"It does. It connects to another tunnel, which is lined with some storage rooms. We think. They were all locked up, but they looked like they'd been used recently, and there were no visible ventilation shafts, just solid doors." He shrugged.

"And the guard situation?"

"Present, but minimal. There were three on shift when we scouted, but one trip doesn't guarantee that it's always that way."

"Right." I drummed my fingers on my thigh, thinking it over.

"Were you able to get oriented to any landmarks inside the cavern? Which side the storage rooms were near—the caldera, the tents, the command building?"

"Mm, closer to the very back of the tents, just past the big bowl." Steve made a cup gesture with his hands.

"I know that tunnel." Chace surprised me by speaking up. "Lyle and I locked up those storerooms when the base camp first went into lockdown."

"What? Why did it get locked down?"

"The captain's people attacked the city, and breached the gate. They've currently got people hiding in their rooms, and are shooting or imprisoning anyone who tries to escape. Though, my intel is now more than twenty-four hours old, so a lot could have changed."

I couldn't stop my grimace at that. The captain was making her grab for power, and she had no qualms about killing anyone who stood in her way. I looked warily around the circle. I didn't want to put a target on our people, or lose anyone. But somebody had to do something, and if it had to be us, we'd just have to do what we could to keep everyone safe.

"What if we split up, gather the rest of the Nightbloods, and then break for the surface with as many UTVs as we can steal? We're far enough from the city here that we'd see reinforcements coming, and we'd have more room to maneuver up top. But if the captain is still inside the cavern, keeping her down here is our best chance of stopping her," I suggested.

"One way in, one way out. I like it," River said, rubbing sleep from his eyes as he joined our circle.

"Nice of you to join us, sleeping beauty," Chace ribbed him, but there was no heat behind it. The two exchanged a fist bump.

Jacie spoke up next. "I could help with the UTVs. Most of them run on a universal key." She pulled a carabiner from her belt, three black-and-silver keys dangling from it. "But I can't leave Morgan down here if the captain has taken over. I've got to find my cousin."

"We won't leave her. But we're going to have to work quietly, and quickly," Chace said. "The spacers have more tech than we do, but if we can take them off guard, some of the city soldiers might step in to help. They'll want to dethrone her, too."

Jacie nodded agreement. "I've got some people I can ask for help. They might not be happy I ran off with you lot, but they'll still help if we've got a plan for taking out the captain and getting the city back under our control."

"The Nightbloods in the camp will add to our numbers, too." Niko spoke up.

"How many more are in your group down here?"

"Ten."

"Okay, so, we've got options. Now, how do we want to split up?" I asked.

Forty

INCURSION

I climbed off the back of Cade's bike in the storage tunnel and waited for him to stash it at the intersection with the feeder passage.

Our group was small, only six; Myself, Niko, and Rahlise had ridden with Cade, Johns, and Isadore from the Red Riders. We were going in first via the storage tunnel, while Chace's group—with Jacie and half of the forces—entered from the main tunnel as a distraction. In theory, that would allow us to slip unseen into the camp and round up the Nightbloods before meeting them at the UTV parking lot. River, his old friend Sax, and the other half of the forces were heading to the command building, where they hoped to find Morgan and her friends.

It made me nervous, the three of us being split between the groups, but I didn't have time to dwell on it. We'd unanimously agreed to charge ahead, rather than giving Captain Jacira time to get further entrenched. Or worse, get to the surface and lock herself inside the city walls. That had to be avoided at all costs.

My nerves felt jangly, like I was a big, old bell that someone had just struck with a mallet. Every part of me was alive, but unsettled. When all six of us were gathered, we moved forward quietly. I was the middle of the formation, as the least skilled fighter. Also, because my ever-present guards insisted.

I had Hema's curved black blade tucked into a weapons belt one of the Red Riders had as a spare, the weight of it both strange and comforting against my lower back.

I'd practiced drawing it a few times with River before we left, enough that I was confident I wouldn't drop it. I was no master, but hopefully it would offer me an element of surprise, should I need it.

As we rounded the final bend, I sent up a silent prayer that I *wouldn't* need it. Two guards came into sight. One had his back to us, clearly relaxed on the job. The other was scanning the tunnels lazily. His eyes lit up, and I knew he'd spotted us. Rahlise and Johns were the front of the formation, and they broke into a smooth run, straight toward the guards.

The guard got out a short shout that alerted his companion before engaging with Johns.

Rahlise took the second guard with ease, their movements so fast that I couldn't track them. The guards never stood a chance against their hand-to-hand prowess.

I winced as the final blows were struck, both guards collapsing within seconds, making awful gurgling sounds as they slumped to the floor. But while I felt sick to my stomach, everyone else was already moving. So I pushed myself to keep up, to not be the weak link in this chain of rescuers. The mouth of the cavern had no more guards, so we dropped down into the depressed end of the cavern on swift feet, cutting across the empty space towards the line of tents.

We almost made it.

"Intruders in the east end of the tunnel! Intruders in the east end! I need backup!"

The sounds of running feet only spurred us to move faster, but they intercepted us at the second row of tents. Our group stayed as tightly formed as we could, but space-suited soldiers were closing in from every angle.

"Nyx, duck!" Rahlise's voice rang out darkly.

I didn't think, just dropped to my haunches as a dark, curved blade spun by over my head. It met resistance with a sick thud, and when I stood, it was protruding from the windpipe of a soldier who had been creeping up behind me.

There wasn't time to process the gore, because the soldier behind *him* was trying to grab me. I kicked out a booted foot, catching him in the side of the knee. As soon as his leg buckled, I bolted towards Rahlise and Niko, who were fighting back to back.

"Get between us! We've got to get backup," Niko ordered, blades flying in graceful, devastating arcs. I ducked under their arms, and they took a step apart so that I was sandwiched between them and their sinister blades.

What few glimpses I caught of the Red Riders showed Cade and Johns holding their own, though they were bleeding from multiple cuts and wounds, and I couldn't see Isadore through the mass of bodies.

There were more space soldiers than I remember coming down on the UTVs, and they were all swarming us at once. My boots were slipping across bloody stone, and the tang of copper permeated the air, clogging my nose. I was inured to the blood, to the pain. Blows to my body melded together, ignored for the sheer push of survival. When I was shoulder to shoulder with Niko and Rahlise, they fought like men possessed. But for every man they killed, another stepped forward.

A few slipped between them, aiming for me. I did my best to help defend, kicking and lashing out with Hema's blade. It warmed in my grip as I fought, occasionally biting the hooked end into a suit's seam.

Even as we fought, we moved slowly, steadily deeper into the sea of blue canvas. When the crowd of attackers grew too great to cut through, Rahlise took up a high, ululating call. Niko joined him, the words foreign to me. It was a deadly battle song, but also a call for help. Shouts and cries rose up from a distance, mixed with the discordant sounds of metal blades crunching into thermal suits.

Through a break in the crowd, I caught a glimpse of why. The Nightbloods streamed out of the main tent, roaring a high, threatening call as they swarmed toward us.

Our attackers' attention split, and suddenly, the tide turned. Where before we were barely defending against an oncoming rush, now, exposed backs were turned our direction as the greater number of Nightbloods fell upon them like unholy terrors.

They seamlessly joined the battle song, and the spacers began to fall back, terror in their eyes at the otherworldly fighters, before turning to run.

With our mission accomplished, our group rejoined and began to press towards the UTVs, where we were set to rally with Chace's and River's groups.

When we stepped out into the main road that cut through the cavern, we were met with an nigh-impenetrable wall of spacers. Their dark metallic suits glinted under the harsh lights, as if they were robots of liquid metal, waiting to surge over us in a lethal wave.

That wasn't what stopped me, though. I froze in the middle of the street, holding up a hand to stop my men as my breath came in short, pained gasps.

The captain herself dragged a man forward by the collar of his thermal suit. He stumbled after her, blood matting his short-cropped blond hair. He was deeply tanned, and when he looked up at her with hatred, it was those familiar crystalline eyes that shattered something in my chest. River's eyes, filled with despair.

Blood bubbled from the corner of his lips, but he was far from tamed. He was furious. She held his back to her chest, the hilt of her favorite blade in her hand, blood oozing out around the blade where it was buried into River's side, right between his ribs.

"You have two options," she shouted at us, but I couldn't take my eyes off the grievous wound, the dark, thick blood that oozed out between her fingers, sending me into spirals of panic.

He was dying. He was dying, and I had to do something.

"You can surrender Nyx right now, and we'll graciously allow you all to live, including this delectable morsel." She leaned in and closed her eyes as she sniffed River's neck, a visible shiver rolling through her at the scent of his blood. He ground his teeth, pure hatred shining from his eyes.

A rumble of angry Greek rose from my men, though none of them moved a muscle.

"Or, I can fillet him like a fish, and let my men finish you off, and then take her from your bloating corpses. Your choice."

River was mouthing something. Something I couldn't quite make out.

Fight.

Fight. He was telling me to fight her, to sacrifice him to take out the psychotic captain.

Everything inside me rebelled at the idea. The words wouldn't form. I couldn't watch her disembowel him in front of me, any more than I could reach into my chest and tear my own heart out with my bare hands.

"We surrender!" I held up both hands, and the angry Greek turned to shouts, though still, they honored my orders to stay still.

I slowly paced forward; eyes locked on River's sorrowful ones.

No, *no*. He was still mouthing the words, urging me to fight, to push. But I couldn't. He may never forgive me, but I couldn't.

When I reached them, I ignored the captain, wrapping my arms around River and pulling him to my chest. She let him go into my arms, and his weight nearly toppled me.

"All of you, kneel! You heard your leader, you're now in my custody."

I let my eyes close against the pain and horror, as River and I slowly slid to the ground.

When I opened them again, River was still mouthing something, but I couldn't make out the words. His face was turning pale from blood loss, as it steadily streamed around the knife blade which she'd left buried in his side. His chest heaved, and his hand rose weakly as if to cup my cheek, but he grabbed my hand instead.

There was something hard and square in his palm, and the words he was trying to tell me finally clicked.

Take this.

I closed my hand around the object, whatever was so important to him, tucking it into my pocket with one hand as I brushed the hair away from his face with the other. I lost the fight holding back my tears and as his eyes sank closed and he lost consciousness. Only the little bubbles of blood and saliva forming at the corner of his mouth showed he was still alive. Sobs racked my body as Jacira loomed over us again, her cold, lifeless eyes lit with deranged glee at my sorrow.

"He needs a doctor. You promised he'd live," I snapped up at her, not concerned about her ire. After what she'd done to River, I'd gladly sink my father's blade into *her* ribs, given the chance.

"Oh, we'll see to it." She snapped, and four of her soldiers stepped forward, prying River's lifeless body from my arms.

Two more grabbed me by the arms, and I watched helplessly as they carried him away from me.

Forty-One

No Return

They took River. He was bleeding from his chest, and they took him.

I was on the verge of hyperventilation, straining as hard as I could against the viselike grips of my captors, but all that earned me was a hard slap across the face. My lip split in a hot burst of pain, but it didn't matter. Nothing mattered.

My ears rang as I stumbled forward, trying not to let the tears fall. There was a coppery tang of blood on my tongue.

Everything had gone wrong. Why had I thought I could do this? Change things?

I was nobody, nothing. A scavenger from the Wastes who barely scraped by, not a strategist. And now River was gravely wounded, maybe dead. I was trapped. I had no idea if Chace was still alive, or in the cavern. My Nightbloods were being subdued, and it was all because I didn't have the grit to keep fighting when my lover's life was on the line.

There was no way they'd ever follow me again if we made it out of this cavern alive. I was a disgrace to Hema's memory. I let my eyes fall closed, shutting it all out. They could drag my limp body wherever they were taking me, for all I cared. I was still breathing, and for now that was all the rebellion I had left.

But then we stopped. When I opened my eyes again we were at the base of a rocky outcropping, narrow stairs carved right into the stone.

"Let's go. Single file from here on out." Alix led the way, while the other guard took both hands behind my back and forced me onto the steps.

I dragged my feet, but we gained height quickly, and it would have been a death sentence to fight this high up with no guard rails.

They'd taken my knife, anyways.

I stared at the back of Alix's knees as we climbed, not letting myself imagine River gasping out his last, bloody breath somewhere alone right now. If I let myself imagine that, the hysteria crept up and drowned out common sense. I wasn't about to follow after him; this wasn't Romeo and Juliet, and dying together wasn't my idea of romance.

The ground leveled off eventually, and I kept my eyes close to the cave wall, not daring to look over the ledge. We were high, high up in the cavern. This lip was narrow enough that I hadn't noticed it before from the ground. But Captain Jacira was already here, smiling her demented smile with her arm slung around one of her space soldiers.

No. Not one of her soldiers. *Guffey*.

But the Guffey I'd last seen pulling away in mole five hadn't been black and blue, face swollen nearly past recognition. If it weren't for his white, tufted hair, I wouldn't have believed he was the same man.

One of his arms hung limply at his side, and his eyes were full of sorrow. He was mouthing something to me.

I'm sorry.

Sorry? What could Guffey possibly have to apologize to me for, when he looked like that? And why had he been beaten? He was no fighter, by any stretch of the imagination.

I didn't have time to puzzle it out before the captain waved us forward.

"Nyx, darling, I'm so glad you could join us. I take it your boyfriend was sufficient motivation? You two are so touching together, really," she cooed, as if she was a warm mother offering me a treat, not a psychopath who'd used my boyfriend's life as leverage to get me to turn on my own people.

That's all I was, all I'd ever been. A tool. Used. Pushed around and owned, in fact if not in name. She was just the latest in the line of would-be users.

The numb horror receded, River's plight fuzzing away into the background miasma of my thoughts, replaced by one central focus; hatred. For this woman, for this world, and for all the dictatorial jerks who'd come before her, thinking only of themselves.

I wanted to burn them all down, but that was out of reach at the moment. So, I did the next best thing and spat a fat glob of bloody saliva across the chest of her shining metallic space suit.

It landed with a wet splat, right across her chest.

Her chipper smile melted away like so much mud, and she let out a terrible screech.

"Ungrateful girl!" The backhand came so quickly, I didn't have time to move with it to lessen the blow. She caught me straight across the nose, and the crack of flesh on flesh rang inside my head. My vision went double as pain burst in my face like an exploding water orb.

I blinked hard, trying to clear my vision. Getting hit sucked, yes. But seeing that look on her face was worth it.

I forced my head back up, glaring at her woman to woman.

"You will stand here and act civilly, or I'll shove you off the edge in front of all your sad little troops. My people can leave this cursed rock, but you never will. Are we clear?"

"Crystal," I huffed the word angrily, but nothing more. I'd made my point, and I was outnumbered.

She reached up and tapped something over her ear, and then turned a beaming smile out over the cavern.

"Hello, lovely people!" Her voice echoed around the cavern, through some sort of amplification system. "As you all know, I'm Captain Jacira. We've made a true breakthrough, and I'm here to tell you all about it today. On stage with me is my crewmember, Guffey. He's a brilliant engineer and a *loyal* servant. Isn't that right, Guffey?" she crooned, rubbing his arm like she cared so deeply.

"Yes, Captain," he rasped, wincing with pain even at the small movement.

"Guffey and I have had a very long talk about the future. Ours, as well as all of yours."

I risked a peek over the edge, and to my dismay, thcrc was a huge crowd gathered underneath us. I quickly looked back up, so the world would stop swaying so threateningly.

"And Guffey here had some brilliant observations. You see, he was part of the expert team who repaired the water generator."

A small spattering of applause broke out from the crowd so far below, and she beamed down at them.

"Yes, thank you. It was exceptional. But more than that, Guffey here has figured out the key." He shot a guilty glance over at me, and I reflexively tried to take a step back. The guards stopped me, and I didn't like where this was headed. Not one bit. She patted Guffey on the hand, and he hobbled back to lean against the safety of the wall.

"Nyx, please step forward." She held out a hand for me, as if we were long-lost friends, and not mortal enemies.

One of the guards planted a hand between my shoulder blades and shoved me forward. I stumbled, and Jacira caught me around the upper arms.

"Oh, so eager," she chortled, and another wave of laughter floated up from the ground. I couldn't not see it from here, we were so close to the edge.

I tried to suck in a deep breath through my nose, but the swelling had reduced my airway to little straws, not sufficient for panic breathing.

"Nyx here is special. I'm sure you've all heard about her, though the commandant"—she said his title with a sneer before letting her falsely cheerful veneer settle back into place—"has tried to keep her exceptionalities a closely guarded secret. Nyx, would you care to share with everyone why you're so special, or should I?"

I didn't dignify that with a response. I stared straight ahead, ignoring whatever the frack strange show she was trying to drag me into.

"Nyx here has a special lineage, yes, but there's more. Somewhere along the way, she's picked up some tech. There are nanites in her blood, and those nanites are the key. With those nanites, we have not only unlocked this water generator, but we can unlock an entire *network* of water generators, already buried and waiting for us to flip the switches. The future of earth as we know it will be changed! There will be abundant water, as we enter this new phase of the future. A *better* phase of the future, under my leadership."

Shocked silence, and then whoops echoed off the cavern walls. Were people really buying this? Bastion City people, or were those only her spacers?

I couldn't let her do this. I couldn't let her take control of Bastion City, and all its weapons and resources. She was dangerous, and capricious, and she would lay waste to what was left of the world, if left unchecked.

But what could I do? I was injured, unarmed, and outnumbered. I was wholly unprepared for the challenge, and there was no hand left in my card deck to play.

Except . . .

"Captain, there's something Guffey doesn't know." She froze, the smile plastered across her face taking on a sour tinge at the edges.

"What is that, Nyx?" The icy words conveyed the threat, even though they were hissed through smiling teeth.

"How to give the nanites to other people. You could have them, and I can give them to you, right now. You could be the one to hold the key to all those water generators. You wouldn't need me, or the headaches I bring with me."

Her eyes glinted at the possibility, but she didn't jump on the bait. "Why would you offer me that, when I could kill you without repercussion?"

"I don't care what you do to me. I want you to guarantee River and Chace's lives, and their freedom. I'll give you this, the nanites, the knowledge—you can have it all, just let the two of them go free. Do we have a deal?" I lifted my chin, showing her my trader face. It might be the last time I ever used it, but it would be worth it.

"Tell me."

"It's so simple, you won't believe it." I reached up slowly, sore from being manhandled and knocked around. But my fingers found the familiar silver clasp, under the neck of my temperature-regulating suit. I undid the clasp, and with all the drama I could muster, lifted Chrysanthe's locket free.

Her eyes locked onto the spinning bauble, full of suspicion.

"You expect me to believe this bit of jewelry holds the nanites?"

"I do. Because it's true, isn't it Guffey? Neither of my parents had nanites. My brother isn't a carrier, and neither is my father. I'm the only one, and that's because I'm the only one who's ever possessed this necklace. It belonged to my ancestress, Chrysanthe."

I held it high overhead, letting it spin and catch the light, small but gleaming, for everyone to see. My palms may have been sweating, but I'd committed now, and there was no turning back.

"Show me," she demanded, the greedy gleam in her eye overwhelming common sense or suspicion. She'd always wanted power.

"All you have to do is hold it." I settled the locket, with its etchings of hearts and leaves, into my palm and offered it to her.

She hesitated only a second before snatching it up. She was holding it in front of her face, examining it for clues, when the noxious green powder began spewing out from inside.

She gasped out a choking cough, turning wide eyes on me.

"That's it! Well done, Captain," I stepped forward, placing both my hands over hers, capturing the locket between our clasped flesh with a false smile plastered on my face.

She sucked in little gasps of air, panic starting to overtake her as the powder took effect.

"There's just one thing, Captain. I'm the only one who they don't kill." Her wild eyes went wide, as if she could feel herself slipping away from consciousness already.

But I didn't wait, didn't take the chance of her somehow surviving the powder. I shoved her hands away from me, as hard as I could. She took one stumbling step backwards, her body already crumpling downward from the poison, but her second step met nothing but air. The locket chain drew taut between us. Her hand was still clawed around it, while I held the locket itself.

It gave way all at once, little bits of silver flinging far and wide into the air like confetti winking under the overhead lights.

I watched as she tipped over the edge, falling like a rag doll to the unyielding ground below.

Forty-Two

RATS OFF A SINKING SHIP

People were screaming on the ground. They were running pell-mell, some heading for the UTVs to escape the cavern, others diving into tents as if the flimsy fabric would protect them. I should care—I should be horrified that I just killed a woman, that everything on the ground was crumbling into chaos.

But I wasn't. The stain on my soul was a small price to pay for stopping her evil.

She would have killed so many more, all the while smiling like it was a Saturday drive to the cactus patch. The faces of all the innocent street children, of the tiny burn victims from the Red Riders ran through my head. I could see so vividly all the evils already wrought on the next generation by Commandant Kieran.

Jacira would have been ten times worse.

A guard grabbed me roughly by the shoulder, and I windmilled back, keeping myself away from the edge as he swung me around. The locket was still clutched in my fist, and I brandished it, the only weapon I had left.

It may have been pretty, but it was also deadly, and now they knew it. The guard took a wary step back, looking at Alix for direction.

His expression was tortured, gaze flicking from the empty cliff's edge to me and back. Was he going to push me after Jacira? I didn't dare look away. If my death was coming, I'd stare it in the eye.

Surely he didn't harbor any love for her, not after she carved him up for no reason other than her own selfishness.

He turned and bolted for the stairs. The second guard hesitated, but then he was running, too. I swayed on my feet, the adrenaline all leaving me at once.

Guffey hobbled slowly to my side, a wary look on his battered face.

"What's your plan now?"

No judgment, no scorn. Not even fear, not really, though he'd stopped outside of arm's reach. Just a question that I had no answer to.

I looked around, forcing myself to assess the scene below and ignore my fear of heights. The Nightbloods were on their feet, fighting free of the space soldiers who were still standing. Some had run to their fallen leader, but even more had run for it, escaping towards the command building.

"Who's next in line to lead when the captain's gone?" I asked Guffey.

He pursed his lips, then winced, running a shaky hand through his hair, making the tufts go askew on the left side. "Alix, technically. But he's just run for the hills, so I think he won't be sticking around to make a claim. I suppose this counts as a battle for leadership, which would mean you. Of course, that would be highly unusual, given you don't actually live on the ship."

I sighed. I didn't need more people to herd. I'd already failed the Nightbloods.

"Who's after Alix?"

"Kindred."

"Excellent. Any idea where he is?" I began the slow descent, being careful this time and leaning hard against the wall for support.

"Command building, last time I saw him. And Nyx . . . I really am sorry. I had to tell her something."

"Don't worry about it. My secrets aren't worth dying for. Do you have someone you trust to go get him and bring him here? I need to see about calling off the siege on the city."

He hummed a sound of agreement but didn't speak again.

Chace was waiting at the bottom of the stairs, stark relief painting his features. And blood, which I hoped wasn't his. There was no censure in his expression, and I was so grateful that he wasn't looking at me differently. I could deal with my own actions, but if Chace had pulled away from me, that would break me.

I picked up the pace on the last few, tripping in my exhaustion. He caught me by the forearms, his grip gentle.

"Thank God," he murmured, inspecting my injuries with a critical eye.

"Don't thank anyone yet. We've got to find River. He's in bad shape, Chace. And the Nightbloods . . . they're probably not going to help us, now."

"You would insult our honor?" Rahlise's words were pained.

I spun to face him, and the gathered throng of men with him. They'd doubled in size, more than twenty men—no, twenty *warriors*—and all of their eyes were on me. They were so silent I hadn't heard them approach, even as they secured this corner as a bubble of safety for me.

"No, I only assumed that you would question mine. I made you kneel."

"We follow where you lead, Aíma." One of the men from the back stepped forward, bowing deeply at the waist.

The rest of them bowed in a wave, and I was overwhelmed with emotion. Gratitude; unworthiness. I didn't know what to say to the show of wholly unearned devotion, so I didn't.

"Where is Sax?" I skipped to the problem weighing most heavily on my mind.

He stepped forward, head hanging as he approached me.

"I have failed in my mission to protect River, Aíma, and I accept any punishment you see fit to give me." He dropped to his knees, kneeling like we'd been made to kneel to save River. His face covering was torn, bloody, and a massive purple contusion was visible on the side of his face.

"Stand up, Sax. I don't want to punish you, nor would I punish a man for being hurt in the line of duty. I want you to help us get River back, and then find yourself a healer to check on that lump. Do you think they'd have taken him back to the command building? Or somewhere else?"

He jerked his chin up, calculating intelligence in his gaze. "I'm not sure, Aíma, but—"

"Kindred has him inside the command building." Guffey's words washed over me in a wave of relief.

Chace squeezed my hand and surprised me by bolting off at a dead run for the command center. As much as I wanted to run after him, I felt every bruise and bump along the entirety of my body. So I just walk-shuffled as quickly as I could, while the Nightbloods formed a protective circle around Guffey and me.

The doors of the command building were propped open, the stark white insides on display, like we'd gutted a great snowy beast, instead of just unlocking a pair of doors.

Exhaustion was doing funny things to me.

But still, I hesitated. Fear held my throat in its claws, sinking into me viciously. Could I walk through the door and face what it might hold?

Guffey rested a hand on my shoulder. I looked over at him, and his face was kind.

"You must think badly of me, now. I killed your leader." Why those words popped out of my mouth, I couldn't say. It was a less sore bruise to poke than the thought of River dying inside this squat, buried building.

"She was never a leader. Jacira was a tyrant, blood-soaked and cruel from the beginning. We should have removed her long ago, and the guilt I bear that we didn't, that we put that burden on you . . ."

I waved a hand, stopping him. "She's gone now."

He nodded, guilt clear even on his puffy, damaged face and in the stoop of his shoulders. I squeezed his hand where it rested on my shoulder.

"I could use a friend for this next part." The words were threadbare. A whisper of weakness.

"You have one." He squeezed my shoulder before releasing it and offering the crook of his arm, instead. I looped my hand through it, and we went inside.

River's tanned face was unusually pale. The dried crust of blood at the corners of his lips made tears well up in my eyes as I crossed the room to his side.

He was so still. But he wasn't dead; there was a scant rise and fall of his chest as he lay on the exam table. Chace stood at his side, looking pensive, while Kindred was a few paces away reading something off a handheld scanner.

I reached for his hand, then stopped, not wanting to hurt him further.

"It's okay, you can hold his hand," Kindred said, smoothing down my fears. "He's resting, and his vitals are stable." He flashed the screen at me, but the numbers meant nothing to me.

"You got the knife out?" I looked down at his side, where a thick bandage covered the wound between his ribs. The knife had nicked his lung, and who knew what else.

"Yep, and he still needs to see a real doctor, but I had some heavy duty med patches in my pack from the ship. They can't fix *everything*, but they can fix a lot. The blood stopped and his breathing evened out, so I'm guessing they successfully sealed off the tear in his lung. His oxygen levels are high, even without breathing support."

The words rolled over me as I gently brushed River's blond hair away from his face. Seeing him so still, so pallid, was terrifying.

I could have lost him. He was almost snatched away from me, and I'd never told him—anything, really. How I felt. How much he meant to me. I'd been keeping him at arm's length, ever since the video.

Deep regret burned in my stomach as I stared down at his still form, now.

Guffey, standing staunchly at my side, said, "Those patches can just about bring somebody back from the dead, Nyx. Him resting peacefully is a good sign." Chace gave me a reassuring smile from across the table.

"It's true, Nyx. Kindred just re-ran the scans when I got here. Everything's stable. He might sleep for a while, but I know there's a doctor down here, if we can find them and trust them to examine him."

I frowned, tracing my thumb over River's knuckles. I wanted nothing to do with the

Bastion City medical staff. They'd proven they didn't have our best interests at heart; only the commandant's.

Frack. We still had to find *him*. I kept a tight grip on River's hand and turned, looking for Rahlise.

"We need to find the commandant as quickly as possible. Can you guys work on questioning some of his people, see if you can find a lead? Send whoever you think is best, but nobody goes alone."

"Consider it done, Aíma." Rahlise nodded respectfully and then paused in the doorway. "One of my men retrieved this for you."

He held out Hema's blade on his open palm. My heart clenched as I stepped over and took it back, holding onto it a moment before slipping it into the holster at my lower back. Rahlise nodded once more and rejoined the rest of my men in the hall, giving orders in a low, crisp tone.

"Oh, and Morgan—" I spun back around to Chace. "Did Jacie find her? I don't know what River found, before he, he—"

"She's with Jacie. River had already located her and about a dozen teenaged workers and sent them to us. He was coming to back you up when the captain caught him."

I let myself fall forward, my forehead dropping to River's forearm as I closed my eyes hard.

I wouldn't cry for him, because he wasn't going to leave me. I'd hunt down every doctor, from every faction until I found one that could fix anything else that was wrong. Whatever it took, he'd wake up so I could tell him what I needed to tell him.

I should have known better than to keep myself apart from him, to keep my feelings hidden. We didn't have the luxury of time, of long leisurely lives going old and gray together.

I'd chosen to ignore the reality and hide the truth from the man I loved. The one who made me better, who held the other half of my soul.

That was a mistake I'd never make again.

Forty-Three

HORROR

"**I** need to talk to her! This is important." The familiar, sassy voice in the hallway pulled me from my vigil at River's bedside.

"Let her in, please," I called.

There was a feminine grumble as the human shield of Nightbloods parted to admit Morgan with her cousin hot on her heels.

"Nyx, I need you. Probably the grumpy group, too. I know you don't want to leave River, but I think I know where the commandant is."

I had to forcibly relax my grip on River's hand. "Where?"

"One of my girl friends is on the janitorial team. Apparently, he's got a hidey-hole behind the storage rooms. She's got the storage keys, but nobody except him has access to that room. But Jacie said there's some cutting tools that the soldiers have access to . . ."

I cast a glance down at River, then over at Chace.

Guffey laid a hand on my forearm. "Let us stay with him, Nyx. We will keep him safe, and you can leave some of your men as guards. Your work isn't done yet."

I nodded acceptance and called for three of the Nightbloods to come in, but still I struggled to peel myself away from River. He was so vulnerable, it felt wrong to leave. Fragile.

"I can go for you, Nyx. You don't have to do this." Chace's words were low, meant only for me.

But he was wrong, I did have to do this. I had to see it through, and River wouldn't want it any other way. He wanted the commandant taken down as badly as I did; for the Red Riders, as well as the Lifesiders who just wanted to be free.

"I'm coming back, River. And you better be here waiting for me when I do." I whispered the words against his forehead before pressing a careful kiss to it. When I turned away, I set my shoulders. "Take us to the storage rooms."

Morgan and I stood back as Jacie wielded the cutting tool like a pro. She sliced through the door's hinges, then the deadbolts, until there was nothing left except molten metal. She counted to three and then pushed it over.

It crashed to the ground with a boom which shook the stone under our feet. We walked across the non-molten middle of the door, into a large safe room. It held a luxurious bedroom suite off to one side—with a full shower, no less—and on the other, a huge bank of monitors. Surveillance video of the cavern from many angles, as well as twice as many views of Bastion City were plastered across every inch of the wall, from floor to ceiling.

"He's not here," Chace groused, kicking an empty chair and sending it skidding across the room.

"He was studying something, though. What is this?" I held up a black and white printed diagram, which I'd found next to a lukewarm cup of coffee. "It looks like pipes."

"Pipes?" Morgan squeezed between us, peering at the diagram. "Those look like the ones where the laborer class works, around the city."

"Yeah, they do," Chace confirmed with a shudder.

"Why would he care about the pipes, with everything else going on? Should he be looking for a way out, or a way to get the city back from the spacers?" I hadn't meant to ask it aloud, but something was bothering me. What was the commandant up to, and where had he gone?

"He doesn't need to look for a way out. He's already got one." Jacie wore a livid expression when we all turned to face her. She was pointing up, above the toilet in the bathroom. "He's got an escape hatch."

Sure enough, there was a man-sized hole in the ceiling, with ladder rungs built into the side of the tunnel leading up and out overhead.

"Do you think he's heading back to the city?" Morgan asked.

"Where else would it go? He's certainly not going to exile *himself* to the Wastes," Chace said.

I walked back to the diagram, something still sticking in the back of my mind. "Can we find out what's in these pipes? He's not going to blow up his own city, is he?"

"He would never," Jacie insisted. "There would be no way to rebuild it. No matter how desperate he was, he would never destroy the city itself. He's too selfish. Those are ventilation pipes, anyway. There's an air purification system built into the dome's ventilation pipes which ensures the air inside the dome stays safe to breathe. It balances the oxygen levels and filters out any toxins that have been blown over from the ocean."

Horror, hot and acidic, flooded my veins. Jacie was right. He *was* too selfish to destroy his own city. But he'd proven plenty of times that he didn't care about the people in it.

"He's going to tamper with the ventilation. Do something to kill off the invaders, and whoever else is trapped in there with them!"

All the blood seemed to drain from Jacie's face as she looked back and forth between me and the diagrams.

"Our families are still inside the city. Thousands of innocent people. Surely he wouldn't wipe them all out—"

"How would *you* clear the city without damaging it?"

"Carefully, by sending our troops through it room to room, like we're trained to do!" She yelled it, panic lighting her eyes.

"He doesn't have his troops! He's cut off, and desperate. Put yourself in his shoes," I argued, knowing in my gut I was right. The commandant was a coward. He would take the coward's way a hundred percent of the time. He'd lost control of his people; then he'd lost face by letting the captain best him. He was going to retaliate, and it would be devastating when he did.

"We need to go after him!" Jacie put one foot on the rungs, as if to go right then.

"Stop! You don't know what's at the top of that tunnel. We *know* there are vehicles here and a safe road from the cavern."

"Fine, but we have to get back to the surface, now!" Jacie was already running, leaping over the downed door and sounding the alarm over her comms device. Chace followed on her heels, leaving Morgan and me to trail behind.

"This is bad, Nyx. Really bad. Those pipes are in multiple parts of the city. How are we supposed to figure out which ones he's using?" She clutched my arm like I could save her; save us all.

I was trying to hurry, trying to run after my brother, but my nose throbbed with every jarring step, and I knew I needed to get back to Kindred. Get him to call the people on the surface, try to get them to evacuate, so all the citizens they were holding inside could evacuate. We didn't know how much time we had, or how far ahead of us the commandant was. Was he alone? Did he have people with him who would get in our way?

There was so much information we needed but didn't have. I gritted my teeth and forced myself to run through the pain. People's lives were on the line.

Morgan and I skidded back into the open hallway of the command building, and the waiting Nightbloods bowed to me as they parted.

I was never going to get used to that. I gave them all quick nods in return but breezed through to the little clinic. My heart was pounding, and the sharp scent of astringent cleaner burned my already-aching nose.

"Kindred. You're in charge of your people now, right?"

"No. No, I'm not in charge. Even with the captain dead,"—clearly Guffey had filled him in while I was gone—"Alix is the one who's next in line. I'm third. *Third.*"

He said it twice, as if that would change anything. "Alix ran. You're up, and I need you to call your people on the surface. Spacers have taken over the city, and they're keeping the Bastion citizens trapped inside their rooms. We need everyone out. Full-scale evacuation, as quickly as possible."

"You've got to be kidding me, Nyx. That's not—I can't just *decide* I'm the leader. There's a committee, an official process—"

"Didn't the last captain kill her own brother and dance around naked in his blood? There's no time, Kindred! Make the call, or they're all going to die!"

"What's happened, Nyx?" Guffey's voice was calm, as he studiously worked on peeling the backs off stickers, for some reason.

"The commandant—he's gone. We think he's going to turn the city into a giant gas chamber. If he poisons everyone inside, he can take back over without damaging the city."

Kindred's face went pale, and he dropped his forehead into his hands. Guffey was less worried, treading the squeaky floor that separated us.

"Look up," he ordered, not addressing the current panic.

"Guffey, we don't have time for whatever this is—"

He grabbed my jaw, tilting my face up and adhering two big white squares to my skin on each cheekbone, skirting the damage of my nose.

"I think this is broken, and it probably needs to be set, but this will take the pain away for now." He released me and wiped the excess stickiness off on his pants. "Now. We'll do what we can, Nyx, but he's right. They won't back off from a direct order without proof the captain's dead, and that will take some time. What's plan B?"

"We've got to get up there and find the commandant." I spun on my heels, shot one last look at River's still form over my shoulder and then hot-footed it back out of the room, heading for the UTVs with Morgan hot on my heels.

"We'll see if we can dig anything else up to help you!" Kin shouted down the hallway after us.

Adrenaline was the only thing that kept me going, though it was either my imagination, or Guffey's miracle patches were already dulling the pain in my face.

Chace waited impatiently in one of the few remaining UTVs, with Jacie riding shotgun. We slid into the back and he gunned it, not waiting for anyone else to jump in—though Niko and Rahlise had no trouble jumping in with it already moving.

We all sat in tense silence as he navigated the eerie tunnel back to the surface, nobody daring to say what we were all afraid of.

That we'd be too late.

Forty-Four

Gas Chamber

Relief at being back on the surface barely cracked the tension that rode us all so hard. It was faster on the way back up, since we drove at break-neck speed and only stopped once for the bathrooms. There was no Bastion City rigidity to the trip; it was raw and desperate, and as soon as our tires kissed sand again, it felt like I was home.

Because for all I loathed the endless sand and the baking sun, the scalding temperatures and the struggles to survive; I knew them all so intimately. They were home, no matter where I went. I knew the rules, I knew how to survive, and I was ready, finally, to take the reins into my own hands.

Jacie was driving, by this point, since she knew the path back to the city better than Chace, and had maps on her water meter to pinpoint the location for us. We didn't have a second to waste, and we could have already been too late.

Jacie kept trying the comms to raise people who were stationed inside the city, but her attempts were unsuccessful. While she hadn't said it, her face was etched with lines of worry, her mouth set in a grim line; there was no good reason for them to not answer.

The stunningly beautiful glass dome of the city came into view, and everyone started talking, the questions we'd held back bubbling out like so much foam.

"How are we going to find him?" Morgan asked.

"Kindred sent me a map. It looks like while there are pipes everywhere, there are actually two mains which control the ventilation to either side of the city walls. The dome itself, obviously, is open to the full interior." I tapped around on my meter until I managed to pull up the holo-map. He'd drawn big, red Xes at either end of the city. They were inside maintenance tunnels, well out of the way from normal foot traffic.

"What if we can't get past the spacers?" Chace interjected.

"There's an access on the lifeside that we should be able to get to. The last report I had showed that the gate stood firm," Jacie said.

"So, do we think the commandant went there, too? Should we all head to that side, or should we split up?" I asked the question, even though I was not willing to ask the one that weighed most heavily.

What if they're all already dead? I wouldn't, couldn't ask it.

"I think . . . I think we have to split up. We can't take the risk of guessing wrong. There's six of us, and four sets of pipes. Two people per pipe—assuming your shadow guards are willing to help—and we can hit three out of the four."

I sighed, already knowing where this was going.

"And how are we supposed to split up? Whoever goes to the parkside is taking a much greater risk, not only of traveling further and possibly getting hit with the toxins, but of discovery."

"And that's exactly why Jacie and I are going to that side," Morgan surprised me with the no-nonsense tone of her voice. "I've spent over a year working in those tunnels. I know every by-way and side route in that side of the city, and even if they spotted us, I don't think they could catch us. You two don't have the home-field advantage. We could run your guards to the one in between, and keep going, just the two of us."

"I agree," Jacie said, tossing a quick smile back at her cousin.

Chace and I were both silent for a beat.

He ran a hand through his hair in agitation. "It feels wrong, sending you two into danger, while I hang back."

I could hear the guilt in his voice. This was probably his worst nightmare; three people to protect and only one of him.

Niko nodded to Chace and said, "We'll go with them. You should stay with your sister."

You could have knocked me down with a gently-lobbed water orb. Niko was volunteering to not only leave me, but follow two near-strangers into danger?

I looked back at where he sat behind us, searching his eyes for any sign of fear or indecisiveness, but found none.

"Thank you, Niko," I said, keeping the low words for him only.

He nodded sharply, then lifted his chin. Apparently the discussion was over. A quick glance at Rahlise showed a bit more hesitation, but he didn't argue.

So that was it, then. We were all splitting up.

I faced forward again as we closed the final distance between ourselves and the city. Jacie was already angling far off to the right side, even though I couldn't see whatever entrance she knew about.

When we were about fifteen yards away, she typed a code into her water meter, and the ground began to give way, sand falling into a hole that hadn't been there seconds before. We drove straight toward it, and then the nose of the UTV was dipping down, and our tires met concrete instead of sand.

As soon as our vehicle was completely enclosed, the ramp began to raise behind us, sealing off the secret entrance. A loud vacuuming sound filled the tunnel, as the sand was sucked back out of the passageway.

"More resources than they know what to do with," Chace muttered under his breath, but we didn't have long to discuss the many excesses of Bastion City. Jacie threw the UTV in park, leapt out, and approached what appeared to be a store room. She palmed the scanner on the door, then held it open for us to follow her inside.

Racks and racks of weapons and body armor lined the walls. Jacie walked straight to a rack of black vests, and snatched the smallest size down off a hook. She pulled it over Morgan's head, then grabbed another and handed it to me. Chace grabbed his own, eyeballing the sizes. My bodyguards stood impassively, arms crossed over their chests and watched as we geared up, apparently content with their own gear.

"The temp control suits are bulky, but they block the electro-net weapons. I know it's hard not to react to the threat, but as long as you protect your head and stay fully suited, they might trip you but won't incapacitate you. These are just extra protection against good old-fashioned bullets, since apparently we need to worry about *that* now." She pressed her lips into a grim line, crossed the room to a drawer, and yanked it open.

She pulled out six pouches, each individually wrapped square barely bigger than my thumb. "These are for the toxins. They help detox the specific things found in the air here. Too high of concentrations will still cause you to have shortness of breath, and eventually pass out and asphyxiate. But, these at least delay the processes by supporting your body's natural detoxification processes. They should buy us three hours of moderate exposure without ill effects."

She handed all five of us a packet, then tore her own open to show us the two large pills inside. She popped them in and swallowed them dry, so we all followed suit. They tasted like chalk had made an ugly baby with peppermint, but it was a small price to pay to avoid asphyxiation.

With that settled, we all chose weapons. I took an electro-net gun, but nothing else. I already had Hema's knife secured against my lower back, and I didn't know how to use any of the specialty items Jacie was loading herself down with.

The whole process probably took less than five minutes, but still it felt too long. Were we breathing in toxins right now? Were our chalky pills being put to the test?

There was no way to tell. We just had to go out there and hope we'd arrived in time. We didn't have time for long farewells at the neck of the hallway, but I took the second to hug Morgan to my chest, anyways. She squeezed me back so tightly, she might have bruised a rib if I hadn't been wearing a bulletproof vest.

"Stay safe, so I can get you out of here, okay?" I said against Morgan's hair.

"*You* stay in one piece so you can teach me cool survival stuff. Your brother tries but he's really not as awesome as you are." Morgan winked at me, and then the cousins were running down the hallway. Niko and Rahlise bowed briefly, and then took off after them, their longer legs eating up the ground.

"Lead the way, sister." Chace gestured toward the opposite hallway, and I lifted my holo-map to double-check the location one more time. My hands definitely weren't shaking, because that wouldn't be bravely dignified.

Okay, so I was shaking like a leaf. But it wouldn't stop me, and that was good enough.

We ran as quietly as we could down the pristine white hallways, stopping at each intersection to check the way was clear of soldiers. Our luck ran out at the third.

"Stop! By order of Captain Jacira!" The metallic-suited man raised a deadly-looking rifle, gleaming darkly under the harsh lights.

But Chace was faster. I closed my eyes when I heard the gunshot, a mere foot from my shoulder. I didn't want to watch him fall, though I heard the lifeless thud of his body hitting the ground.

"Come on, Nyx. We've got to keep moving—somebody will have heard that." Chace tugged my arm, no remorse, only determination in his eyes.

He took the lead, and I was grateful for his stubborn protective streak.

"Left after this one," I whispered as we cleared the next intersection.

He nodded, jaw clenched as he ran.

We were scant feet from the corner when my meter buzzed on my arm, and a message popped up over the holographic map.

It was bright red, marked urgent from Kindred.

DO NOT ENTER THE DOME

Nyx,

I hope this letter reaches you in time to stop you. I found and decrypted communications between the commandant and Leader Sakura. It's not surface toxin. It Zyvlox, a nerve agent. He's planning to pump the entire dome full, and nothing short of an oxygen tank and Level A hazmat suit is protective. It can enter through the skin as well as through inhalation. GET OUT if you are in there. I'll try to send a mass evacuation message to anyone whose meter is enabled.

Kin

Frack.

Frack, frack, frack.

A few things hit me with crystal clarity all at once, even as I ran behind Chace on autopilot.

The surface toxin tablets we'd taken as protection were useless against a weaponized nerve gas. Kindred may or may not be able to get the message to everyone. Even if he did, the likelihood of everyone locked inside their rooms getting out in time was next to nil. And if I told Chace any of this, he would turn around right now and drag me out, instead of trying to stop the mass execution.

The spacer had still been alive, which meant we weren't too late yet.

But could I risk my brother's life, and my own, on the off chance we could stop the commandant?

I might never see River again. He'd wake up alone, and I would be gone.

I bit back a sob, even as I knew there was only one choice I could make. I kept running.

"Clear," Chace whispered as we rounded the corner.

"Straight past the next two cut-offs, and then it's the last door on the right." My voice wavered, so I cleared my throat to cover it up.

He tossed a glance over his shoulder, his eyebrows drawn down in concern, but I kept my mouth shut. If I opened it again—if he knew the stakes—so many people would die.

Armed Bastion City soldiers poured out into the hall in front of us, and dread clawed at my throat. *We don't have time for this!*

Chace's gun was already up, but recognition hit me in the split second before he could fire.

"Nanette!" I hollered, and she whipped her head toward us.

She assessed Chace's firing stance with practiced ease, and her own gun was up before she spoke a word. To my relief, Chace didn't fire, but he also didn't relax or blink as he stared her down.

"You're supposed to be underground, Nyx! We haven't cleared the city yet, and you're not safe up here."

"We need your help, Nanette. The commandant has gone rogue and locked himself into one of the ventilation rooms. He's going to poison everyone inside the city to get control back."

Fletcher swore under his breath at her side. "We've got to stop him."

I spoke in a rush. "That's what we're trying to do—I've got a map to all of the ventilation rooms. We could use help accessing them." I pointed to my palm, guessing there'd be a scanner on the door.

She only wavered for a second. "Lead the way." She stepped to the side, and the four soldiers with her did the same.

Chace sent me a questioning look, but I was already running past him to the head of the group. Every second we spent talking we were a second closer to death, to failure.

I skidded to a stop in front of the solid, unmarked door. Nothing but Kindred's map indicated that there was anything more than a broom closet on the other side, but there *was* a hand scanner.

"Here!" I called for Nanette, and she palmed the scanner. The door rolled outward automatically, a soft *whuff* of air escaping when it opened, as if it had been air-sealed.

Huge metal pipes like white tree trunks littered the room. I held my breath as we crept inside, Nanette, Fletcher, and the team fanning out into formation, while Chace stepped back in front of me.

The door sealed shut behind us, and my eyes flicked closed for the barest of seconds. We were sealed in, and my stomach was full of lead at the implications. Would we die first, or last, being closest to the gas being released?

Movement at the other end of the room caught my eye.

Two people in fine clothing, handling a large canister.

Holy frack, we'd picked the right room. They were both in gas masks, but there was no mistaking them. The commandant wore a white suit, and Sakura, with her straw-straight, jet black hair, stood at his side, dialing something into the pipe in front of them.

"Stop right there!" Nanette barked, advancing quickly through the maze of pipework.

The panel in front of the two of them beeped three times. A feminine robotic voice spoke over the room's speaker systems.

Infusion accepted. Lockdown initiates in ten seconds.

Ten.

Nine.

The two of them ignored Nanette, ignored us. I saw with a sinking stomach that a hose, sheathed in flexible woven metal, ran up from the canister on the ground into a port on the side of the large pipe she'd been programming.

Eight.

Seven.

They ran. The cowards *ran.* Commandant Kieran slapped a square blue button on the wall as they bolted through the back door of the ventilation room.

Six.

Chace raised his gun, aiming at the commandant's back.

"Chace, No!" I slammed into his shoulder, and he jerked the barrel of the gun up.

Five.

The door shut with a hiss behind them, and he rounded on me. "I had him, Nyx! Why would you do that!"

"The canister! Look!" I pointed at the innocuous black tank.

"Nyx, it's just surface toxin! We're good on the tablets for another three hours!" He slammed the gun back into its holster, as Nanette and her team bolted towards the door to run after him.

Four.

"It's not, I'm so sorry, Chace. It's not surface toxin." I sobbed, my eyes welling with tears as the reality hit me.

Three.

"What? What is it, Nyx?" He was shaking me, holding my shoulders, but I was already buried, under a landslide of guilt. It was like the ground opening up and dropping me through the buried roof into the underground mall—only this time, I'd dragged my brother down with me. And there was no way out. We were both going to die, and it was all my fault.

Two.

One.

Infusion beginning.

Forty-Five

Lean Into the Doubt

Nanette cursed a blue streak when the back door was sealed, non-responsive to her palm on the scanner. A thin, clear divider lowered down the middle of the room, separating Chace and me from Nanette and the rest of the soldiers on the other side.

Lockdown complete. The chipper robotic voice sealed our death warrants, and it didn't care.

"Nyx! Talk to me!" Chace shook me again, before dragging my chin around to look at him.

"It's Zyvlox nerve gas. Kindred sent me a message."

"Oh, hell. We've got to get out of here, get to fresh air. Come on," he dragged me to the door we'd come in through, but I already knew there was no way. The commandant wouldn't have just locked *us* down. He'd want to make sure every single person succumbed inside this dome.

Chace yanked and pounded on the door, but it wouldn't budge. When that didn't work he stepped back and took a run at it, dropping his shoulder and ramming the door.

He groaned when it held fast, staggering back and clutching his shoulder.

"Help me, Nyx. We've got to get to fresh air. If we both run at it we might be able to pull the screws out of the hinges."

"Chace, he's pumping into the halls, too."

"I know that Nyx. But the only thing that combats concentrated nerve gas is open air. As much as we can get, dilute the gas to survivable levels. Hell, if we could blow the roof off the dome we might all stand a chance. Come on."

"Oh my God. Are you sure, Chace?"

"Yes! Yes I'm sure. I've seen it in history books. We've got to get outside and upwind. There's a constant breeze this close to the sea—it's our only chance."

I slid my hand into my pocket, the small button there surprisingly warm from riding against my thigh since River had handed it to me as he lay bleeding out on the ground.

He would be so smug if I lived to tell him about this.

I pulled the detonator out of my pocket, and Chace's eyes went wide.

"What's that?"

"A bomb," I said, my voice shrill in my ears. I was going to destroy Bastion City, and everything it stood to protect. But it was that or let it become a glittering mausoleum.

I flipped open the cover.

"Nyx—"

Precious seconds were passing, and there wasn't any more time to think.

I pressed the button and met Chace's wild eyes.

The noise was deafening when it detonated. Chace tackled me to the ground, covering my body with his own as everything around us trembled and went black.

Red lights flashed, but I couldn't hear anything. There was a sharp ringing in my ears, and nothing else. Chace was speaking, shouting something? As he dragged me off the ground, but all I could hear was the ringing.

Was that from the explosion, or the nerve gas?

My addled brain finally realized what he was screaming at me.

Run.

I grabbed his hand, and we ran towards the door.

It had popped open with the blast, and no lights were on except the angry red-and-white pulsing emergency lights. Chace dropped my hand as soon as we were in the tunnel, both of us pumping our arms as we ran at full speed. We backtracked our path from memory, not stopping to check that the corners were clear, not stopping for anything.

Sunlight streamed in ahead, and we bolted for it. It was an emergency exit—the large, rounded archway leading out into the dome's protected scrubby ground. We sprinted through it, running straight through the scratching, grabbing branches of the bushes.

Chace tripped over a cactus, but I grabbed his arm and kept him upright. As soon as we hit glass, Chace lifted his gun and fired at one of thc pancls to the side. The bullet ricocheted off, not even denting the bulletproof glass.

He swore.

"We've got to go to the front. That's where River planted the T-4." I spoke, but couldn't hear myself over the ringing, that infernal bell toll that wouldn't stop.

We ran as hard as we could for the front gate, though my energy was starting to flag, and my lungs burned.

I didn't let myself think about that being an effect of nerve gas. Or that the ringing could mean that my oxygen was already dropping too low, my muscles ceasing to function. I just pushed on, struggling in the ankle-deep sand and dodging the few brave plants that pressed up against the glass.

If the blast hadn't taken out the dome, we'd have to figure out a way to pry it open. But Chace's gun couldn't even shatter a panel, so I doubted we'd be able to break through any other way.

We might still be trapped.

The crunching under my boots changed when we reached the front corner of the city's walls, and a quick glance down showed me fragments of glass.

It worked!

I ran harder, and when we rounded the corner, the flagrant destruction came into view. I paused as my eyes began to sting, blinking at the smoke. It filled the top of the dome, hazy and lingering, pouring up from the destroyed front gate of the city. Little bits and larger chunks of stone had been catapulted from the walls and into the dome itself, which was riddled with holes. The earth was blackened, and flames licked the ground and plants inside the once-protected circle. But to my relief, whole panes of the dome had been blown free, meaning fresh air was pouring into the city by the second, diluting some of the gas being pumped in through the ventilation pipes. Chace grabbed my hand again and pulled me outside the glass, his feet churning in the deeper sand with a lifetime of strength and determination.

Even now, after I'd so recklessly endangered us, he only cared about getting me to safety.

But when he tried to turn west towards the ocean, I grabbed his arm, steering him south, perpendicular to the buffeting, salty breeze.

I wanted to sob with relief when I saw it. There, sitting so proudly in the loose sand. The Bronco.

She waited in dust-covered glory, her proud green paint still peeking through the piles of sand that had built up in her weeks of abandonment. I couldn't dig out the key, since it was hidden in the pocket of my underclothing, but it still opened when Chace hit the button, sensing the key's signal through my suit.

He flung open the driver's side door and dove in, while I did the same on the passenger side. As soon as the door shut behind me, he punched it. And *now* he drove straight east, straight toward fresh air. The sand blew off the hood in undulating ribbons, spinning through the air like a dancer.

When it was clear, he rolled down all of the windows, buffeting us with both sand and streams of air.

When we were clear of the dome, and past the massive, glinting spaceship, he turned us and stopped. We watched the smoky air billow from hundreds of smaller holes in the dome, the smoke illustrating the wind pattern.

To my relief, it was blowing away from us, the strong breeze rushing past us, over the dome, and drawing the dangerous air away.

I didn't know if it would be enough, but dazed, confused people were pouring out of the front of the dome onto the sand, leaving the shattered glass behind and clutching each other as they fell to the sand. Shocked or wounded, I couldn't tell.

"We need to go back and help, Chace."

"No, not yet." My head snapped towards him. I could hear him, just barely. "We need to make sure the gas is clear first. If they're getting themselves out, they're probably okay, or at least they'll survive." He squeezed my hand tightly in his, and we watched in silence for a few short minutes as more and more people poured out, in city clothing and space suits alike. My heart rate slowly returned to normal, but I was still a little shorter of breath than usual.

Something at the other end of the dome caught my eye. A small group of white-clad figures, running from the back of the dome. More refugees, from a side tunnel?

But, no. They weren't running to the sand and collapsing in fear. They were running *straight for the spaceship.*

"Chace, look! It's the commandant; he's trying to escape!"

"Hell no," he growled, punching the Bronco back into motion. But they were already climbing up a ladder and disappearing into a hatch on the side of the ship.

We skidded to a stop when we were close, and flew out of the doors, running hard again for the ladder up to the ship. But we were too late.

A deep blue-red glow and intense heat burst from the bottom, and the still-standing panes of the dome's glass rattled in their frames as the ship slowly lifted from the earth. We were surrounded by a maelstrom and pelted with blinding sand. All we could do was turn our backs and cover our faces as the behemoth ship rose into the sky like a specter of doom.

The commandant was gone.

Forty-Six

ΛΡΤΕΡΜΛΤΗ

Two Weeks Later

Recovery was never a fast process. In River's case, he was two weeks into specialized therapy to help him get remobilized after his injuries.

I watched, my arms crossed over my chest as he cracked jokes with the medic who was instructing him when to twist and when to stretch. The man was one of the Red Riders, the group who were most familiar with assistive therapies, given how often their people had been targeted by the Bastion City leadership.

The *old* leadership, at least. The new leader hadn't been determined yet, after ex-commandant Kieran's escape.

Speaking of which, I checked the time on my water meter. Ten minutes until the meeting, and these two knuckleheads were just getting warmed up.

"But what did the camel say to the sand dune?" Rick, the medic, asked.

"I don't know man, what?"

"Stick with me, and I'll never desert you."

River laughed so hard he gripped his sore side, laughing through the pain.

I snorted and shook my head as I laid my hand on River's shoulder. "You two are *ridiculous*. I feel like somebody normal needs to say that."

"Maybe, but I'm *your* ridiculous." He grinned up at me with those crystalline blue eyes that I still wanted to get lost in.

"Yes you are. I've got the meeting with the new leadership panel to talk about next steps, now that the decontamination protocols are complete."

"Ahh, right. I forgot about that. I can come with you, and circle back with Rick after."

"No, it's fine. You need to stay on top of your therapy so we can get out of here soon." I gave his firm bicep a squeeze, but he rose gingerly from the chair, anyways.

He looped one arm around my waist, and tilted my chin up with gentle fingertips. "If you insist." He dropped a kiss to my lips, the warm, soft feel of him sending tingles shooting through me. It never got old, kissing River. He still lit me up, and made me feel brighter, happier. I twined my arms around his neck and kissed him back enthusiastically until Rick cleared his throat.

Whoops. Forgot he was standing there. I made to step back in embarrassment, but River held me tight.

"I love you," he whispered against my lips.

I smiled, feeling the barest whisper of our lips brushing with the motion, and tugged him a little closer where my hands rested on the back of his neck. "I love you more," I said teasingly, then planted one last, hard, fast kiss on his lips and dodged out of his grip.

"Yep, you definitely need to finish therapy, or you'll never be able to catch me." I shot him a playful wink and bolted for the door.

"Rude, woman!" he called after me, but there was no heat to the words. Only joy. I tried to carry that bright bubble of his affection with me as I walked down the freshly-scrubbed halls of the city, but it was hard.

I could still see it too vividly as it was right after the explosion. Bathed in red light, filled with smoke, and the bodies of those who hadn't gotten out quickly enough.

Many survived, but not all, and this city elicited a deep sadness that I knew I'd never be able to shake off. It was in my bones.

But I couldn't leave it—not yet. There was so much work to do, so many details to pin down.

I spotted Sasha stepping out of her temporary bedroom up in the hall and called out to her.

"Hey, Nyx." She stopped and waited for me to catch up.

"Hey, Sasha."

"You excited about today?" She smiled at me, genuine excitement in her expression.

"Excited? No. Just ready to be done with it."

"Oh, come on. There are big rumors that you're going to be voted the new leader of the city. You could do so much good, taking over here."

I sighed, anxiously picking at my nails, even as I tried to appear relaxed.

"They're not going to vote me in as the new commandant."

"I am, for what it's worth."

"Sasha!" I groaned. "I don't want to lead this city, nor would I have any idea *how* to lead all these people. The way they live, so confined, isn't for me. And it never will be. You're throwing away the vote, if you vote for me."

"Fine, but I still think it's a huge mistake. Who are you voting for, then? I don't know any of the rest of these people well enough to cast an intelligent vote."

"Oh, I don't believe that for a second. Who's next on your list?"

She pursed her lips, refusing to answer until I did.

"Fine," I capitulated. "Yu-riel has my vote. He's a solid leader of the lifeside already, and I think he'll keep a level head with the challenges ahead for the city. Also, I already know he's willing to foster trade with the Wastelanders."

"Wastelanders, huh? Is that what you're calling your people now?" she asked teasingly.

I rolled my eyes at her. "The Nightbloods are still the Nightbloods, as you well know. But they're not the only people in the desert, are they?" I gave her a saucy grin right back.

"No, they are *not*," she agreed crisply as we walked through the door to the conference room. It was nearly full; about half of the original leadership panel had survived the various attacks, and all of them were already present. There were also representatives from the Red Riders; the Sidewinders; and even the spacers who'd been left behind. I officially represented the Nightbloods—though I also spotted Rahlise leaning against a wall, his black clothing blending into the shadowy corner. Kindred gave me a quick chin nod before resuming an argument with Guffey across the way.

"Nyx!" Chace called me from across the room. He sat next to Jacie but had an empty pair of seats on his other side for me and Sasha. It was strange to see him smiling with someone, leaning into her as if waiting on her next word.

But at the same time, it was good. He'd never been so free, so unaware of my every move.

We were settling into a new cadence, one where I was an adult with a serious partner, and he was an adult, free to be his own man. It was every bit as wonderful as it was strange. I knew that though time might create more distance between us, it would never change the bond between us. And no matter what, we would always be there for each other. Even if that was going to look a little different from here on out.

"Have I ever told you that I find it weird how much you like your brother?" Sasha muttered as we sat down.

"The only reason you don't like yours is because he's a wild man?"

She rolled her eyes, but the conversation was cut short by Vander stepping forward. He nodded to his daughter, before addressing the room.

"Thank you all for gathering today. If you'll shut the door, please, we can begin." He gestured to the door, where Morgan stepped in and shut it. She waved at me quickly before focusing on her uncle.

"I want to start by saying that we all appreciate your efforts to help us decontaminate and re-seal the dome of our beautiful city, so that the life within may once again flourish for many decades to come. In our time of greatest need, you've all proven to be true allies."

A smattering of applause rolled over the packed room, but quickly died down.

"Today, we're here to cement the alliance of the new Inter-Community Committee, as well as to vote in a new leader and commandant of Bastion City. We hope that today's actions lead to a brighter future for all, in the years and months ahead." He said it so smoothly, you'd never know how much of a fight the leadership panel had put up about having outsiders interfere in their election procedures.

But when it came down to it, they had faced the possibility of being completely overrun, and having what was left of their city destroyed by the Wasteland groups that surrounded the city at their time of need.

This was a compromise, and one I was very proud of having brokered. Establishing the ICC, so that there was open communication and trade between the city and all the representative groups of the desert, was the greatest deal I'd made in the whole of my life.

It was only a small atonement for the lives my decision to blow the T-4 had taken, but both Chace and River were insistent that opening up the city had saved more people than it had hurt.

The twelve names of the victims weighed heavily on my shoulders, and I saw their faces when I closed my eyes at night despite their assurances. I'd attended their funeral ceremony last week, where pictures of each of the deceased had been displayed. They were burned into my retinas; faces I didn't recognize, but had meaning, nonetheless.

If you'll please take one of these slips, write down your vote, and then someone will be around to collect it in exactly three minutes.

The papers worked their way around the room to where I sat, so I wrote down my selection, and folded it neatly. When the ballot box came around a few minutes later, I tucked it inside, and then waited.

Restless chatter filled the room as the votes were counted at the center table. Once they were finished, a single slip of paper was handed back to the commandant, whose eyebrows went up when he read it.

"The new leader of Bastion City is our very own Frankie Grenkel, son of Frank and Lira Grenkel, our late elders of the lifeside."

A cheer went up around the room, and I breathed a sigh of relief. We were almost free.

Rahlise waited for me outside the meeting room, always in a state of careful awareness. I nodded to the side, silently requesting that he follow me. He immediately dropped into step at my side, and we walked the half-empty halls in quiet contemplation.

I had things to say that he wouldn't want to hear, things that might make him angry. But the time for honesty had come.

"I cannot be Aíma of the Nightbloods." The words tumbled out of me in an inelegant rush.

His steps didn't falter, nor did he jump to argue. Time passed, and we kept walking. Past the point where I could have turned off to pick River up from his therapy, past the point where the Nightbloods were staying in a borrowed barrack.

Finally, when it suited him, he spoke. "You *are* the Aíma of the Nightbloods. It is not a role that can be abdicated. However . . . perhaps it need not mean you are the sole leader, if that is your wish."

Warmth suffused me at his willingness to have the conversation. To bend, for me. "Could someone with more experience perhaps be my co-leader, the one in control of the day-to-day running of the community? I know you all have wives and children back in the south. You've been away long enough, but I'm not going back."

He stopped to face me, those deep, bottom-less eyes searching my face. "One day, I believe you will return. But it is good for young ones to explore, to see what there is to see of this world.

Your father and I did, when we were younger than you are now. He would want that for you."

I nodded, understanding his point. Eventually, they would expect my return. And maybe someday, I would want to see the legacy that Hema had built. But not now, when the pain was so fresh.

The desire for freedom, for open sand and peace, called me out into the wilds with a pull so strong, each day felt like a little piece of me was tearing away to float off in the incessant breeze.

I had to go.

Back to who I was, back to my roots.

And he saw that in me, in a way words couldn't express. Thankfully, he didn't need the words.

"If it is your wish, I will lead until the day comes you are ready to take back the reins."

"That is my wish, very much so." I reached out and gently touched his shoulder, hesitating, waiting for his permission.

Then he opened his arms, and I hugged him. He clasped me tightly, and I squinched my eyes closed for a second, accepting the gesture of friendship, of family.

It was never the family I expected, but it was the one I'd found, nonetheless. And one day, perhaps I would return, when I was ready.

Forty-Seven

Epilogue—True North

Six Months Later

T he water detector beeped on the Bronco's
dash. It was happening more, now that
we were so far north. It also didn't hurt that
Kindred had upgraded it. He and Guffey were
settling in well to life as Bastion City residents.
They never ran out of things to tinker with.

"Ooh, less than a mile, straight ahead." River
rubbed his hands together with excitement.

"You are such a kid at heart." I shoved
his shoulder playfully, and he tickled my ribs
right back. I swerved briefly before successfully
fending off his attack. "Settle down or I'll wreck
us." I pointed an accusing finger at him, but he
just captured my wrist and kissed the back of

my hand. He was completely nonplussed by my pretend anger.

"You wouldn't have me any other way."

"No, I guess I wouldn't. I'm kind of attached to you at this point."

He grabbed his chest, as if I'd stabbed him. "Only 'kind of?'"

"Okay, *very* attached." I tossed him a cheeky grin, which made him shake his head at me.

My water meter buzzed with an incoming comm request, so I held up a finger to pause our lighthearted exchange. River nodded, so I accepted the request.

"Nyx, it's me." Chace's voice came through crystal clear, all the way from Wolf Well.

"Hey, bro. Calling to wax poetic about your lovely lady, and her many finer qualities?"

"No . . . although Jacie and Morgan say hello."

"Good, because that would be gross. And hey back at them. What's up?" River snorted in the passenger seat but didn't otherwise comment on our ridiculous sibling relationship.

"An excursion team reported in to the ICC this morning. Apparently you skipped the weekly touchpoint?" He sounded annoyed, as he always did when he had to chase me down for bureaucratic reasons.

"Sorry. We were occupied."

River waggled his eyebrows at me, pressing another kiss to my palm. I'd keep the details of our occupation to myself.

"Also gross," Chace retorted anyways, but moved on quickly. "They were investigating a report of an attack on a city not far from Wolf Well—"

"The Carthage settlement?" I asked, concerned. I'd met a new survivor group and invited them to join the ICC about three months back. I was glad they'd taken me up on my offer, but not that they'd had an attack.

"No. Apparently Wolf Well has contact with another city a six-hour drive west. It's called Dakota. That's where the attack was."

"Huh, okay. So what did the excursion team find?"

"You're not going to believe it; they found what appears to be a wrecked spaceship."

My grip on the wheel slipped, and my heart started pounding in double time.

"Repeat that?"

"You heard right the first time. The commandant's stolen ship was wrecked. No signs of life, no functional support systems on board."

"Did they find his body?" I flicked a worried look at River, and found his lips pursed in a thin line.

"Negative, no body found. The wreck was old."

I blew out a slow breath, trying to slow my rapid pulse, to think through it. He could still be dead; if they didn't find a body, though . . .

"Are they following up with the citizens of Dakota?"

"Yes, everyone has been told to look out for anyone fitting the commandant's description, and to report to the ICC immediately if he's located. They know he's excommunicated from all civilizations inside the ICC."

"Copy," I replied, but the word was pure habit.

"Stay safe out there, sis. And don't be *occupied* for the next check-in. We'll be heading down to the next generator, so I won't be there."

"Yeah, yeah," I teased. But I would be there. He was making a huge sacrifice for me, in locating and clearing the paths to the water generators while I scavenged; the least I could do was take the ICC calls.

The first one they'd checked, the tunnels had collapsed due to seismic activity. We were hopeful the next one, which was closer to the cast coast, would be open and accessible. Once the way was clear, I would get to face my fears and head back underground to get it running again.

I woke up screaming sometimes, remembering the ceiling collapsing on me. Other times, it was Jacira's face as she fell, or the dead bodies who didn't make it out before the commandant's poison reached them.

Kindred and Guffey were going to come along and study my blood when they did find one that was accessible. Kindred wanted to see if he could get the nanites reprogrammed to someone else's blood so that I could stop going underground. But if he couldn't . . . well, Chace was at least making it so that I didn't have to go until we were sure we could access the generators.

"Nyx—" he growled into the comm.

"I'm kidding, Chace. I'll be there. River will see to it."

"Yes, I will," he chimed in beside me. "She's got a rendezvous with the Nightbloods, too. Something about an annual new year celebration?"

I was finally going to get to visit their home base, meet the women and children the men fought so fiercely to hide and protect.

"Good. Hoss sends his regards and wants to know if you've found any more thrillers out there yet. He's salty about the one you gave him ending on a cliffhanger."

"My regards right back. And no, sorry. Tell him if he's put out about a gift, he can write his own ending. We'll probably go north another few days, then bring back some stuff for him to run through the reclaimer, at least. We're nearly full." We'd been scavenging far, far north into what used to be Cananda, but were now running out of space, even with my handy bumper platform. But Wolf Well was our home base, and where we returned when we wanted a break from the constant travel.

Marl had let me purchase the top floor of her new hotel, putting some of my endless water credits to good use, and providing something I'd never had before...

A place to call my own.

"Copy."

The meter on my wrist buzzed twice, indicating he'd dropped the line. I drove in silence, trying to breathe out the tension that his news had brought. Both about the space ship, and about Chace going back underground. It wasn't as bad as going myself, but it was only slightly better. He was determined to help, though, and it was a good role for him. He had more to take care of than just me, now.

"You know the commandant is probably dead, Nyx. And we may never get that confirmation," River said, his quiet words soothing me slightly.

"I know. He had no survival skills, and no supplies besides whatever was in the ship he stole, and *that* crashed."

"Exactly. And nobody's going to take him in. So, most likely he's out there drying under the sun somewhere, where we'll never find him."

He squeezed my shoulder lightly, and I forced it to detach from my earlobes. He was right.

Thinking about that man was only giving him brain space he didn't deserve.

If there was any justice left in this world, the man was dead.

"Nyx, are you seeing what I'm seeing?" River leaned forward, placing both hands on the dash. His breathless words pulled me out of my funk.

I scanned the horizon, not sure what he was talking about at first, and then I saw it; a shimmer. A pale, blue shimmer, surrounded by the sharply angled green tips that could only mean one thing.

"Trees." I whispered the word with reverence.

"Trees and a lake," he agreed, sounding just as awed as I felt.

I stepped on the gas, all thoughts of the commandant and my responsibilities falling away, replaced by the wonder stretching before us. We'd finally found it; a real, wild oasis. The rest of the world could wait.

Thank you so much for reading Descendants of Rust! For now, this is the final book planned in this world. To stay up to date on any future books, make sure to follow on amazon!

If you're looking for another great read, check out **Marked**! It's action packed, and sure to keep you on the edge of your seat.

What Readers are saying about Marked:

"I was not expecting this to be so good! Love love love this book and series so far!" – Amazon Reviewer

"Another book you can't put down!" – Amazon Reviewer

In the meantime, you might enjoy hanging out with me in my new reader's group, **which you can find here.** Hope to see you there, and keep turning the pages for some fun tidbits/behind the scenes notes about the story.

Forty-Eight

Notes for the Curious

I did a *ton* of research on caverns, cave systems, aquifers, underground temperatures, and even tunnel boring, grading, and digging while writing this book. Far too much to encapsulate in an end note, though you know I love to try. So, instead what I'll do is give you some fun links to the two caves I based my imagery off of:

Mammoth Cave, Kentucky

Tuckaleechee Caverns, Tennessee (I've been inside of this one, personally)

And as for the rest, I'll leave you to wonder where reality ends, and fiction begins.

Forty-Nine

Greek Phrases Guide

It's time to confess that I am *not* a native Greek speaker. However, my editor reads and speaks Greek, as it is a large part of her family heritage. She's helped me to make the phrases inside the book as accurate as possible. Below are the main snippets, in case you were curious:

My child — παιδί μου

Beloved of the blood — αγαπημένη του αίματος

"Beloved" nickname, shortened - αγαπημένη

Goddess in the flesh — θεά σε σάρκα

Nyx's new title among the Nightbloods now that Hema is gone (translates to blood) - Αίμα

May you enter the next life in peace, my friend — Να μπεις στην επόμενη ζωή ειρηνικά, φίλε μου

Before You Go . . .

Thank you so much for reading Descendants of Rust! The Endless Desert world was such a wild ride; I'm a little bit sad that it's over. My husband insists that it's *not*. We'll see in time if he's right, or not. :)

If you enjoyed this book, I would so appreciate you taking the time to **leave it a kind review, or some stars.** Reviews and Ratings help Indie authors like me get found by more readers, and help the stories you love reach more people. So, thank you in advance! I read and cherish every kind word you share with me.

If you'd like to sign up for my mailing list so you never miss a new release, and get fun freebies from time to time like recipes, short stories, and more, you can do so **here,** and receive a free deleted scene from this book! This is a really fun deleted scene where Nyx and River try those MREs they found—I'm always sharing things like these with my newsletter first, so you don't want to miss out!

I've also recently started a **Facebook group for readers, who enjoy YA Dystopian books** (with romance, like mine!). If that sounds like your cup of tea, please **come and join us.**

I am available by email at kagandyauthor@gmail.com as well, if you'd ever like to drop me a line directly!

MORE BY K. A. GANDY

Marked(Populations Crumble: Resurgence, Book 1)
On the run from the men who murdered her parents, there's only one way to save herself; marriage to a genetically matched stranger.

Captive (Populations Crumble: Resurgence, Book 2)

Love and Other Dangers Anthology
<u>Fantasy</u>

Aerthen Sight (An'Loran Chronicles, FREE Pre-quel Short)

The Lost Talisman(An'Loran Chronicles, Book 1)
The Hatchling – Coming Soon (An'Loran Chronicles, Book 2)

About the Author

K. A. Gandy was born and raised in Jacksonville, Florida, and is married with two kids. She has worked as a restaurant hostess, library book shelver, ranch hand, tour guide, Realtor, tech whiz, landlord, and small business consultant, all in addition to pursuing her passion of writing. She likes to write late in the evenings and thinks drinking hot tea and baking great cookies fuels hopes and dreams. If you would like to find more of her works, you can sign up for her newsletter at https://dl.bookfunnel.com/shu7 7m948u. You can also get updates on Facebook at https://www.facebook.com/KAGandyAuth or.